"In detail as rich and colorful as one of her grandmother's quilts, Angela Correll's splendidly woven romantic adventure flies us from New York to Rome, to an unlikely landing in the Bluegrass."

—BYRON CRAWFORD, *Kentucky Living* magazine

"Nestled deep in the woods and rolling hills of Kentucky is a tiny, magical world: The farms on May Hollow Road. You will be swept away by the charming, quirky characters who dazzle you with their wit and wisdom ... to say nothing of their fried chicken and cherry pie dinners. Angela Correll's Grounded is a modern Southern tale with a big, old-fashioned heart."

— LINDA BRUCKHEIMER, author of *Dreaming Southern* and *The Southern Belles of Honeysuckle Way*

"Grounded is a wonderfully captivating novel built on the values of debt free living and contentment. This is a must read. You won't want to put it down."

—HOWARD DAYTON, Founder, Compass—finances God's way.

"Grounded speaks to anyone who has ever lost their way and found it again by going home. Angela Correll captures the simple beauty of life in Kentucky and its particular power to comfort a hurting soul. I am already looking forward to the sequel!"

—JAMIE ARAMINI, Founder, Sustainable Kentucky

"I laughed, I cried and as soon as I finished reading, I missed spending time with Annie and Beulah. These are the kinds of characters I would like to have as next-door neighbors. Angela Correll has done a beautiful job of creating a world that readers will want to return to again and again."

—BETH DOTSON BROWN, author of *Yes, I am Catholic!*

Grounded
by Angela Correll

Published by
köhlerbooks ™
an imprint of Morgan James Publishing

210 60th Street
Virginia Beach, VA 23451
212-574-7939
www.koehlerbooks.com

Publisher
John Köhler

Executive Editor
Joe Coccaro

Habitat
for Humanity®
Peninsula and
Greater Williamsburg
Building Partner

In an effort to support local communities, raise awareness and funds, Morgan James Publishing donates a percentage of all book sales for the life of each book to Habitat for Humanity Peninsula and Greater Williamsburg.
Get involved today, visit www.MorganJamesBuilds.com

For Jess

Grounded

ANGELA
CORRELL

NEW YORK
VIRGINIA

THE FARMS
— on —
MAY HOLLOW ROAD

The Wilder Farm

wall crossing

← To Somerville

Betty & Joe Gibson's

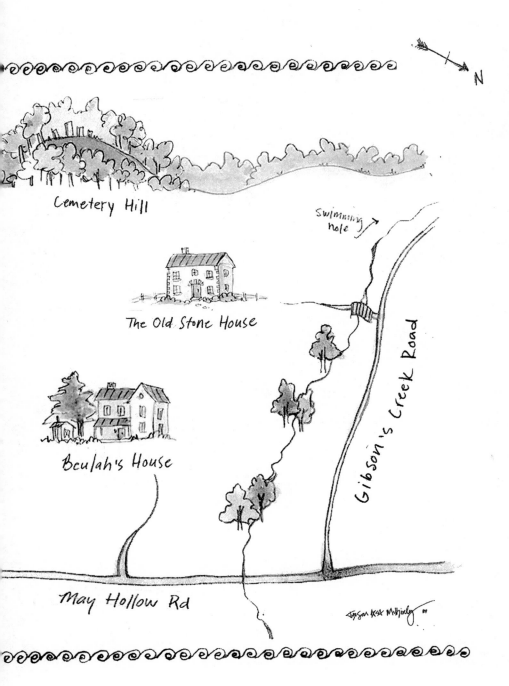

N

Cemetery Hill

Swimming hole

The Old Stone House

Gibson's Creek Road

Beulah's House

May Hollow Rd

Chapter One

ANNIE COULDN'T WAIT to get home. Up from the subway station and into a downpour, she wrestled a book out of her black leather handbag and used it to cover her head. The book made a poor umbrella, but with her other hand dragging luggage, it was the best she could do. Maybe getting soaked would at least wash the red stain off her khaki skirt.

Good rain, good rain. It was something her grandfather used to say years ago on the farm. Annie could see him in her mind, standing at the window of the farmhouse, a contented smile on his face and pipe smoke curling around his white head. But that was when rain was vital for food and income. Now it was a messy inconvenience.

The weather had delayed their landing in New York and added to an already difficult flight. The crew had celebrated her birthday the night before, and she'd had too much wine. A dull headache lingered into the first few hours and then there was the businessman from New Jersey who could not be pleased. As soon as she brought him a newspaper, he wanted a drink. Then he wanted another newspaper and on and on it went. A bossy teenager flying alone complained about the music selection, all the while going through three headsets to find the one with the best sound. What was a teenager doing in first class anyway? And what happened to the iPods that seemed to sprout on every teenager's body like an appendage at age thirteen?

The apartment building in sight, Annie ran the last few yards, her feet bitterly complaining in the high heels. Under the stoop, she unlocked the door and stumbled over the threshold with her luggage.

The air was thick with the rich scent of curry. She hoped it was coming from her Indian neighbors, the Agarwals, and not from her apartment. Her roommate, Prema, also Indian, had taken up traditional cooking lately and their apartment was beginning to smell like the Kashmir Indian Restaurant. Stuart had even smelled it on her clothes and hair when they'd gone out last week.

Nearly to the door, her luggage caught on the grate in the floor, jerking her backward. When she reached down to dislodge the wheel, her purse fell, scattering her phone, hairbrush and lipstick across the floor.

Snatching up the errant items, Annie nearly stuffed her phone back into her bag before seeing a text from Stuart.

"Running late today ... meet me at the apartment?"

She rubbed her temple, working it to release the tension. The last thing she wanted to do was go back out in the rain and ride the subway uptown.

"Annie, you are home!" Prema smiled, her warm dark eyes alight with excitement when Annie finally struggled through the door. "Oh, what happened to your skirt?"

"Tomato juice. We had a little turbulence and a passenger who had too many drinks. It could have been worse."

"Yes, like my flight to Delhi a few weeks ago. A child threw up on me! It was most unpleasant."

Amused at the understatement, Annie hid her grin since Prema was entirely serious.

"You're cooking," Annie said.

"Yes. I invited this son of my father's friend for dinner. He is newly arrived and sounded so sad, all alone." The gold hoops in Prema's ears swung as she moved from the living area to the kitchen, the scarf of her purple sari flowing behind her.

"And you're in traditional dress," Annie said. "Why do I think this is more than just a 'Welcome to New York'?"

"I am only doing as my father asked of me. Jatindre is used to seeing Indian women in their traditional clothing. I don't want to shock him with my American style yet. Can you have dinner with us?"

Annie tossed the book she had used for an umbrella on the side table and picked up her mail. "I'm going out with Stuart, thanks."

"There will be leftovers, I'm sure." Prema pointed to the chalkboard hanging next to the door. "Kate and Evie are gone through Tuesday. Whatever is left is yours. I leave tomorrow for Delhi."

In an apartment of four flight attendants, the chalkboard was the only way to keep up with who was coming or going. Days of the week were listed at the top. To the side each girl's name was written. An "X" meant you were out that day and night. A small "x" meant you were out part of the day. It helped with planning for social activities.

Four women in a three-bedroom apartment had worked out well for the most part, because it was rare for them to all be home at the same time. Annie had the master bedroom, Prema had her own room and the two younger flight attendants, Kate and Evie, shared the third. Annie earned the larger bedroom by being in the apartment the longest, as several roommates had come and gone after getting married or transferring to another city.

Annie tossed the mail on her bed and stripped off her TransAir uniform before stuffing it in the dry cleaning bag that hung from a hook in her closet.

The hot shower enveloped her, washing off the grime of an overseas flight. Breathing deeply, the moist heat eased her clogged sinuses and aching head. Her body relaxed.

She had snapped at two passengers and had bit her lower lip so much it was now as raw as sandpaper. For a couple of weeks she had been on edge, as if a black cloud of foreboding had settled on her. Annie knew it stemmed from the news reports that kept coming out about the airline's financial crisis. She had tried to shake it off but was overcome by the paralyzing fear of losing her job.

The hot shower massaged her skin like a thousand small fingers and she tried practicing the deep breathing she had learned in exercise class. She felt somewhat more relaxed and pried herself from the water cocoon. Annie wrapped a towel around her body and leaned in close to the mirror. She peered at the lines around her eyes. They had gotten deeper since she turned thirty-two. Digging eye cream from one of her toiletry bags, she dabbed a bit in each corner before putting on her makeup then drying her dark shoulder-length hair.

Dressed and left with some extra time, she sat to read through her mail—bills, junk mail, a letter from the airline, and a letter from her grandmother.

"Bad news first," she said to herself and opened the envelope from the airline. It was a letter from the CEO updating the employees on the attempts by a competing airline to take TransAir. Nearly the same as the letter that had arrived a month ago: *We are trying to fight the takeover. We want to continue to provide the routes and services we've been providing since 1969. Please be patient as we work through this with our shareholders ...*

She threw it in the trash.

With full passenger loads on most flights, how can they not make it work?

She reached for the envelope from Kentucky.

Dear Annie,

We sure do miss you around here. Your short visit at Christmas was not enough. Do try to come this spring and stay awhile. We look forward to a wet spring, which we need after last year's dry summer.

There is a new single preacher in town. Evelyn met him in the meat section of the Kroger and invited him to eat lunch with us on the Sundays he doesn't have an invitation from his congregation. Mary Beth White's divorce is final and she's been taking lunch with us on Sundays. She was so pitiful after her husband ran off and left her with those two young children. Evelyn thinks she and the new preacher might be a match, but I don't know if his church will let their preacher marry a divorced woman.

I'm thinking about painting the house, but the Millers moved out of the stone house and I hate to take on a new expense with less money coming in. Maybe if I can find a good renter, I'll do it.

Jake was promoted again by that big bank up in Cincinnati and Evelyn says he's getting right serious with a girl from up there.

Joe and Betty Gibson have a new grandbaby. It's a little girl called Frances Grace. You know people are going for the old-fashioned names nowadays, but I've yet to hear of someone naming their child Beulah.

Love, Grandma

P.S. Don't forget we have a new area code now. We got new addresses five years ago for the EMS. Why they can't leave well enough alone, I don't know.

Annie hadn't been home in four months. Even then it had been a quick visit, squeezing in a ski trip with Stuart on the back end of the holidays. Maybe she would plan a trip this summer and bring Stuart. Annie smiled at the thought of him in his Armani suit and alligator shoes on the farm. Maybe she would buy him a pair of Red Wings for his birthday.

Annie let herself into Stuart's apartment with the key he had given her. His place on the Upper East Side was spacious and neat compared to her cramped quarters in the Village. Chester, the orange tabby a client had given Stuart, pranced, tail swishing in greeting. The cat's soulful green eyes beckoned the usual scratch behind his ear.

"Hey, Ches, did you miss me?" The soft fur felt good on her hand and she lingered, giving him an extra rub down his back.

Annie straightened and put her purse on the low-slung black leather couch. Behind the couch, paintings with geometric patterns in reds, oranges and blacks by the same artist hung three in a row. Metal end tables next to the leather couch and chairs held black lacquer lamps, and, central to any bachelor's apartment, suspended against the far wall was the latest technology in flatscreen televisions.

The only thing that looked out of place to her was the wilting peace lily in the corner of the room. It had been her subtle attempt to soften the room and make it more "homey" but it continually suffered from neglect since its arrival two months before. Stuart had seemed happy with her gift, but clearly plants weren't his thing.

In the kitchen, Annie looked around while she filled a container with water. Not one thing was out of place. Stuart was compulsively neat and his cleaning lady came three days a week. Just once, Annie would like to find something awry, like a dirty glass or plate, even a pair of socks on the floor.

After watering the peace lily, Annie wandered into Stuart's bedroom. A stack of sales books were on the bedside table, a *Wall Street Journal* was folded neatly next to them, and there was his perfectly made bed.

"Chester," she called to the cat. "Does he ever mess up anything?" Chester came to her in the bedroom and looked as if she were telling him something important, his head tilted slightly to the side, his ears pointed forward.

There was a time when he did look a mess, she remembered: the night they met, more than six months ago. Her best friend, Janice DeVechio, had invited Annie to a charity fundraiser for cancer research. She had tickets given to her by an aunt who had married a wealthy Sicilian. Janice firmly believed her new uncle had mob connections, but it never stopped her from accepting the generous offer of tickets to plays, events and shows frequently doled out by the aunt to her favorite niece.

"It's costume, but don't worry. I know what you can wear."

Annie had rolled her eyes. "I'm afraid to ask."

"Jimmy is going as Hansel, I'm Gretel, and you'll be Little Red Riding Hood. You look great in red."

Annie had gone to the party in red tights, a red cape found at a consignment store, and carrying a small basket. Janice and Jimmy danced to Bobby Darin and Annie stood at the hors d'oeuvres table debating how long she would need to stay.

She had decided to get some fresh air on the terrace when a man said, "Not so fast, Little Red Riding Hood." Annie turned to face a wolfman grinning at her, rows of straight white teeth peeking from under pieces of brown fur taped to his face and intense green eyes peering between strands of a long brown wig. She burst out laughing as a piece of fur dropped onto a plate of crackers.

"That is the worst costume I have ever seen," she said.

"This is the worst party I've ever seen. I had to come for business. What's your excuse?"

"I'm with a friend," she said.

"That's too bad," he said, and looked disappointed.

"Not a date—a couple. They're out there dancing." *Who is this man?* She had been immediately intrigued.

"Aha. The story is getting better all the time," he said, grinning.

"I don't know why I'm here. Bad social life I guess."

"Well, since you're not here with another wolf, I think this means we are meant for each other," he said, raising his eyebrows in feigned sincerity.

Annie laughed at him, but something deep within her stirred at his words. It was as if there was a magnetic field around him and she was helpless to fight the pull. His convincing green eyes, laughing one minute and piercing the next, reshaping her belief on the spot that love at first sight was possible.

"Let's go to the bar. We can talk there." He put a hand gently on her back and guided her out of the room. She helped him remove the silly pieces of fur from his face while they talked, telling each other their life stories, right up to how they ended up on that night in that place. The attraction had been seismic.

Annie was so lost in the memories, she didn't hear the lock click and the apartment door open until Chester jumped off the bed to greet his master.

Stuart filled the doorway of the bedroom, one arm behind his back. He was tall, tan with dark blond hair that curled naturally. When he entered a room, it was as if he owned the entire block of buildings, so strong was his confidence.

"Wow, you look great. I missed you," he said, his eyes taking in her whole body and opening his arms for her. Annie responded with a warm and lingering kiss, inhaling the smell of his cologne mixed with the white roses he held in his hand.

"I missed you too," she said. She forgot her irritation at having to come to his apartment. All that was important now was being with him.

"Let me look at you again." His green eyes moved appreciatively down her body. "You are stunning." He handed her the flowers and kissed her again.

"Thank you! I'll put these in water."

He loosened his tie and followed her into the kitchen. "You are never going to believe who I went to lunch with today."

Annie reached for the scissors and pointed them at him. "If it's a rich, young heiress, I'm not sure I want to hear about it."

He grinned and moved behind her, hugging her from the back. "I think it is safer back here."

"Okay, now I'm in suspense. Who?" Annie carefully snipped the ends of each stem diagonally, as her grandmother had taught her to do.

Stuart poured a Scotch for himself and a Chardonnay for Annie.

"Jack Carney." He waited for Annie's reaction.

"Carney the developer? The one who did the big project over in New Jersey?"

"That's him. We hit it off, Annie. He's into poker, loves golf. We couldn't be more alike. I need to work the relationship, but I think he'll invest with me."

"That's great!" She placed the last rose into the vase.

He handed her the wine. "Did you miss me?" she asked.

"Bad. Chester was even worse. He unwound a whole roll of toilet paper then shredded it on the bathroom floor while I was at work."

"You're joking?"

"No, I'm serious. Vera was not happy about the extra work, and believe me, she let me know about it." Annie remembered the first time she met Vera. The older woman made sure Annie knew she worked for Mr. Henderson and no one else. No girlfriend would be giving her orders.

Stuart took her hand and pulled her over to the couch. "I don't know why I ever let that client talk me into taking that cat. But I did get a good sale out of the deal."

"That's why you're so successful—anything for the customer."

Stuart looked at his watch. "I better hop in the shower. I have a car coming at seven-thirty." The dimple in the cleft of his chin deepened with his smile as he leaned in for a kiss. "This is a special night for us. I've got a surprise."

Gino's was known as a restaurant where lovers, both illicit and legitimate, could meet discreetly. The wine list was first-rate, the service excellent and the lighting dim. Like the director of a play, Gino himself attended to the details, giving cues to his staff with a raise of his dark eyebrows or a small hand gesture. Stuart was a regular, bringing clients and friends, and Gino showed his appreciation by giving them the best corner table.

Stuart ordered an expensive bottle of wine. After the waiter poured the glasses, he lifted his to Annie's. "Happy belated birthday!" They clinked glasses and drank.

When he leaned in, Annie thought he was going to kiss her and closed her eyes. Instead, he whispered: "This Jack Carney connection could be huge. He is estimated to be worth half a billion. His friends could be worth even more. He asked me down to Miami this weekend to play golf." Stuart reached for Annie's hands. "I know we were going to spend the weekend together, but this could be the biggest meeting of my life."

Annie leaned back, disappointed. This was the first weekend they could spend together in two months because of her work schedule. As a ten-year flight attendant, she was fortunate to do the overseas flights, but she generally only got the weekend flights, even though she always tried bidding for the weekday, just in case. Occasionally she got it.

"No, that's okay. I know it's important," she said.

Stuart leaned across and kissed her hand. "That's why I love you. You're so free and understanding." Annie didn't feel very *free* or *understanding*. She was bummed out, even a little upset. But it was her birthday celebration and she didn't want to spoil it.

"Anymore news from the airline?" Stuart asked as the waiter placed the entrees on the table.

"Another letter today, but nothing new. I don't think it looks good, but I'm trying not to worry."

"I'll take care of you no matter what happens. Did I tell you how much I missed you while you were gone?" He reached for her hand.

She smiled back. "Yes, but you can tell me again."

"I missed you."

The lemon sole was delicious, but Annie only took a few bites. After the plates were removed, Stuart reached inside his coat pocket and pulled out a small square box, pale blue with white ribbons—Tiffany's signature packaging. She felt as if a flock of hummingbirds fluttered between her heart and stomach.

Annie studied his face as he pushed the box gently across the table. His blond hair looked golden in the candlelight, the short curls highlighted by the aura giving him an almost angelic halo. He was one of the handsomest men she had ever seen. *And to think, he loves me.*

She held the gift in both hands for a moment before untying the ribbon and removing the top. Annie felt her breath catch and wondered if there might be a ring inside? Her heart banged like a gong. *Could he hear it?*

Lifting out the small black box, an eternity seemed to pass before Annie reached the treasure. Glitter spilled out reflecting the candlelight from two shimmering stones. Two diamonds. Two large and glistening earrings.

"Do you like them?" he asked, his words coming from a faraway place.

"They're beautiful! I'm overwhelmed."

He took the box and laid it aside, taking both of her hands in his. "Annie, I've never felt this way before, but I'm finding myself needing you with me all the time. I've never even considered this with another woman, but it seems right with us. Will you move in with me?"

Chapter Two

BY THE END of April, rumors of an imminent takeover swirled around TransAir. According to stories traded in the crew lounge, there were two airlines vying for ownership of TransAir, while the CEO was trying desperately to persuade the stockholders to hold out for another year. Every day it was a different variation of two stories. The deal was already done, according to some. Details were being worked out before making it public. Others were sure the CEO was preparing the restructure plan so it could be announced in time for the stockholders' annual meeting next month. One fact was undeniable: The airline was in trouble and something was about to happen.

Annie's heels clicked against the tile floor, passing the pilots' area and into the crew lounge, where their sound became muffled when she hit carpet. Comfortable chairs were placed in conversational arrangements in one area of the lounge. On a television in a corner, CNN was presenting breaking news from Turkey, where an apartment fire killed more than one hundred people. Behind the chairs, vending machines offered snacks and sodas. A long counter displayed coffee, tea and popcorn. Employment and work related notices hung on the wall alongside FAA regulation changes.

Filling a Styrofoam cup with coffee, Annie headed to the bank of computers against the opposite wall, greeting other flight attendants as she went.

"Hey, Annie," one of the pilots called as he stuck his head in the door of the lounge, "you still owe me a dinner!" He pointed his finger at her and raised his eyebrows, affecting an exaggerated frown.

"I know. We haven't flown together since the Final Four!"

Phillip Miller was from Connecticut and shared a common passion with Annie: basketball. Unfortunately, they were usually at odds since he rooted for UConn and Annie was a Kentucky fan. The regular teasing had gone to a new level a couple of weeks before when UConn played Kentucky in the Final Four. Kentucky lost in overtime, a particularly painful defeat.

Annie picked up her FAA updates out of her mail slot and filed them in her board manual. She checked the schedule and found no changes. She was on for the Sunday-Tuesday Rome flight next week, a break from her usual weekend flights. There was a memo on new price changes for alcoholic beverages and another letter from the CEO saying the airline was working on several options to avoid takeover.

Janice was already in the small briefing room when Annie arrived. She pulled a seat out for Annie.

"What's happening? It's too quiet in here," Annie whispered.

"The union met last night. If TransAir is bought by an airline that doesn't have a union, there is nothing they can do for us. The new airline can take away our seniority and treat us like new employees unless we are protected in the merger agreement. Or worse, we could lose our jobs."

"But isn't it possible they may restructure the company?"

"Not likely now. Everybody is saying Patriot made the deal. The lawyers are drawing up papers."

"Okay, ladies and gentlemen, listen up!"

The two chief flight attendants began the briefing, covering everything from passenger loads to special customer needs and work assignments. Annie was assigned coach on the way over, which meant she would most likely have business class on Tuesday afternoon's return trip.

***

The night flight to Rome was uneventful. Once on the ground and finished with their duties on the plane, the crew was shuttled to the Savoy Hotel off the Via Veneto.

The hotel was like a home away from home for the crew: the sparkling clear Venetian glass chandeliers in the lobby, the familiar Carrara marble steps leading down into a breakfast room below the first floor, and rooms so small there was barely space to walk between the furniture and the bed.

Crew members went their separate ways, but not before setting a time to meet for dinner. Each person had his or her own routine. Some stayed in their room, slept and watched television. Others visited favorite sites or shops.

With the Eternal City only steps outside the hotel doorway, Annie couldn't imagine holing up in a hotel room. Her routine allowed for a three- or four-hour nap to make up for the lost night's sleep. Afterward, she enjoyed viewing historic sites and architecture, people watching on the piazzas and visiting the glorious churches. Like an illicit love affair, the few hours in Rome were never enough but kept her wanting more.

When Janice worked with Annie, they fell into a comfortable habit of going out together in midafternoon. Janice's Italian heritage and fluent language skills helped them find the shops and restaurants only the locals frequented. But on warm and sunny afternoons such as today, it was hard to resist the popular and touristy Piazza Navona.

Navona was built on the site of a first century stadium used for carnivals and circus games. The shape reminded Annie of a smaller racetrack.

In the middle of the oval, Bernini's Fountain of the Four Rivers provided a tablelike centerpiece.

While Janice found a table near the fountain, Annie admired once again the baroque statue with four figures sculpted into the square base and a large obelisk shooting skyward from the center with the waters falling toward the four corners of the world. It was an allegory of grace, she had once read. The four figures receiving the water represented Africa, Europe, Asia and the Americas as the four corners of the world—grace like a river, flowing for the whole world to receive.

"Here, Annie," Janice called.

Annie moved between tables and chairs to join her friend.

"Desidera un cappuccino?" a waiter asked.

"Sì, grazie. Due," Janice said and smiled.

Italians normally didn't drink cappuccinos after breakfast and were sometimes perplexed at the Americans desire for them at all hours. *Maybe similar to our wonderment at them not wanting ice in their water or tea,* Annie thought. Nothing hit the spot like a cappuccino, unless it was a hot afternoon. Then Annie craved a dip of creamy pistachio gelato.

Janice and Annie sat in front of the statue, with the church of Sant'Agnese in Agone as a backdrop. Old buildings in faded apricot, salmon and ocher lined the piazza. Vines hung from the iron terraces above, scattered here and there, as if some designer had placed them just so.

Artists sat on folding stools, easels in front of them while they painted. Finished works showing famous Roman landmarks were displayed near each artist. Annie furnished her apartment with several of the paintings she bought at the piazza. Stuart had dismissed them as "commercial" and told her she should invest her money in one good painting. But she had liked them, and if art was to be enjoyed, then they had done the job for her.

As Annie watched people pass by, she reflected on the many Italian afternoons she and Janice had forged their bond of friendship during the past year when they had both been regularly assigned to the Rome flight.

Janice told Annie about Jimmy's brief affair after the turbulent and traumatic times following September 11, and their struggle to forgive and move on.

Annie told Janice about the difficulty of losing her mother at twelve and barely knowing her father. A friendship was formed and sealed, witnessed by the waiters and notarized by drops of cappuccino or sometimes Chianti.

Annie, the sleeves of her cotton shirt pushed up, felt herself relax, enjoying the silence that lay between them like an old quilt.

Janice lit a cigarette, leaning back in her chair.

"I thought you quit," Annie said.

"I did. But there is something about these Italian cigarettes."

The waiter set two cappuccinos on the table. Janice nodded at the young boy and said, *"Grazie."*

"Do you think we'll lose our jobs?" Annie asked.

"I think some of us will. The way I figure, the new airline has got to have a few of us if they're picking up our routes. I mean, nearly every flight I've worked lately is loaded."

Annie poured a small packet of sugar into the frothy topping of her cappuccino and watched the mound of sugar sink, grain by grain, into the quicksand-like foam.

"They'll keep you," Annie said. "You have a language skill, and you've been with the airline for almost twenty years."

"I hope so. With only one year of college, I don't know what else I could do. They'll keep you too. You've worked hard, taking extra flights. That's worth a lot."

"Yeah, but I only have ten years in. There are a lot of people with more seniority."

Janice took a last drag on the cigarette and stubbed it out in the ashtray. "What else would you do? If you couldn't fly, I mean."

Annie leaned back in her chair, still holding her cappuccino. "Something in hospitality or travel. Maybe lead tours."

Just then a cluster of people clad in yellow neon vests trod past their table. They followed a tour leader who walked backward, a yellow stick high in the air, while she spoke into a microphone that transmitted her words into small earpieces worn by each tour member.

After they watched the tour march by like penguins, Annie looked at Janice, trying to contain a grin.

"And maybe not!" Annie said, both women bursting into

laughter.

In the silence that followed, Annie was drawn in to watching the fountain's spray. The water droplets looked like many pieces of crystal shattered and falling to the sea below. At the base, a young couple leaned on the fence protecting the fountain and stared into each other's eyes. The boy traced the girl's cheek with his thumb, gently lifting her chin and kissing her.

"Isn't it strange how falling in love is so easy for some people?" Annie said. "They meet, they fall in love, they get married and have babies and live until ripe old ages. Others struggle all their lives and never find that right person. Or maybe there's too much baggage they can't let go. Or maybe they love someone they can't have."

"I think it has to do with the person and whether or not they are ready for it. Some people are ready at eighteen. Some people are never ready."

The waiter appeared smiling. *"Un altro cappuccino?"*

"Sì, grazie," Janice said. *"Due per favore."* To Annie, she said, "Speaking of love, when do you change addresses?"

"Tomorrow." Annie reached for her ear and felt the stone between her fingers.

"Are you crazy? You don't get home from work until late afternoon."

"There's not much to do. I'm leaving my furniture with the girls until I need it. I'm just taking my clothes, toiletries and a few books. Prema will be in my bedroom by the time I get home. Kate is taking Prema's room, and Evie has invited one of her friends to move in. We're trying to get it done by the end of the month, which is tomorrow, so there's a clean break."

"Don't you want that antique corner cupboard? I love that piece," Janice said.

"Stuart's not really into antiques. Besides, I don't think we'll be there long. We've talked about getting out of the city soon, and there's no sense in moving furniture twice."

"You mean you suggested it last week, and he didn't shut you down right away?"

"Janice, sometimes I regret telling you *everything*."

The waiter brought the cappuccinos. Annie picked up the cup with both hands and breathed in the aroma.

"I'm your best friend. You're still a fresh-faced farm girl who happens to be ten years wiser for living in New York. I don't want you to get hurt. What if he never marries you? Isn't marriage what you really want? I want you to be as dysfunctional as me and Jimmy," she joked, "and happy at it."

"I do want marriage but Stuart was badly hurt when his mother abandoned him as a little boy. He needs to take things a step at a time and I understand that. He's committed to me."

"Let me tell you a family story."

"This is not another of your grandmother's Sicilian curse stories, is it?"

"No, no. This is what happened to Maria. My little sister dated this guy seriously all through college. He told her from the beginning he didn't think he would marry until he was older, but she thought he would change his mind. At graduation, she expected a ring. Graduation came and went. No ring. At Christmas that year, he gave her a beautiful set of diamond earrings. They were smaller than yours, but expensive for a kid fresh out of school. That night, my sisters and I knew he would never marry her."

"Why? Men don't go spending that kind of money on someone they don't care about."

"Exactly. He cared for her, but he didn't want to marry her. It was a way to give her something of value without committing. Five months later, they broke up."

Janice's voice softened. "I'm sorry, Annie. I can be too hard. Jimmy says I think I know what's best for everybody. But you're my best friend, and I don't want to see you hurt."

Annie drained the last of her second cappuccino and pushed it away with a sigh. "I understand. But trust me, I trust Stuart. I think we're going in the right direction. It may take a little time, but we'll get there."

Janice was quiet. Annie heard the wistfulness of her own voice hang heavily in the air. Needing to break the spell, she said, "Are you ready to go?"

"Mi può portare il conto?" Janice called to the waiter. She dug through her purse and left euros on the table.

"My treat today." She stood up and stretched her back. "I've been cleaning the house, getting ready for Mama DeVechio's visit, and I'm beat. I think I'll head back and relax a bit before dinner."

"When is she coming?" Annie stood and gathered her purse.

"This weekend. She's staying for a month. The visits get longer and longer. I think she might be sizing up the place to see if she could live with us eventually. She keeps saying it's to spend time with the grandkids, but I'm not sure."

"You'll do fine. And you'll be gone half the time."

"Unless I lose my job, then things could get really interesting. See you at eight in the lobby."

***

In the small alleyway off the piazza, sunlight was hidden by the ancient buildings. Passing the Italian Senate, Annie watched as dark Lancias whizzed in and out of the heavily guarded gate. The street was filled with people. Scooters motored between cars and pedestrians, their horns beeping a warning to anyone in the way. A couple walked a few paces in front of her, and Annie watched as the man pulled the woman to the inside of the sidewalk as a car zoomed by. *That is the nice thing about having someone,* she thought. Stuart was there to pull her out of the street when danger was too close; at least he would if he was with her.

Annie pushed her sunglasses on top of her head, using them to keep her fine straight hair off her face. Like a grain of sand in her pantyhose, Janice's questions about Stuart irritated her. Janice had no motive other than concern, but she could be opinionated and didn't mind at all telling anyone who would listen whatever she thought. It was part of why they were such good friends. They were different in that way. Annie had opinions but her Southern upbringing kept her from voicing every thought in her head.

Annie tucked her purse in front of her, holding it like a small pet. *My situation is different from Janice's sister*, she thought. Stuart wasn't a kid out of college. He was a successful adult who could buy her a set of diamond earrings and a ring on the same day if he wanted.

She felt the stone again in her ear, fingering the cuts of the solitaire and the metal setting. Stuart had commitment hang-ups. *Who wouldn't if his mother abandoned the family while the children were so young?* But as they had grown closer, things had changed. They were taking a big step in the relationship. Stuart said it was huge for him, something he had never done with another woman. It was certainly big for her.

A chaperone, looking pale-faced and out of breath, chased along behind a group of teenagers, calling out in a British accent, "Stay together, please!"

She moved down a narrow alley, then suddenly the great Pantheon was in view. The stunning, ancient structure with a columned porch and the great bronze doors nearly two thousand years old stood majestic, as if holding court in the piazza. Annie knew from previous visits the Pantheon stood on the site of a former temple. The architecture was famous for the rotunda having a dome in equal height to the diameter of the circular interior that gave a sense of harmony. She didn't walk inside today, instead choosing to admire it from the center of the piazza. Cafes surrounded the perimeter of the piazza, and a fountain in the middle near where she stood added background noise to the bustling center of activity.

"*Scuzi, dove ...,*" a man asked for directions in Italian.

"No Italiano, sorry!" Annie said.

The question was a compliment, she thought, due in part to her dark hair and the fact that she never wore sneakers like most other tourists. Annie considered taking Italian lessons, but she was never sure how long she would keep the flights to Rome she bid for every month. For international flights, giving up her weekends was a small price to pay for the experiences. Annie had always wanted to see the world, even from her roots in a small Kentucky town. She didn't always get the Rome flights;

sometimes it was Munich or Amsterdam. Janice, much higher
in the line and a dual language speaker, preferred weekends
so she could be home during the week with her children when
Jimmy had to work second shift.

Despite Annie's effort to be optimistic, the airline's prospects
were disturbing. She tried to imagine herself working for another
company, learning new service policies, perhaps having to go
through the entire training process again. Ten years of seniority
was not a lot in an industry where flight attendants worked up to
and more than thirty years. *Would there even be jobs available
with other airlines in New York, or would the market be too
flooded?* A cloud of questions hung over the whole mess.

But for now, she had this moment in Rome. She needed
to enjoy it, soak it in and not worry about the future. Her
grandmother always said today had enough trouble of its own,
and that was true.

She walked up the Piazza della Rotonda with the decorative
iron light posts with mustard buildings and brown shutters and
onto the Via delle Muratte. Annie heard the roar of the fountain
mixed with voices calling to one another, shrieks and laughter,
before she actually saw it. The small piazza was dwarfed by the
Trevi Fountain, eighty-five feet high and sixty-five feet wide.
Salvi's famous creation incorporated the space of the piazza and
the backdrop of the palazzo into the design. She paused to sit on
a stone bench and watch.

Around the sides of the piazza, vendors hawked their wares.
A policewoman blew her shrill whistle anytime someone stepped
into the water. To her right, a Japanese tour group listened as
the guide talked about the fountain, or Annie assumed since it
was in Japanese.

Across the street from where Annie sat, a small balcony was
lined with pots of different shapes and sizes. An elderly woman
sat next to one of the containers and worked the dirt with her
wrinkled hands. Annie watched as she dropped seeds into the
pot and then covered them with the dirt. With a tin can, she
poured a small stream of water over the seeds. Then she pushed
the pot to a corner of the balcony where a glint of sunlight shone.

Something about the woman reminded Annie of her grandmother. This universal need to grow something, even when surrounded by the bustle of the city, was a common thread binding man and woman since the beginning of time.

After an hour of enjoying the scene, Annie decided to take her turn at the fountain's edge. Fishing a coin out of her purse, she turned her back to the fountain as legend required, made a wish and tossed the coin over her shoulder.

* * *

Tuesday morning's flight made Annie wonder how an airline could teeter on the brink of bankruptcy with full flights. Every trip she had worked in the last few months had been either full or near full. Today, the flight from Rome to New York was no different.

"Good afternoon. May I take your coat?" Annie asked the first man who entered the business class cabin on her side. He handed her his sport jacket. A father, mother and two young children entered Janice's side of the cabin together, and Annie stopped on her way to the closet to take the man's leather jacket while Janice situated the children. She hung the coats in order of passenger seats for later reuniting with their owners.

After everyone was seated, Annie offered the passengers orange juice or champagne. She was halfway down the aisle when a heavyset, middle-aged woman stumbled into the cabin with a bulging shopping bag.

Janice intervened. "Can I help you?"

The woman's face was flushed and the dash to the plane had obviously winded her. She handed Janice her boarding pass, too out of breath to talk.

"You're right here in front, the aisle seat," Janice said. The woman managed a breathless thank you and moved to the front, bumping passengers with her bag as she went.

Several minutes later, they were in the air and waiting for the pilot to indicate they were at cruising altitude. Facing the cabin, Annie watched the late arrival talk nonstop to her seatmate, hearing bits and pieces of the conversation. The man kept looking down at his book and, when that didn't work, he plugged in the headphones and hung them around his neck, but the woman didn't get it. As soon as they could move around the cabin, she would try to divert the woman long enough for the poor man to put on his headphones or feign sleep. It worked nearly every time. Once she had a man so happy to be relieved of the talking that he tried to give her a hundred dollars when he exited the plane. She didn't take it, but it was a nice gesture.

When the tone sounded, Annie unbuckled her seat belt and went over to the woman.

"Did I hear you say you're from Illinois?" Annie asked her.

"That's right. Peoria! Are you from Illinois?" The woman's face was wide and smiling. The man next to her shot Annie a grateful look and slid the earphones over his head.

Peoria was Stuart's hometown. It was a good excuse to divert her for a moment. "I'm not, but I know someone who is. I'm sure it's a big place."

"Not that big. Who do you know?"

"His name is Stuart Henderson."

"Stuart Henderson? Curly blond hair? You've got to be kidding. My niece dated him. How do you know Stuart?"

Later, looking back on that moment, Annie could not explain why she said what she did. Before the words could be formed in her mouth, something held her back and kept her from revealing their relationship.

"We met at a charity event."

"He's a piece of work. Good looking, but a character."

"Really? Why do you say that?" Out of the corner of her eye she saw Janice motion for her, needing her help in the galley. She held up her index finger, asking for another minute. Annie was mesmerized by this woman and repelled by her at the same time. Was she talking about her Stuart?

"He and Sandy lived together for four years, dated two before that. Never could make a commitment. Last year, when she turned thirty-eight, she finally got tired of it. Wasted six years of her life with him." The woman leaned in as if telling a secret. "I don't know how Sandy expected anything different. He did the same thing with another girl before he moved to New York. I guess she thought she was different."

Annie held her breath. She must be wrong. Stuart said he had never lived with another woman. Yet the ages matched up. Stuart would turn thirty-nine this year. Her legs went weak, and she crouched next to the woman, unable to move.

"I like Stuart. Charming as they come, successful, a real looker, but he's got some kind of commitment issue. Sandy tried to get him to go to counseling, thought it had to do with his mother leaving when he was little. I don't know. I was glad when she finally broke it off. He would have lived with her forever if she could have agreed to it. You know how some women are."

The woman laughed and her shrill voice bounced around inside Annie's head like a ricocheting bullet.

Annie tried to stand, to say something intelligent. "It's the cat she really misses now, not Stuart."

"Cat?" Annie managed to form the simple word.

"Yeah, a big orange tabby Sandy named Chester. A dog was too much for Stuart, so he agreed to a cat. Her new apartment building didn't allow pets, so she had to leave him with Stuart."

Chapter Three

JANICE COVERED ANNIE'S end of flight wrap up so she could head straight to Stuart's office. She needed to see him, to hear him admit the truth to her, to explain why he had lied.

"Wait, honey, let me go with you," Janice had said, sounding like a mother. "You're too upset."

"I'm okay. Just cover for me."

Annie decided to take the subway since it was late afternoon and traffic would be terrible. She got off at the financial district, after what seemed like the longest ride ever. She rode the elevator to the 20th floor of Stuart's office building, her travel bag in tow. When the doors opened, she flew past the receptionist, who was calling after her as she raced back to Stuart's corner office. Annie had been here only once before, not long after they first started dating, when he wanted to show her off to everyone.

The lights were out. The office was empty. She took a deep breath and let out the last hour of anxiety.

"Annie?"

Annie turned to see a man looking at her over wire-rimmed readers.

"Greg Stein. We met at the Christmas party." He shook her

hand. "Are you looking for Stuart?"

"Yes, I was ..." She couldn't think of what to say next.

Greg shifted his weight. "I think he left for Florida this afternoon. Have you talked to his assistant?"

"No. Is Martha here?"

"Martha left last month. Felicia is the new girl." Greg pointed to a desk near Stuart's office in the maze of center cubicles. "Doesn't look like she's there either. Wait just a second."

Greg stepped deeper into the labyrinth. He asked a woman there about Felicia. "Where is she?"

Annie heard the woman say, "Where do you think? With Stuart, drinking daiquiris in Florida."

Annie's face grew hot. She quickly turned to look into Stuart's empty office. On a table next to a copper lamp was a picture of Stuart in a tuxedo and Annie in a gown, dressed for a charity ball. The perfect couple.

Greg cleared his throat. Annie turned to face him, hoping the color had faded from her cheeks.

"She's not here. Is there anything else I can help you with?" His eyes were kind, and she sensed what he didn't say had more to do with her pride than any desire to protect Stuart.

"No, thank you."

Annie could feel him watch her walk away, pulling her bag. She raised her chin and stepped deliberately.

Annie stared out the window of the subway car, seeing nothing. Instead, she was lost in the memories rewinding in her brain of the day's events. First, the lady on the airplane, blubbering out painful truths while they still had hours of an overseas flight to get through. Annie had done her best, serving lunch and then dinner to the business class customers, getting their extra drinks and hot fudge sundaes while all she wanted to do was lie back in a chair and cover herself with a blanket. Then the trip downtown and into Stuart's office building, looking absurd in her navy blue uniform and pulling her black rolling bag, all in the desire to see Stuart face-to-face and hear him confirm or deny for himself the woman's claims.

Why hadn't he told her about Martha leaving? And who was

this new Felicia, and why was she going to Florida with him? Martha had never traveled with him.

Inside his apartment, Annie found Stuart's note on the kitchen island: *Baby—big invitation from Jack Carney came through at lunch today. Can't pass it up. Will call you. Love, Stu*

Annie dropped on the cold leather couch, letting her rolling bag fall to the floor and her purse with it, its contents scattering when it hit the parquet floor. The escaping air from the leather couch and crash of her bag falling scared Chester off his perch and a flash of orange dashed across the floor.

Her hand trembled when she picked up her cell phone. It wasn't even turned on. She had forgotten to do it in her haste to leave the airplane. There were four voice mails.

Annie, I met the plane, and Janice said you were already gone! Get to my office now! Her boss, Bob Vichy, sounded irritated on the first message.

Bob needs to see you, Annie, Janice said. *I told him you had a family emergency. Better get back here as soon as possible. Call me after you meet with him.*

Annie, where are you? The plane landed an hour ago. I need to see you in my office today. Bob again, this time sounding angry.

The last message was from Stuart. *Hey, babe, thought you would be on the ground by now. Jack Carney invited me and some of his friends down to Miami for some golf and poker. We're at Teterboro loading Jack's G-5. I'll be back on Friday. Call me.*

She dialed the number, but it went immediately into voice mail. She ended the call and tried Bob Vichy. It also went to voice mail. *Bob, it's Annie. I had my phone off. I'll be there within the hour.*

The apartment felt like a shrinking box, with walls closing in and the ceiling crushing down. This place she had loved, because it was Stuart's and she loved him. Now it felt cold and sinister, as if it held secrets she didn't want to know. He had owned it for six years, he once told her. *They must have picked it out together*, she thought, looking around the apartment with a new understanding. Sandy and Stuart together, until it became obvious he wanted nothing more permanent.

In the corner of the room, the peace lily wilted, once again lacking water. The sight of it caused her eyes to well with tears. Annie shuddered, feeling as if the temperature in the room had dropped several degrees. She had to get out, but before she did, Annie took off the diamond earrings and placed them on Stuart's nightstand. They looked so pretty, glistening against the shiny black lacquer.

At the door, Annie took a last look around while Chester's green eyes bored into her. The sight of him reminded her to add food and water to the feeders. It wasn't his fault, after all. "There, enough for you until your owner gets back." She bent down and scratched Chester behind the ear. "Go play with the toilet paper."

In one last defiant gesture, Annie swept the sagging peace lily onto her hip like a toddler before grabbing the rolling bag with her free hand. *I'll come back for the rest of my things later.*

"Another flight today, Miss Taylor? They're working you awful hard," Howard the doorman said as he held open the door and smiled, his eyes on the wilted plant.

Even Howard would have known about Sandy.

***

Annie hailed a cab for the trip back to the airport and her supervisor's office. After swiping her access card, she was admitted into a buzzing hive of activity inside the TransAir offices. Solemn-faced executives moved from offices to cubicles, giving and taking instructions, checking computers, talking on phones and huddling for subdued conversations in the hallways.

Annie heard Bob before she saw him. Dropping the handle of her luggage at the door, Annie shifted the peace lily onto her other hip and waited at the threshold. Bob waved wildly with one hand while he yelled into the phone.

"It's out of my control! There's nothing I can do!" He saw Annie and motioned for her to come in. "Hey, we'll talk about this later. I gotta go." He slammed down the phone and turned to Annie. "It's about time you got here. Where were you? I met the plane and you were already gone. And what is that?" He pointed to the plant as if it were a criminal.

"It's from here. Long story. What's wrong?"

"It's done. Patriot bought us out. Effective immediately. They already worked everything out so when they told the employees, it would be a neat, clean cut. It happened yesterday. My other flight attendants have been told, but I had several planes in the air. When I got to your gate, you were gone. What's that all about, anyway? They're about to go public with the news and I'm in hot water if I can't tell all my people first."

"It was an emergency. I'm sorry. So what are you saying, Bob?"

"I'm saying you don't have a job ... right now, anyway. I barely have a job."

Annie felt her legs give way. She sat hard in the chair.

Bob sighed and walked around to the front of his desk. "Look, there's a chance we can hire you back in a few months after all this settles down. I met with my new boss this morning. Patriot plans to hire back the best down the road, after they combine routes and figure out what they need and what they don't. You are at the top of my list."

"How long?" she asked.

"Three months, six months tops."

Annie felt lightheaded, as if she might pass out. "What about Janice?"

"We managed to save her and a few others who speak two languages." Bob poured a cup of coffee from a dirty Mr. Coffee carafe and handed it to her. "I'm sorry, Annie. I hate doing this. As far as work ethic, you're at the top, but between seniority stuff and Patriot wanting dual language speakers, I could only keep a small percentage. Take time off to enjoy life for a few months. I'll call as soon as I can get you back."

When Annie called Janice after leaving Bob's office, her friend insisted on her coming to stay with her in Brooklyn for a few days.

"Janice, you don't have to do this. I can stay at the apartment with the girls. Prema said there's an empty bed until the weekend."

"Mama DeVechio doesn't arrive until Sunday. I have an empty room until then," Janice said. "Please come."

Janice met her at the door and took the peace lily from her without asking questions. Her brown eyes were full of sympathy as she set the plant down in a corner of her dining room and then went to get water for it.

"What happened to Prema and your other roommates?" Janice asked.

"She's still on. Like you, the second language helped her. Kate and Evie don't work for TransAir, so they're not affected."

"That's good. Do you want something to eat?"

"No, not now."

"The kids have strict instructions not to bother you. If you need anything, let me know."

In the spare room of Janice's house, Annie waited for Stuart's return call, trying to calm herself in the storm of emotions that raged from anger to grief to disbelief. Her phone rang a little after eight.

"Hey, you're back!" His words were slightly slurred.

"Yeah, where are you?"

"On the patio of the golf club. It's beautiful down here. Wish you could have come with me."

"Sounds like there wouldn't have been room. When did Martha quit?"

Silence. "Did I not tell you about that? Yeah, she decided to go work for some charity uptown."

"Stuart, I lost my job today."

"What? You got fired?" He sounded incredulous.

"No, I got laid off." She felt irritation rising up. "Patriot bought us out."

"Babe, I am so sorry."

"I can probably go back in a few months."

"Good. You don't have to worry about paying rent. I can take care of you until you get back on your feet."

She took a deep breath and plunged in. "I met Sandy's aunt on the plane today. She told me all about you and Sandy. I remember you talking about the girl before me. I didn't remember the part about you living together, or the part about the cat being hers."

Silence. Then she could hear his hand muffle the phone. "Hey, guys, wait one minute." Silence again. "Honey, I'm sorry. I should have told you." His words lost their lazy slur.

Another deep breath. "Why would you lie about that, Stuart?"

"I was planning to tell you. It wasn't that big of a deal with Sandy."

Not a big deal. She could almost hear him talking to his next girlfriend about her. "It wasn't that big of a deal with Annie," he would say.

"Come on, honey, let's not mess things up while they're so good. We can talk about this later."

"I haven't messed anything up. You have."

"Okay, you're right, but we'll work it all out when I get home on Friday. I'm not thinking clearly right now."

"There's nothing to work out."

"Annie …?" She hung up the phone and turned it off.

In her mind, a memory arose with vivid clarity. They were walking around Battery Park last fall, early in their relationship, when the subject came up.

"I don't know if I ever want to get married," he had said.

"Maybe you haven't dated the right person," she had coyly responded.

"Maybe." They had both laughed, and Annie had felt at the time that he was laying down a challenge for her. It was as if he wanted her to change his mind, and she knew that she could. She would be the one he would want to settle with, to make a family with. She had known it to be possible, and so she had not given the exchange another thought until now.

That night in bed she lay staring at the ceiling of the DeVechio's guest bedroom, thinking about Stuart. The love blinders were off and she began recollecting flaws in his character, little things she had overlooked. Only two weeks ago, he had talked about fudging on his tax return. "Uncle Sam doesn't need it like I do," he had said.

Then there was the time she'd said no to an expensive bottle of wine. "Don't worry about it," he'd said. "The company's paying for it."

"Why would they pay for us to have dinner?"

"Annie, in this business, you have to look successful to be successful. If I don't look the part, no one will invest with me. There's a man here tonight I've been trying to get in to see. With a generous tip to the maître d', I got a phone call this afternoon and knew what time his reservation was. I'll stop by their table on the way to the restroom, say hello, have a brief chat, and I guarantee you I'll get in the next time I call."

It all seemed so staged, she had thought, but what did she know about his business? He lived in a world of lies and illusions. Why wouldn't he lie to her about his past? Worse, why wouldn't he lie to her about the future?

One minute she was weeping, and the next she was beating her fist into the pillow. She was angry with him—and herself. Denial and then disbelief had been her pattern with guys, starting with her high school sweetheart, Brett Bradshaw. He was the quarterback on the football team, the one who sealed her popularity and the one who moved on when he found a prettier cheerleader.

Then she met Bryan, the perfect anti-venom to Brett, who she dated throughout college. He was loads of laughs, someone she could really enjoy life with, until a string of DUIs made him decidedly not fun anymore. He was a drunk in the making.

After Bryan, there was Mike, the Texas businessman she met on commuter flights to Dallas. He seemed to have it all, until she found out about his wife, quietly wasting away in a nursing home with a brain injury. Stuart followed Mike.

And here she was: thirty-two, single, no children, no home and no job. She was empty. Poured out, emotionally parched.

On Friday, with Janice waiting below in the car, Annie went to Stuart's apartment to remove her few belongings before he returned home. For a few happy months, she had grown to

know his living space as if it had been her own. There were bits
of knowledge she would no longer need, like the name of the
mailman, the extra tug the door needed to lock and the day the
exterminator sprayed. There would be no need to worry about
a surly housekeeper or whether she had left something out of
place.

Refusing his calls and deleting his voice mails left Annie
with no knowledge of his plans, but he was never home during
the day. When he opened the door at the sound of her key in the
lock, she was surprised to see him. He was unshaven.

"Well, well. Coming back to the scene of the crime?"

"What crime?" she asked, dropping the empty bag.

"You stole my heart and ran away."

"You're drunk."

"Maybe. But, you're wrong to leave," he reached for her and
tried to pull her close.

Annie stiffened and pulled away. Her eyes scanned the room,
trying to remember what she left. She found jewelry, toiletries, a
few pieces of clothing and a couple of books. She threw them all
in the bag, hoping to leave as soon as possible.

"Aren't you going to take these?" he asked, holding the
diamond earrings in his hand. "I gave them to you, after all."

"Give them to Felicia."

"Oh, I see how it is. Pretty self-righteous for a girl who dated
a married man once."

Annie turned on him, heat rushing to her face.

"I told you, I didn't know he was married. As soon as I found
out, I broke it off." She jerked the bag and it flipped on its side.
She struggled to set it upright while Stuart laughed. Infuriated,
she lashed out. "I was completely honest with my background,
good and bad. Don't you dare try to use that against me."

"I'm only saying, neither of us is perfect."

Annie scanned the room and saw an afghan her grandmother
made and stuffed it in the bag.

"Annie, I'm sorry. Don't leave like this. Can't you see how
much I'm hurting?"

Annie zipped up the suitcase and pulled it to the door. She

pushed strands of hair out of her face and looked at Stuart.

"What I see is a self-centered, narcissistic, lying cheater." Chester rubbed against her leg and meowed.

Stuart's face twitched, as if he were fighting a grin.

"You're making a mistake."

Without responding, she slung her purse over her shoulder and pulled the bag to the elevator. Like Lot's fleeing family, she didn't look back for fear she would turn into a pillar of salt.

Chapter Four

BEULAH CAMPBELL THOUGHT everything had a purpose. This was instilled in her by Miss Mecie Tarter, her first Sunday school teacher at the Somerville Baptist Church. Miss Mecie would declare in her high, shrill voice, "God has created everything for a purpose. You too, dear children, have been created for a purpose."

When the rain came in torrents on the particular Saturday she had intended to buy plants for her garden, she decided it must be meant for her to clean house and prepare Sunday dinner instead. Tying a brown apron around her ample waist, she set to work seasoning a roast, washing potatoes and carrots, and placing them evenly around the roast in the pan. Sliding the pan into the refrigerator, she marked that off her list.

It was her week to host Sunday dinner for the single folks, a tradition begun after she was widowed and that she shared with Evelyn, her friend and neighbor for some thirty-odd years. Taking turns fixing the dinner after church made the work lighter on each of the widows. Everyone knew the rotation routine, and since the two women owned farms next to each other, all a guest had to do was drive up in one of the driveways and see where the cars were. The leftovers were never wasted and always went home with the younger folks, happy to have another home-cooked meal stashed in the refrigerator.

And younger folks were the regulars at Sunday dinner. The oldest was Woody Patterson, a fortysomething farmer and horse trader from over on Puny Branch. He nearly married once, years ago, but canceled at the last minute. He had proceeded to scandalize the town by going on his honeymoon anyway.

Sunday was a day for families to be together. For single folks, it could be right lonely. How well Beulah knew it, after losing Fred two years ago. Dear Fred. Her childhood sweetheart, the only man she ever loved. She still missed him something awful. During the week, a body could keep busy with work, going here or there, buying this or selling that, but when the quiet of Sunday came, she felt the lonesomes more than any other time. Church service and fellowship helped, but gathering around a table afterward with a tender pot roast put a salve on the wound like no other.

Beulah put on a pot of water to boil, then set about stirring up the cheese mixture for the macaroni. "As long as I'm able, we'll have food on the table," she always called out to admirers enjoying the feast. Everyone laughed at her rhyme, thinking she had created it on the spot. Truth was, it was something her grandmother said years ago, and Beulah had taken it for her own.

Most of the work for dinner was done on Saturday. She didn't believe in running around on Sunday with your tongue hanging out, disrespecting the Sabbath and disobeying the Lord's command to rest. Only the basics were left to do on Sunday morning, and when her guests straggled in after their respective church services, they knew to help set the table, pour tea, or clean up so the workload was spread lightly among them.

The green beans were cooked, and all that was left were the pies. She eased back in the wooden chair at her kitchen table and sipped black coffee, holding the mug with both hands. The sound of rain hitting her tin roof nearly lulled her to sleep. She sure hoped they weren't getting this downpour up in Louisville. She could picture all those women at the Derby, strutting around with their feathered and flowered hats, only to get doused with a downpour and looking like plucked chickens afterward.

Good rain, good rain. Fred had said it forty-leven times in their married life and it would be good for her garden. Beulah never put anything on her garden except a little manure for the soil—organic, they called it nowadays, although it was just common sense to her. She figured the bugs could have their fair share.

Beulah shifted in her seat to relieve an ache in her sore hip and thought about what was left to put in her garden. Heirloom seeds of Kentucky wonder beans, Roma beans, and sweet corn were already in the ground. The plants could be set in a week or so, depending on the forecast and the moon—stone and oxheart tomatoes; red, yellow and green peppers; yellow squash; zucchini; mushmelons; and if a filly won the Derby this year, eggplant. It was not a superstition, simply a frivolity she would allow herself. There was no way of explaining it, but her garden did better if a filly won the Derby, and Beulah had always wrestled so with eggplant.

The first time she discovered this phenomenon was in 1980, when Genuine Risk won the Kentucky Derby and her eggplant won first prize in the county fair. The next seven years were disastrous, until 1988 when a filly called Winning Colors won the Derby. That year, Beulah grew an eggplant the size of a watermelon. Word got out, and the weekly *Somerville Record* took a picture of her holding her prize like a baby. It was plastered on the front page, below the fold fortunately, so her face didn't peer out from every newspaper stand across the county for an entire week. Beulah decided from then on she would keep the size of her vegetables to herself.

The harvest-gold wall phone rang in the kitchen, jarring her thoughts.

As soon as Beulah said hello, Evelyn started talking.

"Beulah, I was catching up on the news this morning and saw that TransAir was taken over by another airline. Isn't that the one Annie works for?"

"Why, yes." Beulah knew this well for keeping her ears

perked as to any airline disaster, always concerned it could be Annie's plane.

"Well, they said a lot of people were laid off. Have you heard from Annie?"

"No, but she usually doesn't call until Sunday. No news is good news."

"That's right. See you tonight."

Beulah poured herself another cup of coffee and mused over the information. Truthfully, she worried about her granddaughter. In the last two years, Annie had called less. When she did, their talks were strained and distant. It didn't help that they hadn't seen each other for a year, other than a quick visit at Christmas. Annie blamed it on her schedule, which required more and more overseas flights, but Beulah sensed it was more than that.

Just Wednesday, Beulah had gotten a funny feeling that she needed to call Annie. Over her seventy-odd years, she'd learned to obey those promptings. When she dialed the number, an electronic voice answered, and Beulah hung up. She wasn't one to leave a message with a robot.

That night, Beulah's across the road neighbors, Joe and Betty Gibson, picked her up in Betty's pink Cadillac, the one she won several years ago for selling cosmetics. Betty had long gotten out of the makeup business, but the Cadillac still ran like a racehorse, hauling them to the Country Diner every Saturday night for supper.

Beulah grabbed her pocketbook and her plastic rain scarf and threw a heavy-knitted shawl around her shoulders. The rain had stopped, but the clouds looked as if they could overflow at any moment.

Joe opened the back door for her, and she slid in beside Evelyn. Beulah always felt a little sorry for Joe on the Saturday night outings. He chauffeured two widow women, held doors open, and sat quietly while they chattered like magpies with his wife, unable to get a word in if he wanted.

"Beulah, did you hear about Bob and Christine Gooch?" Betty's round face was anxious to tell the news she and Evelyn had obviously been talking about.

"No, what happened?"

"Well, they were sittin' in their recliners this afternoon watching that antique show, and a fellow walked right in the front door and demanded money. Bob didn't have time to get his gun, barely had time to lower the recliner when he heard the door open," Betty said.

"What happened?" Beulah asked.

"He gave him everything in his wallet, and that was near five hundred dollars."

"Land sakes," said Evelyn.

"Feller went right back out the front door, like he came in. His car was parked out on the road, so they didn't get the license plate number."

"I swan," Beulah said.

"Police said it was probably for drugs. You know that ox cotton and meth are gettin' awful around here." Betty shook her head.

"News people call them 'home invasions.' I believe that's the third one I've heard about this month. Do they think it's the same person?" Evelyn asked.

"Police don't know. The descriptions are different, but it might be a gang working together."

"Girls, you better keep your guns loaded and handy," Joe said.

Later, Joe's words echoed in Beulah's mind as she was getting ready for bed. It sounded like something Fred would have said, had he lived to hear about such things. If she'd heard it once, she'd heard it a thousand times: "Every woman needs to know how to load, shoot and clean a gun. You might need it for food, or you might need it to protect yourself."

In her nightgown, she got down on the floor, wincing at the pain in her left knee, while her hand searched for the shotgun that stayed under her bed. Pulling it out and blowing off the dust, she loaded it with shells from her nightstand drawer, then placed it right under the edge of the bed where it would be handy. It was nearly ten, past her bedtime, and when she finally did get to bed, she slept easier knowing the shotgun was loaded.

Thunder woke Beulah well after midnight. She listened to the storm at its worst and stayed awake as it abated, leaving only the patter of rain. Her knee might be going out, but her hearing was still crackerjack, she thought, hearing the refrigerator kick on from the kitchen. And above the gentle rain, she heard what distinctly sounded like a car door. Sitting up on the side of the bed, she listened intently. Another sound she couldn't quite make out. On alert now, Beulah reached for the gun.

She tiptoed into the second floor hallway, barely daring to breathe. Loud thumps sounded beyond the front door, as if someone was dropping something on the front porch.

From the top of the stairs, the full length of the front door came into view, thanks to the dim light of the downstairs lamp she had taken to leaving on at night after Fred died. Then there was another thump, followed by the sound of metal on metal as if a key were sliding in the lock.

Lifting the gun to her shoulder, Beulah spread her feet apart and steadied the barrel, drawing a bead just above the doorknob. Her mouth was dry as cotton batting.

The door cracked open. Beulah sucked in her breath, hearing Fred's words echo in her head: "Steady now, steady does it." A shadowy figure slid into the opening. The gun clicked as she cocked it, ready to fire.

"Hold it right there," she said.

The figure jerked, sending the vase perched on the hall table crashing to the floor. Two hands rose in surrender.

"Grandma, it's me!"

"Who?"

"Annie, your granddaughter!"

Beulah dropped the shotgun to her side, her arms suddenly feeling like Jell-O, and flipped on the light. "Law have mercy, child! What in the world are you doing sneaking around like a thief in the night? You like to have scared me to death."

"Well you scared me too!"

Beulah eased the hammer down and laid the shotgun next to the steps, barrel pointing away. Her heart was pounding so hard, she was afraid it might explode. *For heaven's sake, what was that child thinking?*

As Beulah made her way down the steps, she saw Annie's white face and knew her granddaughter had learned her lesson. But just to be sure, she said, "You should have called. What else was I to think when I hadn't seen hide nor hair of you for months."

"I did call, but no one answered," Annie said.

"Didn't I tell you the area code changed? I thought I wrote it in my last letter."

"I forgot, there was just so much going on."

Beulah noticed the puffy eyes and the strain around her granddaughter's pursed mouth.

"Well, we're up so we might as well have some tea."

While Annie slept late the next morning, Beulah wrapped herself in a thick cardigan and took her steaming cup of black coffee on the back porch. Settling herself in the painted metal chair, she looked about her and breathed in the crisp morning air.

These first days of spring were like sweets to a dieter, and she was greedy for as many as she could enjoy. Beulah admired the maples and the shagbark hickory, their leaves finally unfurled in an impressive mass of foliage. The only ones still standing naked were the walnuts, which was fair enough since they kept their leaves longest in autumn.

Annie was home. Usually Beulah was thrilled over Annie's visits, but she found herself a little miffed this morning. If she had known, she would have aired out the bed in Annie's room, baked chess pies instead of chocolate, and stocked up on groceries. She felt like the anticipation had been stolen from her, and on top of that, she nearly shot the child! A chilling shudder ran from her shoulders to her spine. What else was she to do when there was all this talk about home invasions? And Annie, dressed in black, using the front door like a stranger. Beulah shook her head and shuddered again, then whispered a prayer of gratitude that nothing more than a vase had been broken during the episode.

Beulah pulled the sweater tighter around her and puzzled over

Annie's situation. It made sense for Annie to come home, what with no job for a spell—Annie had broken the news to Beulah last night—but why come so sudden? On top of that, she had rented a car and drove all the way from New York City by herself. It seemed kind of desperate to Beulah, like she was running from something or somebody. Time would tell the truth of it.

Wiggling her toes, she felt the bunion on her right foot press against the soft leather of her shoe. It wasn't hurting today, which likely meant a dry spell coming up. Her neighbor, Joe Gibson, had already clipped the grass a couple times this spring but here it was, ready for another. If her knee didn't bother her so much, she had half a mind to start up the old mower out in the shed and do it herself. It was a hard thing, being a widow, but the infernal reminder of her dependency on others was the worst of it. Joe didn't mind, of course, but she couldn't stand to think she was ever a nuisance to someone.

They had worked out a deal for Joe to lease the farm after Fred died. He needed more land to graze his cattle and cut hay. She needed someone to tend to it.

"Mowing your yard is part and parcel of the bargain," Joe had said, but Beulah still felt like it was secret charity.

She looked at her watch and saw it was time to get ready for church. Annie was still in her bedroom and Beulah was glad she couldn't see how the stairs pained her knee. When she reached the top, she knocked on Annie's bedroom door and waited.

"Time to rise and shine. Sunday school starts in an hour," Beulah said, recalling the same line she'd used when Annie was a teenager. Back then, there was never a question of Annie going to church as long as she lived under their roof. Beulah still thought it was the respectful thing to do, but there was no sound coming from inside her granddaughter's room.

In her own bedroom across the hall, she tugged on her pantyhose and new floral dress she had bought at Penney's end of summer sale last year. With her Bible in hand and her tithe check in her pocketbook, she gave one last knock on the door of Annie's bedroom. Beulah frowned at the closed door and wondered how often her granddaughter missed church these days. Well, she would not alter her routine, visitor or no visitor. It was the Lord's Day, after all, and He deserved the first fruits. Annie could be dealt with later.

Beulah was surprised to see Annie's door still closed when she arrived home from church. After changing into her housedress, she made her way down the steps, not bothering to knock on her granddaughter's door. *If she slept through church, she might as well sleep through dinner*, she thought.

Evelyn was already in the kitchen moving around it with the familiarity they shared in each other's homes. Evelyn, nearly twenty years younger than Beulah, was elegant as usual in a pale pink suit, looking for all the world like she was taking lunch at the Idle Hour Country Club up in Lexington. As was their routine, Evelyn gave her the news from the Presbyterian's prayer list, and Beulah shared the concerns of the Baptists. In a small town, many of the prayer requests were the same, but there was always something new to talk over.

While Evelyn tied on a new apron and Beulah fished the vegetables out from the pot roast, she told her about the near disaster of the night before.

"Law have mercy, Beulah!" Evelyn said, clicking her tongue. "Thank the Lord you always leave that light on downstairs!"

"Somebody's here. Can you see who it is?" Beulah asked, hearing the gravel crunch in the drive.

"It's Woody. He must have worshipped in the great outdoors this morning. Looks like he just came from fishing," Evelyn said.

"For someone who likes the outdoors, he does manage to bring himself inside for food," Beulah said, chuckling.

The back porch door banged open. Woody stood with a string of fish in each hand, water dripping on the linoleum.

"Ladies, I've got you each a string of the finest blue gill and crappie my pond can produce. I'll even clean them for you if you tell me where to get started."

"My goodness, did you catch all those this morning?" Evelyn asked.

"They were biting like piranhas. It was hard for me to tear

myself away, but when I remembered the good meal waiting for me, it came easier."

Beulah thought Woody wasn't a bad-looking fellow, except when that unruly upper plate popped out of his mouth when he talked too fast. He never cared to clean up much either and one flap of his overalls usually flopped down on his chest.

"There's a bucket in the smokehouse. Put them in water, and I'll see to them later," Beulah said.

Shortly afterward, the divorced teacher Mary Beth White arrived in the same car as Lindy Childress, the young lawyer who came home to work in the family practice. Both attended the new Grace Community Church.

Lindy flopped her purse down in a corner and looked around the room. "Beulah, who's here with New York plates?"

"It's Annie's rental car. She came in late last night."

"I don't think I've met her before," Mary Beth said quietly, placing her purse next to Lindy's.

"Likely as not," said Beulah. "She hasn't been around much since she got out of college and moved off."

"She left about the time you moved here," Lindy said to Mary Beth. "I remember her from school, even though she was about five years older than me. Didn't she date Brett Bradshaw?"

Beulah nodded, not caring much to pursue that subject.

Woody came in from the back porch. "I went ahead and gutted them. All they need is a good scalin' and the heads off."

"You made fast work of it," Beulah said, shaking flour and water in a small jar, then adding it to the beef juices.

"Scott's tied up the next two Sundays eating with church members," Lindy said. "He wanted us to tell you not to throw his plate out. He'll be back."

"I'm glad the parishioners are taking care of him. I hope he's getting home-cooked meals and not something from a drive-through lane."

"Well, it is a young church," Lindy said, grinning at Beulah and pushing her dishwater blond hair out of her small face.

"I don't know what's wrong with these young people. My generation raised several kids and cooked their own food from what they grew. It was a pleasure to host the minister for Sunday dinner and everybody took turn' about doing it," Beulah said.

Evelyn rinsed the roasting pan and set it on the rack to dry. "Nowadays, all the women work. It's a different world."

"They're working because they want too much stuff. Live on less and be happy with what you've got; that's how I was raised."

Lindy put her arm around Beulah while she stirred the beef gravy. "Beulah, look at it this way. If the church members fed Scott like they should, he wouldn't be here with us so often, and you and Evelyn would miss out on promoting ecumenical harmony. Instead, here we are, Baptists and Presbyterians and … what are you, Woody?"

"An occasional Methodist," he said, pulling a piece of meat off the roast before Evelyn could smack his hand.

"An occasional Methodist. What do you think?" Lindy grinned at Beulah before kissing her on the cheek.

"I believe that university up in Lexington turned you into a slick-tongued lawyer, that's what I think."

"What can I do to help?" Mary Beth asked, her pretty auburn curls pulled back in a twist.

"You can put the green beans and the macaroni and cheese on the table. Lindy, you can pour the tea. Woody, grab that basket of rolls."

While Evelyn set the platter of roast beef, potatoes and carrots on the table, Beulah poured the gravy into a bowl.

"Is Annie coming down?" Lindy asked.

"I doubt it. She seems bent on sleeping all day." Beulah sat down and reached for Mary Beth's hand on her left and Woody's on her right.

"Woody, would you say grace for us?" Beulah said, catching Evelyn's sideways glance before they closed their eyes. It wouldn't hurt Woody to pray a little.

"Uh, all right, I reckon I can. God, thank you for this beef and the cow who give it up for us. Thank you for the taters and the carrots, the gravy Miss Beulah made, and the bread to sop it up with. Amen."

Chapter Five

ANNIE OPENED HER eyes and looked around the room, confused for a moment about where she was. Then she remembered the hours of driving, the midnight arrival, and finally climbing into bed in her old room. Sunlight slipped in, muted by lace curtains. Yellow- and white-flowered paper covered the walls. She had selected the pattern when she came to live with her grandparents after her mother died. Between two windows, an antique chest of drawers stood. On the other wall, a dressing table with a chair covered in pale pink chenille balanced the room. In the corner next to her bed was a round bedside table painted white. Nothing in the room had changed since she left for New York City, ten years before.

The long drive was tiring, but it was how she had wanted it.

"Why don't you call Bob and see if he can get you on a flight? That's the least he can do," Janice had suggested.

"No, I don't want to fly. I want to drive home and enjoy the scenery. It should take around twelve hours, not including stops, and if I get home late, so what?"

On Saturday morning, Annie had felt like a child leaving for school under Janice's mothering attention.

"Here's coffee in a thermos with cream, exactly how you like it. I don't have any muffins, but I put a banana in there. There's also a turkey sandwich packed with some carrot sticks and three bottles of water. Are you sure you want to do this? You've barely driven yourself in the last ten years. Is your driver's license up-to-date? I wish I had more to give you. I have to go to the store today, and I'm low on everything."

"Don't worry. I'll call you. Give the kids a kiss for me when they wake up and tell Jimmy thanks."

That was yesterday morning. Since then, she had driven miles of endless gray road, calling her grandmother's number with no answer, forgetting all about the area code change, and finally getting to the farm late at night in the middle of a rainstorm. Annie had parked out front because the back porch didn't have a roof and she wanted to get as close as she could to unload her things without getting soaked.

After the shotgun scare, Annie was too exhausted to go into more detail other than to tell her grandmother she had lost her job and was home for a visit. The rest of the story could wait. When they said goodnight after tea, Annie fell into the deepest sleep.

She awoke refreshed and relaxed. She folded her arms behind her head and stretched, enjoying the softness of the ragged quilt that had been on her bed as long as she remembered. Then she snuggled back into the aged and frayed cotton, not wanting to leave its comfort.

A few moments later, a savory smell seeped through the quilt, stirring up growls from her stomach. Voices and laughter filtered through the cracks in the hardwood floor. Stomach rumbling even louder, Annie forced herself to leave the warm nest. She dressed in dark jeans and a black cotton shirt. In the mirror, dark circles shadowed her brown eyes. Her hair needed a wash, but that could wait.

The clatter of silverware and plates masked the creaking stairs as Annie made her way down the steps and through the dining room. She stood outside the kitchen door, listening to the conversation, not wanting to disturb the pleasant din.

"Did y'all hear about the Gooches getting robbed?" a man said with a heavy country accent.

A female voice replied, "Detective Harris said the drug problem is the cause of the robberies lately."

"Is that Will Harris, Brian's son?" Evelyn asked.

"No, Will is Buddy's boy. Jeb is Brian's son," Beulah said.

"Oh yes, he's the one that works for the state police," Evelyn said.

"He's married to the girl from up North."

Annie couldn't bring herself to break the flow of conversation.

"Not married anymore," a girl said. "She left six months ago. In fact, the divorce is almost final. Jeb said she never liked it down here. When they couldn't have kids, she took it as a sign they should never have married and left. I think they've had trouble from day one."

"When I first got married, I thought it was the worst mistake of my life," Evelyn said. "I grew up in Lexington, and when Charlie wanted to bring me down here, I thought I had fallen off the edge of the earth into a terrible sinkhole. I didn't know the first thing about keeping house, much less anything to do with the farm. My parents were against the marriage and did everything they could to get me back home. If it hadn't been for Beulah helping me through that time and teaching me how to make a home and life on the farm, I wouldn't be here today. I've been without Charlie for five years now, but I couldn't imagine going back to Lexington."

Tears sprung to Annie's eyes, surprising her. She gathered herself and decided this was as good a time as any to make her entrance.

"Annie!" Evelyn's arms wrapped around Annie before she made it three feet into the kitchen.

Annie wanted to speak but the words choked in her throat. Instead, she enjoyed Evelyn's motherly embrace. When Evelyn released her, she turned to the others and said, "Annie is Beulah's granddaughter, but I feel like I partly raised her. She and Jake were together so much, it was like they were brother and sister." Evelyn squeezed Annie's hand.

"Hi, everybody," Annie said. She looked around the room and took in each person as Beulah made the introductions. Woody Patterson reminded her of a gangly teenager in his overalls, with his red hair, wild and curly. Mary Beth White was a pretty girl with a shy smile and Lindy had wide dancing eyes in a pixie face.

Woody stood. "Take my seat!"

"Woody, grab another chair there from the dining room," Beulah instructed. During the commotion, Evelyn poured her a glass of iced tea and Beulah filled a plate with roast beef, soft potatoes and carrots cooked in the juice of the meat, and tender green beans cooked for hours in fatback. Annie's mouth watered with the smell and sight of the food. It was no time to be concerned with fat grams and cholesterol.

Lindy sliced the pie and passed the dessert to the others while Mary Beth poured coffee.

"How long will you be here?" Lindy asked, sliding into her seat, her eyes bright.

"Close to a month. I'm waiting to get rehired by the airline that bought mine out," Annie said, shifting in her seat at the half-truth.

"I always thought flight attendants must have an exciting life," Lindy said. "I'm a lawyer. Mary Beth teaches at Somerville Elementary and Woody is a farmer. And that about sums up every occupation in Lincoln County."

Annie laughed with the rest of the group and then said, "Evelyn, how's Jake? I heard he got another promotion."

Evelyn delicately wiped her mouth. "He was offered another promotion a few weeks ago, but he turned it down. They wanted to groom him for the CEO position."

"But that's huge! Why would he say no to that?" Annie said, her fork in midair.

Evelyn glanced at Beulah, and Annie saw knowledge pass between them.

"Jake wants to pursue some other options. He's learned so much, but enough to make him realize he doesn't want to spend his life in banking. You can hear the rest from him. He's taking quite a bit of vacation over the next couple of months to decide what's next."

Annie put her fork down, suddenly feeling full. *Jake, home at the same time, after all these years.*

Evelyn reached for the percolator. "Who wants more coffee?"

"Can I get started on the dishes? I need to pick up the kids at three, and I promised them cookies when we got home," Mary Beth said, standing.

"I'll do your part this week," Lindy said. "You better get a move on if you have to be in Rutherford by three."

"I'll owe you one. Thank you both so much. Annie, it was nice to meet you," Mary Beth said before waving goodbye.

"Annie, if you want to go riding, all my horses are shod and ready to go," Woody's loud voice reverberated through the kitchen.

"Thanks," Annie said.

"Speakin' of horses, I better get going." He gulped down a swig of coffee, setting the mug hard on the wooden table. "I'm due over at the Barretts' at two for my saddle club's Sunday ride. Beulah, I'll bring you over the tomato plants this week. I've got to get mine, so I'll get yours too."

"Wait. I'll send you home with some meat," Beulah called, but Evelyn was already hunting out a Tupperware container from the cabinet.

Lindy washed the dishes and Annie dried, while Beulah and Evelyn fixed up another meal for Woody to take home.

"Maybe we can go to a movie sometime," Lindy said to Annie.

"That would be nice."

"There's also a coffee shop in Rutherford where they roast their own beans. You'll feel like you're back in New York," Lindy said. "As long as you have a good imagination."

After Lindy left, Annie folded the dish towel and draped it over the edge of the sink to dry. She filled her coffee cup and Beulah's and sat down at the table with the two other women.

"Evelyn, how do you feel about Jake turning down that promotion?" Annie asked. "It seems like a big opportunity."

"I think he made the right decision. He's worked hard in the last ten years, taken little time off and saved most of what he made. Now he wants to take a break and examine the possibilities of how to best use his skills and passions. Taking that promotion would have set his life on a course he didn't want."

"Not many young people think that hard about things," Beulah said, both hands cradling her cup. "Most just take what's doled out without a question of whether they should or not."

"Jake always was a deep thinker," Annie said.

"He may spend awhile thinking on something, but once he's decided, he'll give it his all," Evelyn said. "The next couple of months are critical, and Camille plans to spend some time down here as well, so it will be a good opportunity for us to get to know each other better."

"So you've met her?" Annie said.

"Only once since they started dating last fall. But Jake has known her father for years. He's been a mentor to Jake through the banking connections."

"At least he knows he likes the family," Beulah said.

"Yes, he certainly does." Evelyn stood and slowly untied the apron and folded it, staring out the kitchen window deep in thought.

"If you all do this every Sunday, shouldn't you think about getting a dishwasher, Grandma?"

"I never minded washing dishes," Beulah said.

"But it would save you so much time."

"I do some of my best thinking while I wash dishes."

Annie saw the faint trace of a smile on Evelyn's lips. "That's what I always told Suzanne, then I finally did break down and get one a few years ago."

Suzanne was Jake's dark-haired sister, five years older than him. "Are they still in Phoenix?"

Evelyn nodded while she put on her coat. "She and Steve are doing well. The kids keep them busy." Evelyn paused at the door. "I'm glad you're home, Annie. I hope you and Jake can spend some time together while you are both here."

After Evelyn left, Beulah settled into a kitchen chair. "It feels good to be off my feet," she said.

"You shouldn't do all this cooking every Sunday, Grandma.

You could take everyone to a restaurant instead. It would be so much easier." Annie refilled her coffee, added real whipping cream to it and started to look at the nutritional value, but decided against it.

"I enjoy it, and so does Evelyn. We help each other, so it's not too much work. After all, what else do I have to do on Saturdays? It gives me something to look forward to. I love to be around these young people. They lift my spirits."

"Couldn't you enjoy them at a restaurant?" Annie asked.

"Oh, maybe every now and then, but they look forward to a home-cooked meal. Most of them eat out all the time. This is a treat for them. And it's a gift Evelyn and I can give. The arrangement suits us."

Annie knew that was the end of the conversation.

After a few minutes of silence, Annie spoke. "I heard the conversation about local robberies before I came in for lunch. I can see why you were on edge last night. Are you locking your door now?"

"At night. I'm here during the day, other than running to town for this or that. I leave it open when I do leave, in case Joe needs to come in for something to drink."

"Have you thought about selling the farm and moving to town? You could get a nice one-story with a pretty lot and old trees. It would be easier to take care of. I bet Joe would buy this place from you and keep it agricultural, if that's your worry."

Annie thought her grandmother looked very tired when she brought up the subject of selling. It was almost as if a yoke had been dropped on her shoulders. This place was weighing her down. The burden of it was spelled out on her face.

But when she responded, Annie was surprised by her steely tone. "I would rather be a little uncomfortable in a familiar place than comfortable in an unfamiliar place. I plan to stay here as long as the Lord allows it."

Annie sighed. "At least consider a security system. If this drug problem persists, and it will in all likelihood, things will only get worse."

"We'll see," she said, and once again, Annie knew that was

the end of the subject.

Annie remembered with full clarity why she had hardly been home in the last two years. She couldn't agree with her grandmother on anything. Her grandfather had been the bridge between them, the peacemaker, and now he was gone. After less than twenty-four hours in the same house, Annie felt their vast differences. But now, there was no Grandpa to fill the gap.

Might as well get it over with, Annie thought. *Throw it all out there on the table.*

"Grandma, there's more to why I'm here than losing my job. I gave up my apartment with the intentions of moving in with Stuart. The day I was planning to move, I found out he lied about some important things—things I couldn't ignore."

Annie waited for a reaction, but her grandmother sat there with the usual stoic look.

"Anyway, I broke it off with him. I could have stayed in New York with friends, but I wanted to get out awhile and clear my head." Annie fiddled with the handle on the coffee cup. It was blue willow, a pattern her grandmother had had as long as Annie could remember.

"Well, you should know a man's not likely to buy a cow if he can get the milk for free."

The words stung her. It was high school all over again, and Annie felt the weight of her grandmother's calm disapproval, heavier than a tongue lashing.

It took her back to the summer after her junior year, climbing out of her bedroom window onto a branch of an old maple and sneaking off to meet the waiting car out on the road. The party in Von Linger's field lasted most of the night. The next morning, her grandmother roused her from a short sleep. A long list of farm chores had to be done that day—not the normal things, but cleaning out the chicken house and moving the manure pile. Without saying a single word, her grandmother's penetrating stare told her she knew it all and was dishing out the punishment.

Annie failed at controlling the irritation in her voice. "You're right, Grandma. But times have changed. It's hard to make it in the city without sharing living space. Besides, it's unfair and extremely politically incorrect to refer to people as cows."

Beulah reached across the table and covered Annie's hand with her own. The gesture surprised Annie, diffusing the anger. She couldn't meet her grandmother's gaze, instead staring at the older woman's hand. Skin thinning, with age spots and calluses; it was the hand of an active person. Years of using hoes, stripping tobacco, cooking and cleaning had marked them. They weren't pretty hands, but they had character, as if they could tell their own story apart from Beulah.

"People aren't cows. They have precious souls that can be easily damaged when too much is shared too soon." She removed her hand and laid it firmly on the table. "Now, you are welcome to stay here as long as you like. Frankly, I'd be grateful for the help. We're in the midst of putting out the garden, and I'm not getting around as good as I used to."

Annie nodded. The dread of truth-telling gone, surely now the worst was over.

Chapter Six

BEULAH GAZED OUT the window while she washed the evening's supper dishes. Long shadows spilled across the grass from the setting sun. The white blooms hung heavily on the locust trees out in the field, and the scent wafted in through the window screen. A rainy spring meant a good first hay cutting and it bode well for her garden. Seeing everything so young and green, with the full anticipation of summer stretching ahead, made her brim with hope and promise. It reminded her of the verse in Jeremiah she had taken for her own so many years ago: *"For I know the plans I have for you," declares the Lord. "Plans to prosper you and not to harm you, plans to give you hope and a future."*

If only the knowledge would take hold of Annie. She slept late her first few days at her grandmother's and didn't want to leave the house, other than to return the rental car. Annie hadn't even bothered with television, even though the TransAir merger was all over the news: jobs lost, lawsuits popping up right and left—a regular mess. Having dozens of TV channels was something Annie surely enjoyed about big city life.

Beulah remembered when Annie first moved in with them at age twelve after her mother died.

"Grandma, why can't you get cable? I'll pay the difference with my money."

"I've never seen good come out of watching television."

"But there are educational programs, even a travel channel, more than we get now. *Please*?" Annie had clasped her hands together and looked longingly at Beulah.

"You didn't have cable at your other house, and we're not going to have it here," Beulah had said, hoping that was the end of it.

"But we couldn't get it back there, and you can here. Jake has it, so if it comes to his house it would come here."

"Just because a body can do something doesn't always mean a body should. We don't need the extra expense, and you need to save your money for college."

"Grandpa wants it too," Annie had said, stomping off.

Fred hadn't wanted it, of course, but he never knew how to say no to Annie or her mother, Jo Anne, for that matter. It had always fallen to Beulah to hold the line on discipline. Losing Jo Anne had broken her heart. It would have been easy to give in to Jo Anne's beautiful daughter, the little girl who lost her mother and, for all intents and purposes, her father, but Beulah knew it would do the child no good in the long run. More than once, she had wished Fred had been stronger with Annie and Jo Anne. It was a man's duty, but not all men took to it. All in all, she never held it against him. Fred was a fine Christian man who loved and provided for her, Beulah reasoned, and that was what mattered.

Oh, how she missed Fred! He balanced her out, facing the world with a grin and a laugh. Losing him had created a vast hole in her heart these last two years. Worse still, he left her without any way to reach Annie. They were two different kind of people, she and Annie, and Beulah could not imagine what went on inside Annie's head. It was plain to see Annie felt the same about her. The visits from her granddaughter had nearly stopped altogether, like a well run dry in the middle of summer.

And what would Fred say now? He would be heartbroken to

know Annie had nearly moved in with a man before they were married. She wondered if Annie would have even considered such a thing if Fred were alive.

The similarities between Annie and Jo Anne were hard to ignore. Beulah wrung out the dishrag and hung it on the faucet, recalling the night Jo Anne came to tell them she was pregnant. She came by herself, even though she and Eddie had already gone to Tennessee and married. Beulah could still see her long brown hair, parted in the middle and hanging in her face. Part of her had wanted to reach out and push the hair back out of her face, but another part of her wanted to slap her child. Beulah felt a deep hurt and anger at her only child, throwing her life away like that.

Beulah had cautioned her against Eddie Taylor. He was a handsome fellow, but he came from a family full of liars and rakes. The saying was, "If a Taylor said it, don't believe it." But as is the way in this fallen world, they were a fine-looking bunch of smooth talkers, and her Jo Anne was not the first to fall under their spell. The whole county had believed Eddie's uncle when he ran for the state legislature. It had all gone fine, until the FBI found him to be siphoning off campaign donations.

But they had married, and she had hoped Eddie would be different. He wasn't. In less than a year, he was gone, and Jo Anne never saw him after that.

Beulah pulled out a red, blue and yellow checked towel from a cabinet drawer to dry the dishes. She liked color; it made her feel good. That was what Annie needed, she thought: color. She was always dressed in black. Who in the world wouldn't be depressed, wearing mourning clothes all the time?

"Why don't you wear that pretty red sweater?" Beulah had suggested before they went to church last Christmas.

"You don't like what I have on?"

"We are celebrating the birth of our Lord, not his death," Beulah had answered.

"It's just black, Grandma," she said. And so they trotted off to church, Annie in solid black and Beulah in her cream sweater with the gold Christmas tree pin that Fred had given her one

Christmas years ago. Annie needed color but Beulah would not suggest it again.

She might never have the relationship with Annie that Fred did, but she did know how to pray for her. And pray daily she did. It was no accident Annie was here. Beulah believed it was nothing short of divine providence.

With the colorful towel, Beulah dried the last dish and put it away. Then she went through her nightly ritual of filling the percolator basket with Maxwell House and the pot with water so it was ready to plug in when she got up. The quicker she could get that first cup of coffee, the better.

Her knee ached worse than usual—must be another big storm coming through. She winced with pain as she climbed the steps. That doctor was on her about getting it fixed, but it would have to wait. "Big storm comin' ...," she said aloud as she reached the final step, pulling herself up with the handrail.

Chapter Seven

ANNIE WAS RELIEVED when the voice mails from Stuart tapered off. She had left the ringer off, not wanting the temptation to answer.

One morning, finally feeling rested, she went out on the back porch and called Janice. Her friend was upbeat, a stark contrast to Annie's own dark funk.

"I think I'm going to like it better than TransAir," Janice said. "I'm on a route to Milan, and the other flight attendants are super nice. One girl is from Tennessee and she sounds like you."

"I want to get back so bad, I can't stand it!"

"Why? Do you know how many people would love to get a month in the country? This is a huge gift. Enjoy it!"

"Yeah, I guess. But it reminds me why I got out. I forgot how quiet it is. I feel like I might go crazy," Annie confessed.

"Just think about all the fresh air you're taking in," Janice said.

"Uh-huh. You mean that sweet air wafting over from the silo and the cow pastures?" Annie glanced at the silo, as if she could almost see the scent of fermentation coming her way.

Janice laughed. "Something like that. You should make the

most of it. Go fishing or snipe hunting or whatever it is you do in the country. Look up an old friend from school."

"Actually that may be easy to do. My friend Jake is coming down later this week." Annie traced a crack in the concrete with her finger. "We used to be really close, but we haven't been around each other in a long time."

"There you go. It's looking better already."

After the call to Janice, Annie returned Prema's voice mail and was updated on Prema's new roommate's strange fascination with David Bowie.

"It is very odd, Annie," Prema said. "She has plastered her side of the room with posters from the 1980s. Evie is disturbed by her friend's behavior and does not know what to think, waking up to a man with spiked hair and makeup every morning."

Annie had laughed with Prema, but when she hung up the phone, nothing seemed funny anymore. She missed her friends. She missed the bagel shop around the corner with the toasted everything bagels, rolled in seeds and spices and served with flavored cream cheese, and the rich Colombian coffee. She missed the horns honking, sirens wailing, the rumble of trucks, and the invisible pulsating energy that permeated the city. She missed the ethnic restaurants with the scent of exotic and faraway places blowing out of the exhaust fans on the sides of the buildings and the rare bookstore she could get lost in for hours.

Sitting on the back porch, Annie could hear nothing except the creak of the metal chair when she moved slightly to the left. She hadn't noticed the silence when she first arrived nearly as much as she did now. Maybe the city noises were still swirling around in her head the first few days but now they were gone and the quiet surrounded her like a padded room.

If there was something I could do, Annie thought. *A project. Something to make the time pass.*

Annie looked at her surroundings with the eyes of a newcomer in search of a job. The garden was one way to keep busy. Unfortunately, it was still too wet from the rains and it would be days before the soil dried. In the meantime, the plants

Woody had dropped off sat in trays next to the back door, looking like displaced refugees.

Her eyes wandered from the plants to the other side of the door where a pair of her grandfather's old work boots sat, exactly where he used to leave them at lunch, or dinner as they called it on the farm. After his funeral, a well-meaning neighbor had suggested Beulah leave them for strangers to think there was still a man in the house. Annie had to admit it did give the impression. It made her think her grandfather might be inside sitting in his recliner, watching a silent basketball game on television and listening to the radio, taking slow puffs on his pipe.

If the house was her grandmother's domain, the back of the house had been her grandfather's. He had puttered back and forth between the garage, house and equipment shed, firing up tractors in the gravel drive beyond the back porch and smoking his pipe under the maple tree in an old metal chair. The familiar feeling of grief clutched at her throat and made it hard to swallow the coffee she sipped. That was the trouble with being here. Everywhere she looked was a memory of her grandfather, of her mother, of her own disrupted childhood.

Annie flung the remnants of her coffee on the grass. It was weak, likely some cheap grocery store brand her grandmother had bought by clipping coupons. She stood and put her coffee cup in the chair. She raised her arms over her head and felt the muscles stretch down the side of her body.

She eyed the run-down outbuildings that used to be painted and repaired as often as the house. Like chicks with the mother hen, the buildings were smaller than the farmhouse but made with the same clapboard. "Dependencies" she'd heard them called one hot summer in Georgia when she took a plantation tour. The smaller buildings supported the work of the farm, but now they were in disrepair from lack of use. There was certainly work to be done, but it seemed overwhelming to Annie. They needed a carpenter, a painter, maybe even someone to lay stone. Not an out-of-work flight attendant.

She stepped off the porch onto the limestone steps that lay

even with the grass and led to the smokehouse. It was a perfectly square structure with a small chimney that poked out of the center of the roof. Annie could not think of a time when anything was smoked in there, but she did remember several country hams hanging by strings from the rafters to cure through the summer sweats.

With no windows to shed light, the inside was as dark as a cave. It took her eyes a few moments to adjust, but she instantly smelled the scent of animal fat that still lingered. A long wooden bowl, shaped like a bathtub, sat next to the wall on the dirt floor. It was used for rubbing the salt on the meat years ago, her grandma had told her. On hot summer afternoons, when the cool of the smokehouse offered a respite from the heat for two young children, it became a canoe for Annie and her friend Jake Wilder.

"Let's 'tend like we have to pick up supplies, and Indians are shooting arrows at us," Jake had said. They both hopped in the canoe and pretended to row and dodge arrows. After they tired of that, Annie offered another game. "Let's 'tend like we are going down Cumberland Falls!" They acted that one out and on and on it went until they were called in for supper. Some adults still played pretend, she thought, never growing out of the desire to be someone else.

She walked outside and behind the smokehouse to the tool shed. A riding lawn mower and push mower were parked under the shelter next to a weed eater, rakes and snow shovels. Various gardening tools hung from the wall. The rototiller was in the front, next to various cans of oil, gas and diesel.

Next to the smokehouse was the chicken house, empty now for how long she couldn't remember. On the far wall sat the rows of nesting boxes where the hens laid their treasured eggs. Gathering eggs had become one of her chores even before she moved in with her grandparents.

Annie felt a shiver run up her spine at the memory of the flogging she got one time from an old rooster. She could still feel the talons scratch at her arms and the wings so close to her head she thought it would eat her alive. Soon after, they feasted on rooster for supper. The meat was tough, but Annie ate her share, if only to spite the old thing. A younger rooster more scared of Annie replaced him, but the fear rose up when hens protested with cackles and squawks. Sometimes she left the eggs under the hens who gave her trouble, figuring it wasn't worth the fight. This worked until one day when her grandmother broke an egg and found a half-formed chick inside, and she had gotten a good switching. The only time she could get out of her egg duties was when Jake came over. He would reach into the nesting box without flinching and gather eggs from under a hen even as she pecked furiously at his hand. The Wilders only had dairy cows, so chickens were a novelty for him. The Campbells traded eggs and frying chickens to the Wilders for fresh milk, an arrangement that went on for years.

"Don't they hurt?" Annie used to ask Jake when a chicken would peck his hand.

"Nah. It's a lot better than getting stepped on by a Jersey," Jake would say, grinning and pulling out eggs as fast as her grandfather.

Behind the outbuildings and the garage, a plank fence separated the backyard from the barn lot. In the lot, the stock barn stood with its angled roof, setting it apart from the larger tobacco barn, just down the lane. Annie climbed the white plank fence, paint slipping off in paperlike sheets, and sat facing the back of the house. It was so familiar to her, yet in years past her visits never provided the time, or maybe she never took the time, to really look at this place with new eyes.

What she saw was work. There were many needed repairs on the outbuildings and the barn, certainly paint on everything, and who knew about the roofs? As her grandparents had aged, so had their ability to tend to the many aspects of a farm. The aesthetic qualities were secondary to the economics of running a farm, especially as human energy was a gradually diminishing commodity.

"The farm is paid for. I'll be all right," her grandmother had said to Evelyn after her grandfather died; but it was obvious there was little extra money to do any fixing up. Annie tried to persuade her to move to town after her grandfather had died, but Beulah would have none of it.

"I was born on this farm, and I plan to die on this farm," was exactly how she put it to Annie. And now, two years later, it sounded as if she hadn't changed her mind. Her grandmother was stubborn, but so was she. It might take time, but Annie made it her goal to persuade her grandmother to sell.

With a sense of resolution on at least one issue, Annie breathed deep the scent of honeysuckle and locust blooms wafting from the pasture. *Fresh air*, Janice had said, and Annie took another deep breath and then another.

Annie hopped down from the fence and carefully picked her way across the barn lot, trying to keep her good tennis shoes clean. The mystery of the hayloft was irresistible to her as a child, even though she had countless warnings about being careful not to fall from the loft. Placing her foot carefully on each ladder rung, she climbed to the top, not sure what she would find. But when she arrived, it was the essence of summer, rolled into square bales of hay, drawing her to it with the promise of comfort.

It had been years since she had hidden out here in the secret fort under the hay bales where no one could find her. She was glad to see this one thing still continued from the working farm she remembered. Annie stretched out and lay back on the bales, feeling the gentle pricks all over her body from the haystalks. Putting her hands behind her head, she stared at the open rafters above.

It was here she had prayed over and over, "Please God, heal my mother. Help her to feel better." He had not answered her prayer. Or maybe he hadn't heard it. Either way, her mother had died.

Other times, she had come here in the midst of the angst of growing up and over her frustration at how strict her grandmother was.

"All the other girls are going to the dance with a boy. Why can't I?" she had asked when the eighth-grade dance was announced at school.

"Because you are too young." Her grandmother had continued to peel the potatoes in the kitchen, her back to Annie.

"You're punishing me for what Mama did. It's not fair!" she exclaimed, stomping across the kitchen toward the back door.

Her grandmother turned at this and pointed the potato peeler at her. "This has nothing to do with your mother! If you don't straighten up, I'll cut a switch off that willow tree. You're not too old for a spanking, missy."

At that, Annie had fled to the barn loft and cried with the barn cats for comfort. She'd planned to stay there all night and catch pneumonia. Then her grandmother would be sorry. About dusk, the bats left their sleeping perches in the rafters of the loft and swooped down for their evening feast. When one fiendish creature swooped close to her head, Annie had decided a bed inside was worth foregoing her pride. She had crept in to find her grandparents already upstairs asleep, but a plate of food left warming on the stove. The next day *it* was never mentioned, but Annie knew she would not be going to the dance with a boy.

When she was here two years ago for her grandfather's funeral, she had not thought about going out to the barn. Instead, she'd cleaned the house, done laundry, scrubbed floors and windows, swept porches, washed the many empty casserole and cobbler dishes left by neighbors and helped her grandmother write thank-you notes. The activity had made the time pass. When all the chores were done, she went back to New York without ever grieving her grandfather in the places he spent so much time.

A breeze lifted a piece of the tin roof up and laid it gently down. Barn swallows scratched around in the rafters, making nests. A cat meowed from somewhere down below. Maybe it wasn't so quiet here after all.

Chapter Eight

FRIDAY MORNING, BEULAH piddled around the house, dusting furniture and doing a little laundry. About midmorning, she heard the wheels of a car crunch the gravel in the driveway. Evelyn came in carrying a Tupperware container while Beulah held the door.

"Your cinnamon rolls—how nice!" Beulah said.

"I couldn't resist. Annie looks like she needs fattening up."

Beulah reached for a coffee cup while Evelyn took off her jacket. "Well, Jake is coming down this weekend to meet with some farmers over in Rutherford. Camille has to work again and won't be able to join him."

"That's too bad," Beulah said.

"I do hope he brings her soon before they get too serious."

Evelyn sat down at the table, the air seeming to go out of her with the effort.

"I had everything ready, flowers in the guest room, fruit and whole grain waffles for breakfast tomorrow morning. This is the third time she has canceled. What do you make of that, Beulah?"

"Probably nothing. You know the young folks don't think much of commitments."

"I suppose, but it makes me wonder all the same. Are you still going with us to Old Mill for dinner tomorrow evening?

Jake said to invite Annie. With Camille not coming, he won't even have to change the reservation."

"Where are we going?" Annie asked as she entered the kitchen, taking a mug out of the cabinet and pouring herself coffee.

"I was just telling Beulah, Jake is coming down this weekend and has made plans for us all to go to the Old Mill on Saturday night for dinner."

"Last time we all went there together was Jake's graduation from college. What's the occasion?"

"It was Jake's idea for Mother's Day," said Evelyn, "and we thought it would be a nice place to take Camille."

"Is she coming?" Annie said, her voice trailing off as she eyed the cinnamon rolls.

"Not this time."

Evelyn pulled a cinnamon roll out of the container and put it on a plate for Annie. "I believe you still like these, unless your tastes have changed."

"There's not a bakery in Manhattan that makes anything close to your cinnamon rolls," Annie said. She pulled a small piece of the dough and stuffed it in her mouth. "Mmm. They're still warm."

Beulah was heartened to see Annie interested in the sweet bread. Her appetite had been poor since she'd been home.

Evelyn reached across the table and took Annie's hand. "I'm so sorry to hear about your job, dear. And your boyfriend."

Annie swallowed and let out a sigh. "I think I'll get my job back in a few months. I don't want the boyfriend back."

Evelyn leaned back in the chair, folding her arms and looking at Annie through narrowed eyes.

"Now, Annie, we have some fine, eligible bachelors here in town. You met Woody, and there's also Scott. They are both single. I'm sure we can come up with a few other prospects."

Beulah laughed. "Now, Evelyn, you know Scott and Mary Beth are sweet on each other, even though they haven't figured it out."

"I'm out," Annie said, rolling her eyes. "Even if I were interested, the odds are terrible for meeting someone here in Somerville. Everyone is married."

"Odds, schmodds!" cried Evelyn. "It's not quantity. It is

quality, and we've got quality here." Evelyn waved her hands as if to take in the entire county. Annie giggled, and Beulah realized it was the first time she'd heard her granddaughter laugh since she came home.

"Either way, here you are, and we are glad for it." Evelyn squeezed Annie's hand and smiled.

Right after Evelyn left, Beulah answered the phone while Annie wiped off the long farmhouse table.

"Hello, Bill," she said, wondering why the local diner owner was calling during breakfast, his busiest time of the day.

"Beulah, there's a woman here looking for a furnished place to rent for a couple of months. I knew the Millers moved out of your stone house awhile back. You interested?"

"Well, I might be. Is she from around here?"

"From up North. Says she's looking for a place to write a book and needs privacy. Offering cash up front for a couple of months. Want me to send her out?"

Beulah thought about the stone house, which had been sitting empty since March. It didn't do for a house to be without dwellers. Even checking on it regularly wasn't the same; and she could use the extra money to paint this house.

"I'll talk to her. Tell her to come to the back door."

Beulah hung up and stood for a moment, her hands on her hips.

"Who was that?" Annie asked.

"Bill said a woman's at the diner looking to rent a place. She's coming out so I can talk to her."

"How much do you normally charge?"

"Well, the Millers paid six hundred dollars a month, but they left furniture when they built their new house. Now I've got a furnished house and it seems like that ought to be worth a bit more."

Minutes later, a silver Focus pulled into the driveway. They watched from the kitchen window as a slightly plump woman got out of the car and pulled a green cardigan tightly around her, crossing her arms over it. She pushed her glasses back on her nose with one finger and studied the ground carefully for the stepping stones. *You would think she was walking through a minefield*, Beulah thought, even though they were level with the ground and offered no danger if she missed one. As she made her way to the house, red hair in flyaway frizz whipped around in the spring wind.

"Come in. I'm Beulah Campbell," she said, opening the back screen door.

"Stella Hawkins," the woman said, pulling her cardigan even tighter.

"This is my granddaughter, Annie Taylor," Beulah said, and then led them to the kitchen. "Would you like some iced tea, Ms. Hawkins?"

"No. The man at the diner said you have a place in the country that might be furnished."

Beulah pointed to a seat at the table and sat down herself but Stella Hawkins remained standing.

"I have a small stone house on back of my farm. There are two bedrooms upstairs, two rooms downstairs and a kitchen and bath built onto the first floor. It's very old, built around seventeen ninety. There's a small yard, fenced to keep the cows out. It's furnished, but it's nothing fancy."

"Is it private?"

Out of the corner of her eye Beulah could see Annie grin, but she purposely did not look at her.

"Very. There's only one other farm back that way and no houses."

Stella nodded. "I have … two thousand in cash. I don't know how long I'll need it. Maybe two or three months," she said, her eyes blinking a nervous rhythm behind the glasses. "Are utilities included?"

Beulah retrieved the key from a nail next to the wall phone. "Why don't you look at it first before you decide. Here's the key. It's probably unlocked, but in case you take it, this is the key you can use. And yes, utilities are included."

"I need privacy," she said, taking the key.

"Bill said you were working on a book?" Annie said.

"Oh, yeah … well, I'd rather not talk about it if you don't mind." The woman's pale cheeks reddened. Beulah wasn't sure if it was embarrassment or frustration.

Annie arched her eyebrows and started to say more, but Beulah cut her off.

"You can have the house if you want it, Ms. Hawkins. Go back out to May Hollow Road and take a left out of my driveway. Take the next left on to Gibson's Creek Road. You'll take another left a quarter mile back. You'll see a bridge going over the creek. The house is just beyond the bridge. The other way is a dirt road straight back here behind this house, but I'd prefer you to use the paved road. The utilities are still on, so everything should be in working order."

Stella Hawkins nodded and pulled a thick white envelope out of her handbag.

"Thank you," she said, laying the envelope on the table.

Beulah wrote her name and number on a piece of scrap paper and handed it to her. "Here's my number if you need anything."

"Where are you from, Stella?" Annie asked.

"Here and there, up North lately," she said. "Okay, thank you." She backed a few steps away then turned to go, nearly running into the doorframe before she found the handle to the door.

After the woman left, Annie said, "That was weird, Grandma. Something is not right with that woman. You should have counted that money in front of her. It may be a wad of newspaper!"

"Now, Annie, this woman will be living on our farm, and I don't want to start right off showing her we don't trust her." Beulah laid the envelope on the kitchen table.

"Well I don't trust her," Annie said. "I've lived in the city too long." She sat down and started counting the bills.

"Looks to me like she just needs a new pair of eyeglasses. Probably ruined her eyes with all the book writing."

"Maybe," Annie said, and laid the last bill in the stack. "It's all here."

"People usually become who you think they are. I want her to believe that we trust her and will keep our end of the bargain. And, this money will go a long way toward painting the house."

Chapter Nine

ANNIE STARED AT the pile of clothes on her bed and fingered the faded colors and out-of-style fabrics, kept for what reason she didn't know. The mound of shoes on the floor contained everything from her first pair of pumps to a worn pair of work boots. Still waiting for the garden to dry out, she threw her energy into cleaning out her bedroom. But now that most of her old stuff was out of the closet, she slumped on the bed and faced the formidable task of deciding what to keep and what to throw away. On top of that, there seemed a hazy memory attached to every single item she handled.

Both prom dresses hung protected under a plastic cover by a hook on the back of the closet door: the long blue-satin dress she wore to her junior prom and the yellow chiffon she had worn her senior year. Both dates were with Brett, her high school sweetheart. Smoothing the skirt of the yellow chiffon, she remembered the crush she had had on Brett since the seventh grade when she first saw him in the middle school library. He never cast a glance in her direction until she made the cheerleading squad her sophomore year.

He asked her to Homecoming and from then on they were

an item, until he moved away to college and dumped her for another cheerleader. Her pride took a hit, but in a way it was a relief. Then there was nothing holding her back—no ties to Somerville other than her grandparents.

Annie's cell phone rang and jarred her back to the present.

"What's up?" It was Janice.

"I was cleaning out my closet, looking at old prom dresses and thinking about a high school boyfriend. How are you?"

"Speaking of old boyfriends, Stuart called to check on you. He said you won't return his calls. He wants to know where you are."

"What did you tell him?"

"I said you were at home, but don't worry. He thought I meant your old apartment, and I never corrected him. Good news! Beverly Enlo has an opening first of June, but you need to get your rent to her ASAP. She's got several girls lined up behind you."

"Great! Her place is just a few blocks from my old apartment." Annie scrambled for a pen and paper while Janice gave her the address and amount. "I'll get it in the mail today. How's it going with Mrs. DeVechio?"

"She's having a hard time adjusting. My kitchen is completely inadequate, according to her, and she keeps rearranging my drawers. But she's good with the kids and doesn't mind babysitting."

"And work?"

"Crazy. Bob said he's on the fast track to getting you back on. We need the help. They've got us selling bags of peanuts for five dollars!"

"No! Does anybody buy them?"

"Of course. You know how people are."

Annie smiled. Yes, she did.

"Alright, gotta go. I'll talk to you next week when I get back from Milan."

Annie barely knew Beverly Enlo, but apartments in Manhattan were hard to find. She didn't know Prema at all when they moved in together and she had become one of her best friends. If it didn't work out, she would hunt another situation, a thought that made her tired. Annie eyed the bed and ran her fingers through her hair. A quick nap would be nice. But her bed was covered with clothing, so back to work it was.

A garbage bag soon bulged with torn or stained clothes and miscellaneous trash. Another bag was filled with items for the Goodwill. The rest was placed back in the closet. In the process, she had found old jeans, T-shirts and tennis shoes that would be suitable for working around the farm.

A charcoal set she had used in a college art class caught her eye, and she left it out in case she might want to draw later. It had been years, and her relationship with art had gone from creator to admirer.

Suitcase finally emptied and stuffed under the bed, Annie stood and stretched. How long since she had gone for a run, or exercised at all? It was time, even though she would rather sleep. She wrestled the two full garbage bags down the stairs and into the kitchen.

"Well, looks like you've cleaned house," her grandmother said. She was sitting at the kitchen table in her print housedress, mixing sugar with flour into a yellow crockery bowl.

"I've made a start at least," Annie said. "I'll put these bags out here until we can get them to town if that's alright."

"Joe hauls garbage off on Mondays. The rest is fine to sit there."

Annie filled a glass with tap water and drank it down. "I forgot how bad the water tastes here," she said, grimacing. "Next time we're in town, I'll get some bottled water."

"Only get what you want. I'm used to it."

"I'm going out for a run," she said and was out the back door before her grandmother could reply.

Annie started off at a slow jog down the long drive. Lethargic after days without exercise, she tried distracting herself by taking in the surroundings.

Broken planks hung cockeyed from the fence behind the trees, reminding her of a man whose glasses were knocked sideways on his face. Her grandfather had kept it manicured, the maples and oaks lining both sides of the gravel like great escorts to anyone entering the farm. Now weeds grew between the trees and the fence.

At the end of the drive, she picked up her pace and turned left down May Hollow Road. The road was named after her grandmother's family and was the reason for Annie's middle name. For years she was called by the double name Annie May until she finally dropped the May in high school so it would sound more grown up.

Falling into the rhythm of her feet pounding against the macadam road, Annie felt better as the blood coursed through her veins and the oxygen pumped through her lungs. She ran for a couple of miles, only seeing two cars, before she turned back. Both drivers waved, and Annie waved back as a courtesy.

Nearing home, she turned right down Gibson's Creek Road, leaving the open rural road for a shadier tree-lined private road that separated the Campbell farm from the Gibson farm. Only the old stone house, the May family cemetery, and another entrance to Joe Gibson's farm were off this road. It dead-ended at the swimming hole, a section of Gibson's Creek wide enough and deep enough for a pool.

Annie had intended to go on home, but the stone house drew her and she had to see it first. It was where she had lived with her mother until her mother grew too sick to live on her own and they had both moved in with her grandparents. The house had always been occupied during her visits over the last several years, and she had not seen it empty since she was in college.

Annie slowed to a walk as she approached the entrance to the old stone house. It sat back off the road a thousand feet or more and was accessed by a wooden bridge that crossed Gibson's Creek. Sycamore trees lined the creek, their wide leaves providing so much shade the sun had a hard time poking through.

"You know, trolls live under that bridge," her mother's voice replayed in her head. "I'd keep away from there if I were you." It was her mother's way of keeping her off the bridge for safety, and it had worked. Instead, Annie spent hours behind a monstrous sycamore tree, waiting and watching for the trolls to appear.

Moving past the bridge entrance, Annie had a view of the old stone house through the trees. Stella Hawkins's silver car was parked in the gravel next to it. Annie examined the house and noted little had changed from her childhood. The plank fence still surrounded it, keeping cattle out of the front yard. Flagstone steps led from the parking place in front of the fence up to the front door. She wanted to go in, to see each room and remember the happy times with her mother, but with someone living there now, that was not possible.

Movement in an upstairs window caught her eye. She moved behind a tree and watched from around the great trunk. A blanket fell over the upstairs window and was adjusted with unseen hands. *As if there's anyone around to look in the windows out here in the middle of nowhere,* she thought. Annie watched a few more minutes as the downstairs windows were covered and never once did she see Stella Hawkins through the window. It was as if she took great care to stay out of the light. She would keep her eye on this Stella Hawkins. Something was off, but Annie couldn't put her finger on it.

The run back went fast as Annie fell into a rhythm. After stretching her legs again next to the shagbark hickory in the front yard, she plopped down on an old tractor tire that served as a flowerbed.

The tire was surprisingly comfortable. Leaning back to look up, she tried to take in the house from a newcomer's perspective, perhaps Stuart's if he had ever visited with her. It was a two-story Victorian farmhouse, white paint chipping from the clapboard. A paint job would do wonders, but it was nothing like the spacious mansions Stuart eyed greedily whenever they traveled together.

No, he would not like this place. He would have been charming to her grandmother, all the while making excuses about why they could only stay a couple of hours.

Annie could almost see it back when she was young, painted and cared for, her grandfather sitting on the front porch swing and smoking his pipe. It was another favorite outdoor spot, second only to the metal chair under the maple tree out back. After supper, he gravitated to the porch for his evening smoke while her grandmother cleared the dishes and prepared for the next day.

The porch ceiling was still painted sky blue. "It keeps the birds and wasps away," her grandfather had told her. "They think it's the sky."

It was also where she and her grandfather broke beans in the summer. They had sat gently swinging, a metal pan for the strings and ends, a pan for the broken beans between them, and a sack of freshly picked green beans from the garden. Annie looked at her fingers and remembered how sore they got after breaking beans several nights in a row. But that's how it was with a garden. When the food was coming in, it had to be dealt with or go to waste. Neither of her grandparents liked to see anything wasted.

Annie hadn't really minded the work, but she'd griped like any normal teenager. Sometimes they worked on the back porch if her grandmother was helping, but Annie's favorite times were in the swing on the front porch, working to the rhythm of katydids and the bullfrogs grunting dirges from the pond.

During those times, they talked like two friends. He listened without judgment, unlike her grandmother, who always seemed to want to teach her something, making a lesson out of everything.

When she told him about wanting to see the world, to do the things her mother was never able to do, he said, "I believe your mother would like that," a twinkle in his eye. "But don't forget to come home every now and again." It was wholly unlike her grandmother's response: "There's nothing out there you won't find right here. You'll do better to get an education and a steady job."

They seemed always at odds, she and her grandmother. But her grandfather had been the buffer between them, drawing both of them to him, and in effect, to each other.

"You two are just alike," he had said again, not long before he died.

Annie couldn't understand. "How can we be alike when we are total opposites?"

He chuckled, his lips quivering in amusement under his thick white moustache. "You'll see it one of these days."

Annie missed him terribly. The pain was as fresh as the day she heard he was gone. Evelyn had called her in New York. She was between trips and able to get a flight to Lexington almost immediately.

When she got home, she heard the details.

"I saw him plowing the front field earlier that morning," Joe Gibson had said. "Then near lunchtime, I noticed the tractor turning circles." Joe's voiced choked and it took him time to get the rest out. "I found him slumped over the steering wheel. He was already gone."

Her grandmother had gone to town that morning, and in the only time Annie had ever seen her cry, she allowed Evelyn to hold her while she said over and over, "If I had only been at home ..."

Annie pushed herself off the tractor tire and tried to shake off the darkness that fell on her with the remembering. It had to get better. If it didn't get better, she would have to leave.

Chapter Ten

BEULAH WOKE UP thinking about the two thousand dollars hidden in the freezer. It was in a coffee can, tucked behind a frozen chicken and a loaf of bread. *I need to get that money in the bank,* she thought, *what with the break-ins and robberies of late.* Beulah wrapped a robe around herself and started down the stairs, holding the handrail and taking one step at a time. The early morning was quiet. Annie was still in bed, and the morning light had yet to break over the horizon.

Her left knee ached. Dr. Bright had given her a prescription for the pain, but she had never been one to take much medicine. If it kept on, she might need to move herself down to the small room downstairs, at least until autumn when she could get that surgery. If she did, she would wait until after Annie left. There was no need to make a big deal out of all this in front of her.

In the kitchen, she plugged in the percolator before calling Betty Gibson. The invitation to the Old Mill meant they wouldn't be going out with the Gibsons to the Country Diner, their regular Saturday night plans.

Betty was hepped up this morning, torn to pieces over her cousin Bobby's troubled marriage. "It's a mess, Beulah, a terrible mess. His wife's done gone out and got a tattoo and a piercing in her belly button and her, a forty-year-old woman! Poor old Bobby Ray don't know what to do. A full-blown midlife crisis is what it is, plain and simple. She had them babies too young, and now she's awantin' to live her teenage years all over again." Beulah listened another few minutes before finally breaking in and telling Betty she had to get off the phone. Betty could go on and on when it came to her family.

Beulah brought out her grocery list and looked it over. There were also a few things she needed at Walmart, much as she hated spending money at a store owned by a big corporation. If there was any other place in town to buy the things she needed, she would. Why, she had even taken to buying smaller rolls of toilet paper at the locally owned grocery to avoid patronizing the big chain. It was either that or drive all the way over to Rutherford for more of the same big corporations.

A new hoe from Duke's Hardware was also on her list, as was gassing up her car and running it through the car wash. There was no weekly wash-and-set at the hairdresser for her. Every woman in town who went to the Snip and Curl had the same look. No, she could do just as well washing her own hair and rolling it herself. That was one less errand and expense on Saturday morning.

"Good morning," Annie said, stretching and yawning in the doorway.

"You're up mighty early," Beulah said.

"I'm ready to tackle the garden," Annie said, pouring herself coffee.

"It's plenty dry enough now. Woody has the rodatilla gassed up," Beulah said in her deep country accent. "You put it on choke, let it have gas, then pull the starter. It should start right up, but you might have to give it another pull."

"Choke, gas, pull the starter. I got it," Annie said, sat down across from Beulah at the farm table and wiped the sleep out of her eyes. "I remember watching Grandpa run the rototiller, but I never used it."

"No, you were too young then and by the time you were old

enough, you were gone most of the summer with church camp, cheerleading camp, practices and such."

"I do remember picking tomatoes and beans, and breaking beans until my hands hurt. But you always did the canning."

Beulah had wondered at times if they had done the right thing with letting Annie run around so much in her youth. She seemed to thrive with all the social activity and it was hard to keep the child sequestered on a farm with two old people, especially after losing her mother. As a result, they had slacked up on her chores, especially in the summer when there were so many other opportunities for young people. But she was here now and ready to learn. Maybe it wasn't too late to impart some of the things her own parents had taught her and even to expect help from Annie while she stayed here.

Beulah took a breath and plunged in. "You'll see where I already planted beans and corn in the first four rows. Nothing is planted beyond that. Till everything past those four rows. Next week we can plant tomatoes, peppers, zucchini and squash. We'll plant more beans and corn in a couple of weeks so everything doesn't come in at once." Beulah shifted in her chair, finding a more comfortable place for her hip. "I am pleased to have you here, helping in this way."

"It's good to have something productive to do," Annie said, gulping her coffee before getting up to refill her cup. "More?"

Beulah handed her the cup. "I'll be back from town by lunchtime. If you have the garden tilled up and ready, I'll show you the rest. If we have to finish up on Monday, that's all right too."

"I could work on it tomorrow afternoon," Annie said.

Beulah looked at Annie sharply and started to speak.

"I know, I know," Annie said, a smile spreading across her face. "It's the Sabbath. 'Work on Sunday, come hard on Monday.'"

Beulah felt a big grin stretch across her own face to hear her father's word's come out of Annie's mouth.

***

Beulah parked the Marquis on Main Street, a few doors down from Duke's Hardware, her first stop. She was easing herself out of the car, hoping her left knee would cooperate, when she heard her name called out. When she turned, she saw it was Jake, grinning and coming toward her.

He was in blue jeans and a blue collared shirt, setting off the color of his eyes. "When did you get into town?" she asked as he offered his arm. He had fine lines around his eyes that crinkled when he grinned.

"Just a few minutes ago. I've got a lunch meeting at the diner with some friends. Where are you headed? I do door-to-door deliveries."

Beulah laughed. "I'm going right here to Duke's, so you've already delivered me."

"Mom said Annie's back. Will she be home this afternoon?"

"Should be working in the garden," Beulah said.

"Well now. That I would like to see. I'll stop by a little later," he said, walking backward for a step or two then turning to cross the street.

He reminded her so much of a young version of his father Charlie, tall with dark hair and a confidence that put everyone at ease.

But he has Evelyn's blue eyes and some of her soul, Beulah thought.

Chapter Eleven

CHOKE, GAS, STARTER. Annie leaned down and pulled hard on the starter chord. It didn't start. She pulled again. Nothing. Hands on her hips, Annie stood and tried to think of what to do next. Then she saw a black pickup ease up the drive and stop.

Betty and Joe Gibson got out and Annie met them between the garden and the drive. Betty waved excitedly while Joe trailed behind her.

"Law have mercy, our little Annie here at last!" Betty Gibson pulled Annie into her comfortable folds of flesh.

"It's good to see you," Annie said, trying hard to get her breath from Betty's tight grip. When Betty released her, Annie turned to Joe, who tipped his hat. He was a wiry, little man, the polar opposite of his wife both in appearance and demeanor.

"Child, we are so glad you're here! I declare, I could nearly pinch myself."

"You still flying?" Joe asked.

"Not right now, but I'll start back in a few months."

"Oh law," Betty said. "Joe, fetch those pies out of the car, please. I plumb forgot what I came for."

Joe returned carrying two pie plates, each covered with a kitchen towel.

"Are those your Derby pies?" Annie asked, her mouth watering at the thought.

"Yes." Betty grinned. "Except we can't call them Derby pies anymore because of some trademark business. Now we call them Kentucky nut pies, but we all know what they are." Her full lips outlined perfectly straight, white teeth, and her blue eyes grew big and she leaned in as if to tell a secret.

"We had a pie auction at church last Saturday night, and don't you know my pies went for fifty dollars each? Course, it was for the youth's annual mission trip up in the mountains, so it was for a good cause, but I declare, I never heard tell of sellin' a pie for fifty dollars. Tickled me pink, I must admit." Betty glanced up to the sky meekly. "Lord forgive me."

"Come on in," Annie said. "I've got some coffee on."

"No, no, we have to go," Betty said. "We've got to run to town for some groceries."

"I'll get your tiller started for you," Joe said. "Sometimes it needs a little gas poured on the carburetor."

In less than a minute, Joe had the motor roaring. He turned it over to her and she yelled her "thanks" above the engine noise. Annie waved and waited until they left before allowing the machine to inch forward by pulling the bar below the handle. She settled it into the row she wanted to till, then pulled the lever to lower the tines. Steadying the machine and trying to direct it in a straight line meant a strong hold on the handles. Great for upper body conditioning, she thought, as she felt the muscles in her arms tighten.

As she guided the machine slowly down the row, black dirt was tossed like a salad behind the twirling tines. It looked so rich and loose, she regretted having to leave her footprints in the soil as she walked over the newly worked dirt.

She released the tines, moved out on the grass, turned and went back into the garden. *Release, turn, engage, forward,* she thought. It was almost rhythmic, like a familiar song she hadn't heard in years. *Release, turn, engage, forward.* It felt good to do something physical, something outside in the sunshine rather than closed up in a fuselage or a tiny apartment.

At the last turn, Annie saw a man walk around the corner of the house. She felt slightly irritated. How did anyone get any work done with neighbors stopping by all the time? She made the turn and ignored the approaching man behind her, determined to finish the row. Before the next turn, she flicked the off switch and let the motor purr to a stop.

"Annie May, Beulah said I'd find you in the garden but I didn't really believe it."

"Jake!"

And without speaking another word, they embraced.

When they released each other, Annie suddenly felt self-conscious. She was sweaty and dirty after all. And Jake smelled so clean and looked so grown up with a day's growth of beard and his T-shirt stretched over broad shoulders.

"You look great, like always," he said.

Annie smiled back and noticed the tiny scar over his left eye, the one he had gotten playing baseball, and the familiar smile with the one front tooth that turned in slightly. She knew his features as if they were her own, and yet he seemed so different. The boy she had known was gone.

"I'm sure I'm a mess," she said, pushing the hair off her face with the back of her hand. "I forgot how much hard work this is!"

"Hard on the body, but good for the soul," he said, shoving his hands in his pockets. "Wanna take a break?"

She nodded and they moved to the old maple and sat down under its shade.

"I guess banking hasn't been too good for the soul lately, what with the economy and all," Annie said.

"Crazy. It's unbelievable how much debt people took on, and the banks were right there feeding the addiction. You know what Fred always said: 'Debt is bad, saving is good.' "

Jake waited for her to finish.

" 'Giving is fun, stuff is meaningless,' " she continued, laughing. "Remember that summer when he made us memorize it? We were helping him paint the fence, over and over."

"It stuck with me. Simple wisdom is the best," he said, fiddling with a small stick. "And what about you? Mom said you're waiting to be rehired by the new airline. How long will you be here?"

"A couple of weeks at least, maybe more," she said. "Although I won't get rehired that fast. I have some things I need to work out as soon as I can, like where to live."

"Sounds like you hit a little turbulence," he said, his eyes on the stick he twirled through his fingers.

"Yeah," Annie said. "I guess that's a good way to put it."

He tossed the stick and stood. "How about I give you a break and finish the last row? I need something to brag to Beulah about tonight when we go to dinner."

Annie smiled back at him. "You don't have to brag. She already thinks you hung the moon."

"Misguided, but I'll never set her straight!" he said.

Annie laughed, remembering how Beulah never acknowledged Jake's mischievous side, a quality well known to the rest of them. When they were twelve, Jake shot his .22 rifle into their chicken house and killed one of the chickens. Annie was sure he was in for it from her grandmother, but Beulah had defended him completely, saying, "I was about ready for a fried chicken dinner, and it was a nice clean shot."

Inside, Annie poured each of them a glass of sweet tea. She watched through the window as Jake finished the last row, handling the machine as if he had done it a hundred times.

The last time they were together was his father's funeral. With hoards of people gathered, they had stolen some time during the meal at his home. But they were soon interrupted and then she had to go back to New York.

When her own grandfather had died, Jake was in Asia and unable to get home in time for the funeral. When he did come to pay his respects to Beulah, Annie had already gone back to work. There had been phone calls from time to time, just to keep in touch, but very little time together.

He turned the machine off, wheeled it into the storage shed, and strode toward her on the back porch. She handed him the glass of tea and they sat down on the metal chairs.

"What about you? Evelyn said you were deciding what to do next. Any ideas?"

"Lots of ideas. Camille's dad—Camille is my girlfriend— wants me to go into the hotel business with him. But my real passion is farming. I want to spend the next few weeks exploring that option first."

"You know firsthand how hard it is, Jake. Nobody can make a living anymore without a big operation."

"That's exactly the point. The land has to be managed in a way that makes it sustainable and not part of some big food machine." He ran his fingers through his hair, a sign of frustration Annie recognized from their childhood. "Things have to change, and I want to be a part of it. As it turns out, there are some guys over in Rutherford who are thinking the same way. We're meeting this week to talk."

"What does your girlfriend think of all this?"

A dandelion was growing between a crack in the concrete porch. Annie bent down and picked it.

Jake leaned back in his chair and thought for a few seconds.

"Naturally, she would like to see me go into business with her father. He was actually a friend of mine before I met Camille," he said. "But she's supportive. I think she'll come around, especially after she spends some time here this summer." He looked at his watch. "I better get home. Mom needs help moving some furniture. Wanna walk to the crossover?"

"Sure," Annie said.

"Good. So you can tell me about this guy."

Annie felt her chest tighten. "There's not much to tell. I made a stupid mistake. Now that I'm away from him, I don't even know how I fell for him in the first place. My same old pattern."

"Sounds like it," he said. She stopped suddenly, surprised he agreed with her.

"I don't mean it that way," he said, grinning and steeling himself for her punch in the arm. "I mean it is your same old pattern, but it's because you pick guys you can walk away from."

"I don't exactly see you settled down either," she said.

"No, but I'm getting close. Camille could be the one," he said.

"Really," she said. "It's kind of weird to hear you say that."

"I think it's the first time I've said it, out loud anyway."

They came to the entrance of the long tobacco barn and stopped at the open doors. "You better get her down here quick to make sure she knows what she's getting into. Maybe arrange for some tobacco work, something to break her into farm life," Annie said.

Jake laughed.

"I'm not sure I can see her doing that. A few of those tobacco worms would send her running into the house. Anyway, that's history, so we'll have to come up with something else."

"Remember all those hot summers, breaking off the tops, row by row?" Annie asked, looking up at the barn.

"And the cold winters in the tobacco stripping room? You bet I do. I can still smell it."

They were both thoughtful for a moment.

Annie noticed the barn was still in good shape, its long, slim openings on the sides closed now because there was no tobacco to air out. Inside, the tier poles crisscrossed up to the vaulted tin roof, where men balanced precariously when the tobacco was strung onto sticks and hung to dry. From man to man to man, they took the tobacco to the top first and through the assembly line, working their way down until the entire barn was filled with the sweet-smelling plants. Annie was usually on the wagon, handing the sticks loaded with green and yellow leaves to the next person in line. Jake was always with the men in the tiers, close to the top.

The barn had not been used for years since the tobacco buyout had ended the Depression-era subsidy. But for generations, Kentuckians had been dependent on the crop and lives were planned around its seasons just as a brown thread might be woven through a tapestry. It was part of Annie's heritage, no matter her thoughts on the end product.

"Kind of sad for it to sit empty, but it was built for only one use," Annie said, still lost in her thoughts.

"I've heard of some farmers doing innovative things with their barns, like goat dairies, farm-to-table restaurants and even lodges," Jake said.

"It seems a waste sitting here empty, but I doubt my grandmother has the energy or money to try and make anything useful of hers. She needs to sell the farm and move to town."

"Whoa, wait a minute. Then what would she do?"

"Well, same thing she does now, but on one story and with neighbors close by."

"She has neighbors here. The house is big enough for a first-floor bedroom. What else?"

"She worries about it financially. You've seen the place, Jake! Everywhere you look something needs to be repaired or painted. In fact, she rented the stone house to a complete stranger because she offered two thousand in cash for the summer."

"Sounds like a good business deal to me," he said, grinning.

The banter was a game to him, and Annie refused to let him win quite yet. "It's too much for her age."

"She's barely over seventy. That's the new fifty," he said.

Annie shoved him gently, both laughing as if they were kids all over again.

When they reached the rock fence separating the Wilder farm from the Campbell farm, Annie hung back. Stone steps built into the wall had allowed an easy climb over. Ivy grew over the steps now, and they were barely visible, but they had once been a worn gateway into each other's world.

"See you tonight," Jake said, climbing the wall steps and jumping off the other side.

Annie walked home alongside the rock fence, thinking back over their time together. Jake was like a brother to her, yet the years had pushed them apart. Being with him again reminded her of their easy relationship, of how he made her laugh and his positive view of life.

It was strange, this feeling of not missing someone until you were with them, then wondering how you had gotten along so many years without them.

Chapter Twelve

"NOW, TAKE THE yardstick and measure three feet from this last row of beans," Beulah said, pointing out the distance with her finger. "Good. Use the sticks to stretch the rope and make a guide for your row. Then plant the tomatoes along that row, three feet apart."

"How deep?" Annie asked.

"Deep enough to bury the plant up to the first leaf. Put the plant in the hole, fill it with water, then cover it over with dirt."

Most folks never planted tomatoes deep enough, Beulah thought. Annie had assured her she wanted to do the work, so Beulah sat in the metal chair at the end of the garden and supervised.

"We'll need to stake them in a couple of weeks, or else they'll fall over like rag dolls come July, and all the tomatoes will rot on the ground."

Beulah's knee was as bad today as it had ever been. She had half a mind to take one of those pain pills, but she thought it might make her sleepy. Enduring the pain to get this garden out was worth it. She was keeping faith with the land, as she had done all these years. Never had she missed a year putting time into the garden, even when she was heavy with her two pregnancies. Fred helped break the ground in March and did the rototilling to get the soil ready, but it was Beulah who planted, weeded, harvested and canned the produce. Fred was proud of her work and the food she preserved every year, but for Beulah it went much deeper. The garden work ministered to her body and soul, much like the oxygen she breathed every day.

Before starting, they had gathered everything they would need: plants, seeds, hoe, trowel, yard stick, tobacco sticks, a rope for making straight rows, hammer and a five-gallon bucket. Beulah had put the bucket under the pump on the back porch and filled it halfway.

Annie had fetched the wheelbarrow stored in the smokehouse and they packed it full of the gardening equipment, seeds and plants. Beulah carried a tray of tomatoes and set them down at the edge of the garden.

Annie was working on the last plant, doing a fine job. Ignoring the discomfort in her knee, Beulah bent down to the ground and scooped a handful of the black dirt in her hand. It was the richest soil in the Bluegrass, with nothing like it for miles around. South of the county, the soil turned to red clay, but here it was black and fine as coffee grounds. She lifted it to her nose and inhaled the earthy scent. Beulah shut her eyes and breathed again, remembering in an instant her childhood, laughing and running from her brother Ephraim, as he chased her with a frog in his hand.

When Beulah opened her eyes, Annie was watching her, grinning. "I never saw anybody smell dirt," Annie said.

Beulah laughed again, feeling a deep contentment inside her take hold. She pushed herself up, trying to hide the struggle with her knee from Annie.

"This dirt holds our history. It's like a time machine for me. I never know what memory will play out when I smell it."

Annie bent down and scooped a handful and brought it to her nose. "Smells like dirt to me."

"You don't have as many memories here as I do. It'll come to you one day." Beulah reached for the hoe and used it to steady herself. "Land sakes, you worked the ground up so fine, it's almost like sand. We better put the zinnias and marigolds on this outside row." She pointed to the edge of the garden. "I left room when I planted that first row of beans. They'll keep bugs out of the garden and make nice cuttings for the kitchen table."

Beulah scattered the flower seeds and showed Annie how to rake the soil over them with the hoe. Annie finished the row of flowers and waited for the next instruction.

"Let's start another row here and put in more green beans. This time, you'll make a furrow with the edge of the hoe, like this," Beulah turned the hoe at an angle and dragged it a few inches so Annie would see what she meant. "Tighten the rope, three feet from the last row, and use it as a guide."

Beulah watched as Annie dragged the corner of the hoe the length of the garden. "That's good." A good straight row meant a person cared about her work.

"I remember dropping the seeds in, but how far apart?" Annie asked.

"Two or three inches. I'd rather have to thin the plants than have a sparse row."

Annie covered the seeds after dropping them. Beulah watched as she did another row of beans and then two rows of corn.

"We'll leave this space in the middle for more beans and corn in a couple of weeks. We don't want everything coming in at once or we'll be worked to death. On this end of the garden, we'll put our squash, zucchini and pepper plants."

Annie fetched plant trays for the final two rows.

"Space those out about four feet each so the vines have room to wind around," Beulah instructed.

She watched Annie on her knees, digging a hole for the plants with the trowel. It was then that Annie disappeared and instead, Beulah imagined it was Jo Anne digging the hole and dropping the plant in it, as she had done many times years ago. A red bandanna held her brown hair back from her face, her creamy skin a little too pale and her brown eyes seeking Beulah's for approval.

"Am I doing all right?" she called.

Beulah, transfixed by the image of her daughter, couldn't answer.

Jo Anne stood, dropping the trowel, and walked to her. "Grandma, are you all right?"

"Jo Anne ... Jo Anne," Beulah repeated.

"No, Grandma, it's me, Annie ... your granddaughter. Come sit here next to the smokehouse," Annie said, leading Beulah by the arm. "I think the sun might be too hot." Beulah followed and then sat hard on the stack of concrete blocks next to the smokehouse wall.

"I'll get you something to drink," Annie said, leaving her to puzzle out what had happened.

For a moment, Jo Anne was there. Beulah saw her plain as she saw the brown dirt in the garden. But Jo Anne was gone, having died at nearly the age Annie was right now. But she saw her, Beulah knew it.

"Here, drink this." Annie handed her a cold glass of sweet tea. "You look like you saw a ghost!"

"My knee's bothering me. Must be the pain," Beulah said.

"How long have you had pain in your knee?"

Beulah heard Annie, but the effort to respond was too much. "We're finished anyway," Annie said. "Rest here for a minute and then I'll help you back to the house."

Finished. *Finished gardening today or forever*?

The vividness of the vision faded, although the impression embedded itself in something tender deep within her.

After a few minutes of rest, she stood to go in the house. When she did, a searing pain ripped through her knee, and the smell of earth came full in her nostrils.

Chapter Thirteen

ANNIE'S EMERGENCY TRAINING as a flight attendant took over when her grandmother fell. She was by her side in an instant, relieved to see she was conscious and able to answer Annie's questions.

"My knee," her grandmother said, but Annie wanted to be sure it wasn't something more serious.

Worried it was sunstroke, or something worse, Annie said, "I'm calling an ambulance."

"Absolutely not!" Beulah called before Annie made it two steps away from her. "I'll not have sirens wailing up my driveway, scaring all the neighbors. It's my knee. Call Evelyn and see if Jake can come and help me get to the house."

Within minutes, the Wilders arrived. Evelyn held the door while Jake and Annie carried Beulah to the living room couch.

Jake positioned her across the faded polyester couch, and Evelyn threw a hand-knitted afghan of orange, green and gold yarn over her legs.

"I'll put away the garden equipment," Jake said.

"Thank you," Beulah replied.

"It's time for that medicine, Beulah," said Evelyn, and there was no question in her voice.

"It's in the cupboard next to the phone," Beulah said.

"What medicine?" Annie asked as she tucked the blanket around her grandmother's legs.

"Pain pills."

Evelyn brought the pill bottle back with a glass of water, and Beulah took it.

"What's wrong with your knee?" Annie asked.

Beulah looked up at Evelyn and Annie saw silent information pass between them.

"What? Somebody, out with it!" Annie insisted.

"Beulah, tell her or I will," Evelyn said.

"Oh, all right. I need a knee replacement. I'll do it this fall."

"Why does it have to wait? Why can't you get it done now?" Annie asked.

"Good question, dear," Evelyn said, folding her arms over her chest.

"Oh good heavens! In fifty years, I've never gone one summer without raising a garden or canning my own food. I'm not starting now, and that's the end of that. This is just a bad spell. It will ease off, and I'll be able to get around."

"But Grandma, you're in serious pain!" Annie protested.

"I'm not having the surgery now," Beulah said.

"Just rest, dear, and let the medicine start working," said Evelyn in a soothing voice.

"Evelyn, I'll have to take a rain check on the Old Mill, but Annie can go."

"No, I'll stay here with you," Annie said.

"We'll see you at lunch tomorrow if you're feeling better," Evelyn said, patting Beulah on the arm.

Beulah was relaxing and her eyes drooped, the medicine taking effect. Annie followed Evelyn out to the back porch.

"How long has she had this?" she asked.

"Dr. Bright referred her to a surgeon over three months ago. She won't do it until after summer. I've already tried."

"Why is a garden that important to her?" Annie asked. "I went to the cellar last week to get something for her, and there are still canned fruits and vegetables from a couple of years ago."

Evelyn sighed, her eyes following Jake as he pushed the

wheel barrow toward the equipment shed.

"Many reasons, some even I don't understand. But I do know food is her ministry. It's how she takes care of people. The garden is an important part of that. I think it also marks the seasons in her life. If she goes a year without doing it, then maybe it's the last time, which means she's growing old. It's a part of her life, a part of living on the farm. I think it's somehow tied to Fred too."

"Grandpa? How's that?"

"Fred used to brag and brag to anyone who would listen about Beulah's garden vegetables. Every Sunday in the summer, he would tell everyone at church how many quarts of beans she had put up, how many bags of corn she had frozen, how many quarts of tomatoes, on and on." Evelyn slid into the passenger side of Jake's SUV. "He was proud of her and her work. I think Beulah doesn't want to let go of that memory either."

"I put everything in the storage shed. Anything else we can do?" Jake asked.

"No. Thank you both for coming." Annie felt a grateful affection for both mother and son.

"We'll check on her later," Evelyn said before they turned around and headed down the driveway, the rear bumper bouncing as tires dropped into deep potholes.

It was after dark when Annie heard a quiet knock on the back door.

"Hey!" Jake said, after Annie answered. "How's Beulah?"

"Resting well. She must not take any medicine on a regular basis. That pain pill knocked her out! How was dinner?" Annie held the door, but Jake stood outside.

"Not the same. Can I offer you a fence post?" he asked.

Annie laughed. "Sure!"

She followed him out to the other side of the drive where the plank fence posts were positioned several feet apart. Annie and Jake selected two next to each other and climbed up to sit. No clouds obstructed the stars, and a full view of the spring night sky stretched above them.

"Ah, this is much better than sitting at the kitchen table," Annie said.

"Unless it's mealtime. Then there's no better place to be than Beulah's table," Jake said.

Annie sighed. "I'm going to have to do something about her bedroom. That couch is hard as a stone bench. And how has she climbed those stairs all this time?"

"She's tough."

"And stubborn."

"Reminds me of someone else."

"And who are you referring to?" Annie asked in mock sarcasm.

"Not many girls from Somerville have headed off to New York City after college. That takes guts and a strong will. I always admired that in you."

Annie soaked in his words and enjoyed the warmth it gave her.

"Thanks," she said quietly. "But I never looked at it that way. After college, I wanted a new start, away from everybody knowing my business. New York was the total opposite of Somerville."

In the easy silence between them, Annie rubbed her hands together, feeling the blisters below her fingers on the palm of her hands. Tenderly, she felt each one and thought about the hard work she had done today.

"So when are you hoping to make a decision about your future?" Annie asked.

"Hopefully by midsummer. If I decide to leave the bank, I want to give them as much notice as possible."

"Haven't you already decided to leave the bank by turning down the CEO track?"

"Not exactly. They've offered me a job with their foundation and I guess that's somewhat attractive."

"And where would you live if you moved back here?" Annie asked, wanting to know all the details of Jake's plans, maybe if only to make sure he had thought of everything.

"Probably the guesthouse. When Suzanne comes back to visit with the kids, she likes to stay in the house with Mom anyway so it's not used all that often. Then I can tramp mud all over the floor and not worry about Mom's garden club luncheons or whatever else she might be doing."

The guesthouse was a separate structure on the Wilder farm, built for servants in the late eighteen hundreds. Evelyn had remodeled it, adding a kitchenette and bathroom for her family to use when they visited from Lexington.

Annie had to ask him the question that had been on her mind since they talked that morning. "Jake, what is it about farming that you're so passionate about? It's hard work for a fraction of what you make in banking. I know how city people can idealize it, but you and I both know it can be a hard way to live."

She studied his face, dimly lit from the barn's security light, his brow furrowed, his eyes intense.

"Camille's dad invited me to tour one of his convention hotels in downtown Cincinnati a few months ago. When we got to the kitchen, he asked the chef to show me around while he returned a phone call. There was this huge walk-in freezer full of frozen meat, any way you like it, cooked, breaded and seasoned. Frozen vegetables ready-mixed with sauces. Outside the freezer were massive cans of processed cheese and other sauces to make up for the lack of flavor in the meat. In that moment, it was like all the dots connected for me. Everything I'd been reading about caring for the land and our food production from Wendell Berry to Michael Pollan all made sense. Farming has been reduced to ruining the land, the animals, and the produce in order to mass produce cheap food that is ruining our bodies." He took a deep breath. "I want to change that, Annie. Even if I don't do it full time, I want to start making a change on our farm. To start stewarding the resources God gave us the way they're meant to be."

The passion in his voice, no—his whole body—convinced Annie. Jake needed to do this thing, no matter the cost.

"Then you should do it. If you feel that way about it, you should do it no matter what it takes."

He looked at her then as if she had handed him a bar of gold straight from Fort Knox.

"Do you really think so?"

She nodded. "I'm just jealous that I don't feel that passionate about anything. I wish I did."

"Don't wish for it. It's made me miserable a few times this past year. I keep thinking I'm crazy for wanting to leave a great job, and nobody around me gets it. I can't tell you what it means to hear you say that."

"I do get it," she said. "And I wouldn't mind reading some of those books if you can give me some recommendations."

He laughed. "I can do better than that," he said, jumping off the post. "I'll bring you my copies when I go back to Cincinnati."

He held his arms out to help her down from her perch. "If you need help moving Beulah's bed downstairs, I'll be glad to lend a hand before I leave tomorrow."

When Annie lay in bed that night, the last thing she saw before falling asleep was her grandmother's twisted and pale face as she fell.

For all her mother's physical frailties, her grandmother had been the very opposite: hearty and tough, strong of mind and body. Annie believed her grandmother would always be there for her to push against. If her grandmother said something was black, Annie claimed it was white, while her grandfather mediated between the two.

After he died, Annie hadn't wanted to forge a new relationship with her grandmother. It was easier to ignore in New York where life traveled at the speed of light. But here, in the quiet and stillness of the country, the truth was plain.

Thinking back over the years past, she understood now that her grandmother had tried in the best way she knew how: phone calls, letters, requests for visits, admonitions when needed, and love in the way she knew how to show it. Annie, on the other hand, had focused only on herself, what she needed and what felt good to her. Annie had given nothing back. Even worse, she had pushed her grandmother away these last two years, when they needed each other more than ever.

There were no excuses now, no reasons not to do what was right. For once, she needed to put her grandmother's needs before her own. The decision settled, Annie finally gave in to a deep and peaceful sleep.

The next morning, Annie was up before her grandmother. She plugged in the percolator and was already into her first cup of coffee when her grandmother hobbled into the kitchen, using one of her grandfather's canes for support. Still in her nightdress and slippers, she looked older and weaker, Annie thought.

"How do you feel?" Annie asked.

"I'll be fine as soon as I get some coffee and take my pills. Don't believe I'll go to church today. First time I've missed since the weekend after Fred died."

"Sit down, and I'll get your coffee for you."

"Now, there's no sense in making a fuss," Beulah protested.

"I'm not making a fuss, only getting your coffee."

Reluctantly, Beulah sat down.

Annie talked as she poured. "Why don't we call that surgeon on Monday and make an appointment to see him?"

"Annie ..."

"Look, Grandma. I thought about it last night. I don't have a job right now. I can stay here and do the gardening and canning until you get back on your feet."

"Annie, you're going back to New York soon. We won't even get in to see the surgeon before then."

"Grandma, I can stay here as long as necessary. I might get my job back in three months, but it might be six. This is really a good time for you to have the operation."

"That's sweet of you, but your life is up North. You'll soon tire of caring for an old woman."

"Grandma," Annie leaned in. "I want to do this. Let me do something for you for once. You gave up your life to finish raising me. Now it's my turn to do one small thing for you."

There were tears in her grandmother's eyes, a rare thing indeed.

"Now, I don't remember anything about canning and not much about gardening, so you'll have to teach me. But I can do it."

"I've always wanted to teach you, but I couldn't figure how that would help you in New York City." Beulah laughed.

"It will help me more than you know."

Chapter Fourteen

BEULAH SIPPED HER coffee, trying to figure out what was different. She had told Annie how many scoops to put in the percolator basket, but it seemed much stronger. Personally, she always liked strong coffee, but it seemed a waste to run through a can too fast.

Sitting on the edge of her twin bed brought down from the spare bedroom upstairs, Beulah looked around her new bedroom, amazed at the miracle Annie and Jake had worked in only a couple of hours Sunday afternoon. They moved her sewing machine and table upstairs along with all the material and other supplies and moved the bed, nightstand, Bible and a lamp down the steps. Some of her clothes were now in the small closet where yards of material used to be, and lickety-split, she had a bedroom on the first floor.

Thank heavens Fred had the foresight to add a full bathroom onto the closed-in back porch when Annie entered her teenage years. He had taken to using that one, giving Beulah and Annie full control of the upstairs bathroom. Knowing Fred, he had probably also been thinking it would be a handy addition for their senior years, although he never said as much.

Last Sunday was the first time Beulah had missed church in years. Church attendance wasn't compulsory to being a Christian, Beulah knew that, but it was like the hand being separated from the arm: Missing church just didn't feel right. However, it was awful nice to rest, and what with the funny way those pain pills made her feel, it was better not to be in the church house and saying things a body wouldn't normally say.

Thinking of arms, Annie had become those for her these last couple of days. Arms and legs.

"Thank you, Lord," Beulah said the words out loud from an overflow in her heart. "What would I have done without her?"

Her granddaughter had called the surgeon on Monday and made her an appointment for later in the week. She must have worked some magic with the doctor's office. First they said it would be a couple of weeks, but Annie offered to bring her any time, even if it was a last-minute cancellation, and sure enough, they called back and changed it to Friday morning.

In the meantime, Annie had asked them about something to help Beulah walk until the surgery. They ordered her a brace, which, aggravating as it was, did steady her quite a bit.

Beulah reached for it, trying to remember how all those pieces of Velcro worked. Positioning her knee just so, she put the brace around it and studied which piece went in which loop. She heard the screen door slam and tried to hurry, not wanting Annie to think her a helpless old fool.

"Land sakes," she muttered when she missed threading a strap through a particular loop. "Looks like an ACE bandage would do as good."

"Need help?" Annie asked, popping around the corner.

Beulah sat up and sighed. "I reckon I'll get the hang of this thing, but you might need to show me again."

"It goes like this," Annie said, flipping the brace around so the straps fit easily into the loops. "You had it backward. Now, all finished."

Annie stood up and handed Beulah her cane.

"Thank you." Beulah steadied herself and hobbled toward

the kitchen.

"Where are you going?"

"Thought I'd make Ms. Hawkins a chicken casserole and coconut cream pie. She's been here over a week, and we haven't heard a peep out of her."

"That's a good thing, isn't it?"

"I just can't get her out of my mind. All hunch-shouldered and looking like the weight of the world was on her. It might be a way to check on her."

"Sure you're up to that?" Annie asked. Beulah could hear the doubt in her voice.

"I'll take it slow. You go on back to doing whatever you were doing," Beulah said, determined to take back control of her kitchen. Annie turned her face away, but not before Beulah saw the start of a grin.

"Okay. I'll be outside cleaning out the shed if you need me."

Before getting her hands on the chicken, Beulah peeked inside at the percolator basket, trying not to burn her fingers.

"Law have mercy!" she exclaimed. The basket was two-thirds full. "No wonder that coffee was strong."

With a deep sigh, she replaced the basket top and the percolator lid. *It's worth it to have Annie home*, she thought.

With old recipes she knew by heart, her mind was free to muse over the strange vision in the garden a few days ago. It was as if she had a visit from Jo Anne for a few moments, more vivid than any dream. Maybe it was only the combination of heat and pain in her knee, but it was as real to her as the ground beneath her feet. Of all places to see Jo Anne, the garden would be the spot. Her passion was growing things, and she would have felt plumb left out to look down from heaven and see both Beulah and Annie planting together.

Beulah slid the dishes in the oven and sat down, thinking of her precious girl, gone these many years. How time had gone by. Jo Anne died on July 15, coming up on twenty years. She never allowed herself to ask why it had to be Jo Anne. *If a body starts asking why the bad things, then you have to ask why the good to be fair.* Why did she have good health for seventy-odd years?

Why did they live in this beautiful countryside with food and with shelter over their heads? Why had she married the finest man in all of the Bluegrass when she was only eighteen? There would be no end to that line of thinking.

When Annie came in to clean up, she said she would ride over with Beulah and carry the food to Ms. Hawkins's door. The uneven flagstone steps to the front door of the stone house were hard to manage, even for a person with good knees.

"I'm ready," Beulah called upstairs.

"Be right down," Annie called back. In a few minutes Annie came down the steps in faded jeans and a blue T-shirt, carrying old pictures in her hand.

"Look at these," she said, and moved next to Beulah to look at the pictures with her. "Here we are with Mom in front of the stone house."

Beulah looked at it. "That must have been taken right about the time Jo Anne was diagnosed."

"Here's one with you and Grandpa, Evelyn, and Charlie, taken on Evelyn's front porch. You're all dressed up and wearing corsages."

Beulah knew immediately when that was taken.

"We were celebrating our anniversaries. It was our fortieth and Evelyn and Charlie's twentieth. We both married in October, twenty years apart."

"And there's another one of Jake and me, sitting on the plank fence by the corral. We must have been about ten."

"Now that's a rare picture. You two were never still long enough to get many pictures."

"I'd love to get these copied and framed."

"Wyatt's Drug Store does a good job on film development. It's right downtown near Duncan's Hardware."

"Good! I'll take them next time I'm in town." Annie carried the casserole wrapped in dish towels, still warm from the oven. Beulah carried the pie.

"Grandma, I can take it over there by myself if you don't feel like going."

"Heavens, no. I want to get out as much as I can while I can.

I'll be confined soon enough."

In a minute or two, Annie was pulling into the drive to the stone house and crossing the wooden bridge of the creek. The silver car was there. Blankets still covered the windows, like Annie said. *Why would this woman want to be shut up in a dark house on a sunny day like this?* Beulah didn't know a thing about how a person wrote a book. Maybe this was what it took.

Annie got the casserole dish in one arm and the pie in the other and carried them to the house. She had to set one down to knock on the door. Beulah noticed movement in one of the upstairs windows as if someone had peeked out. She watched as Annie knocked again. Another minute went by and finally, the door opened a crack. Annie was speaking through the door opening and trying to hand the food to her. The opening widened and she saw Stella Hawkins accept the dish and the pie.

Annie smiled at the woman, but the door was shut in her face as soon as Annie let go of the dishes. She turned back and raised her eyebrows at Beulah when she walked to the car.

"What was that all about?" Beulah asked when Annie got in.

Annie started the car and backed out. "I don't think she appreciates Southern hospitality. She said she was busy right now."

"Law, law," Beulah mused. "I've never heard of a body not appreciating home-cooked food. I guess she's not sick."

"What is that?" Annie said, slowing the car on the other side of the bridge.

Beulah peered at the tree Annie pointed to. There was a small brown square with a round circle in the middle nailed to an old oak. Annie stopped the car when she got across the bridge and got out to look.

Beulah waited on her to come back, wishing she could jump out and do things like she used to. In the rearview mirror, she could see Annie looking at the strange piece of plastic with what looked like a small antenna stuck on top. Annie didn't touch it, and Beulah noticed she was careful to stay on the side of it.

"What is it?" Beulah asked when Annie got back in the car.

"I think it might be a sensor that beeps when someone passes through. That's what it looks like anyway."

"I swan," Beulah said. "You mean it beeps in her house when somebody comes into the driveway?"

"Yep. Maybe Stella wants a warning. She might be a little afraid out here by herself. In fact, it wouldn't be a bad idea for you to have one. It would give you time to load your shotgun."

Beulah cut a sharp look at Annie and saw the grin on her face. She laughed.

"Well, you might be right about that. I might discover the first good use of all this technology."

Chapter Fifteen

THAT NIGHT, WHILE her grandmother watched a rerun of a Billy Graham special, Annie prepared the coffee, adding two heaping scoops more than her grandmother's instructions.

"Need anything before I go up?" Annie leaned around the base of the stair rail.

"Nothing dear. I'm fine."

Dear? When had her grandmother ever called her Dear? Evelyn always said it, but terms of endearment from her grandmother were rare as four-leaf clovers. She liked it.

Undressing in the bathroom, Annie turned the squeaky faucets in the clawfoot tub and let the water heat up before plugging the rubber stopper into the drain. A bottle of bath salts brought to her grandmother from a long-ago trip sat dusty and unopened on the shelf above the tub. Annie poured a generous amount under the hot flowing water.

While the tub filled, she mindlessly traced the rust stain that stretched from the spout to the drain. Gently, she climbed in and eased down into the water. Leaning back against the curved back of the tub, she let her mind roam over the events of the last couple of days.

Jake had called to see if they had gotten in to see the doctor. He was with Camille and made phone introductions to both her and her grandmother by speaker. Camille, or Cam as he called her, sounded nice enough, as much as one could tell over the phone.

Stella Hawkins, on the other hand, was not adorable. She was out of it, high on something. Her eyes were glazed and she slurred the words, "I'm busy" and seemed to take the food only to get rid of her.

Annie was glad she could keep an eye on the stranger for the next few months and curb any of her grandmother's neighborly overtures.

She pulled a wet washcloth over her face and let the heat open her pores. It reminded her of the day of spa pampering she enjoyed as part of Stuart's Christmas gift. Those times seemed so long ago. In quiet moments, she thought of Stuart and wondered what he was doing, what he was feeling or thinking.

Did he miss her, regret anything? Maybe even that was pride on her part. The best thing for her was to move forward and leave it in the past. The lump in her throat and the tightness in her stomach eased as each day went by in this place far away from him.

Annie reached for her cell phone perched on top of the commode.

"Annie, I'm glad you called!" Janice said. She could hear the clinking of dishes in the background.

"Are you in the middle of dinner?"

"We're cleaning up. Mama DeVechio fixed ravioli tonight." Her voice fell to a whisper. "She's cooking all the time. You know I told you she wasn't adjusting well. It all had to do with the kitchen. Once I turned it over to her, she has done wonderful! She feels like her job is to take care of feeding all of us!"

Annie laughed. "You wouldn't believe how much I've been eating these last few days. Every time I turn around, somebody is cooking a big meal."

"Listen to you—you're picking up that accent!"

"Really?" Annie was pleased. "It will be thick by the time

I get back. I'm staying a while longer to help my grandmother through a knee operation."

"Good!" Janice sounded happy, even relieved.

"How's the peace lily?" she asked.

"Great! Mama DeVechio told me I was watering it too much, so now she's in charge of that too."

"I'm glad something survived the relationship," Annie said. When Janice was silent, she asked, "Is something wrong?"

"Why am I always the one to break bad news to you?"

"What Janice?" Annie felt her heart sink.

"Stuart kept calling me about you. Turns out, it came down to wanting to know where to deliver the rest of your things."

"What things? I thought I got it all," Annie said.

"Some box you put in a closet to unpack after you moved in," Janice said.

"Oh," Annie said, remembering the box of journals and books she had brought over ahead of time.

"Anyway, I told him you would be living with Beverly Enlo when you came back. I'm sorry. I should have had him bring the stuff to me."

"No, that's okay. He would know soon enough, anyway."

"That's not all."

"Yes?" Annie waited.

"He took the stuff over last weekend. Apparently they ended up going out together that night."

"What?" Annie was stunned. "Beverly Enlo? She's not even cute!"

"It gets worse." She heard Janice take a deep breath. "They went out again Sunday night. Beverly said they want to see more of each other, and she knows it won't work with you living there. She is bringing your stuff to me later this week with your voided rent check."

Annie felt the breath leave her chest and for a moment was unable to take another.

"Are you there?" Janice asked.

Breathe, she told herself. "I'm here. But what about Felicia?"

"Who's Felicia?"

"Stuart's new secretary ... never mind."

"I told Beverly everything I knew about Stuart, what you found out about past girlfriends, your experience. It went right over her head. She was afraid to call, but wanted your e-mail address."

"I haven't laid eyes on a computer in two weeks, and my phone is spotty."

"Annie, I'm so sorry. When you come back at the end of the summer, stay with me until you find something. I'll keep looking in the meantime."

Annie said goodbye to Janice and hung up the phone. *So this is how he deals with it. Find someone new to take away the pain. Feel better, replace what was lost and grow something new on top of old roots.*

And she had thought he was calling because he missed her. Annie laughed out loud. "That son of a ..."

The next morning, Lindy called to see if Annie could meet for lunch at the diner. While Annie gathered her purse and keys, her grandmother moved slowly over to the shopping list next to the telephone. With her glasses held at a certain angle, her grandmother studied the list. "Bring me a five-pound bag of sugar and a pint of heavy whipping cream. I'll get my purse."

"No, I've got it. Call my cell phone if you think of anything else."

"Oh, wait a minute. Get that two thousand dollars out of the coffee can in the freezer. I've been keeping it in case that Ms. Hawkins changed her mind after staying there, but I'd better get it in the bank."

"You keep money in the freezer?"

"That's one of my hiding places. I'm not sure I remember where all I've stashed money over the years. If anything ever happens to me, go through everything before you sell it all off."

Annie tucked the wad of bills in her purse. Rolling down the windows of her grandmother's car, she took in deep breaths of the sweet scent of honeysuckle. Pulling out of the driveway and onto the two-lane road, Annie left the windows down, feeling a sense of freedom a closed car couldn't give.

She drove slowly, listening to the bobwhites call from the roadside forest as she followed the winding creek which led into town. The dense wilderness, thick with cane and trees, unfolded into flat farmland once again before reaching the town limits of Somerville, the county seat.

It was noon. The Somerville National Bank was next to the County Attorney's office, and Annie found a parking space on the street in front of both. She had hoped to get the money in the bank as soon as possible, but she didn't want to be late for her lunch with Lindy. When plans were firmed up over the weekend, she remembered Lindy saying she had to be in court right after lunch.

The law office was in an old Victorian building. The tall ceilings and wood floors lent an air of old-time lawyering. The secretary rang Lindy's office, and she appeared dressed in a crisp navy blue suit.

"Want to see my office?" Lindy asked.

"Sure," Annie said, following Lindy back to a beautiful room featuring a gas log fireplace and restored to its original woodwork.

"This is beautiful!" Annie said, admiring the painted woodwork and rich wood floors partially covered with a Persian rug. "I never dreamed these old buildings had such character."

"Dad owns the building, so he decided years ago to take it back to its original glory. I think he did a pretty good job."

"It's surprising," Annie said. "I wouldn't have thought these buildings could be so attractive on the inside."

"Time, work and money, but restoration is worth it," Lindy said as she led Annie back to the foyer. "If you're ready, we'll walk down to Bill's."

Just two blocks down the street, a red-and-white-striped awning marked the entrance to Bill's Diner.

"I remember the awning being blue and white when I worked here," Annie said as they approached.

"It was. He changed it last fall and upset everybody in town. Now that they have gotten used to it, I think they like it better."

Lindy pushed open the plate glass and metal door, which jingled the bell above. Several customers looked up to see who was coming through the door.

"Well, if it isn't the prodigal child come home!" Bill rubbed his hands on his white apron and bounded around the counter like a Saint Bernard. Annie met him and they hugged.

"Hey, Bill, how are you?"

She looked at him and noticed he had gained a few pounds, but for the most part, he looked the same.

"Ornery as an old hornet!" And to Lindy he said, "This girl was my star waitress for four years. Annie, can I interest you in a job?"

"Bill, I have waited on people from here to Singapore, and I'm taking a break. Thanks anyway. I'll let you know if I change my mind."

"Now, see! You've had a stellar career in the service industry and all because you got your start here. That airline ought to pay me for your good training." He went back to tending the hamburgers sizzling on the grill.

"What can I get for you two?" he called back.

"BLT," Annie said.

"Cheeseburger and fries for me," said Lindy.

Bill's BLT had been Annie's favorite sandwich for years. He piled on lots of bacon, ripe tomatoes, a generous piece of crisp lettuce, and a dollop of mayo on homemade sourdough bread.

Lindy chose a booth along the front window and they scooted in, Annie feeling a rip in the blue vinyl upholstery rub against her leg.

Looking around, she saw new red-and-white-checked curtains in the windows at each booth. Hissing sounds came from the grill where Bill dropped the bacon on it. Smoke rose as an exhaust fan sucked it out while Bill clattered around, pulling the other ingredients out for the sandwich.

The sounds and smells carried Annie back to her waitressing days in high school and college. Bill hired her to work the breakfast and lunch shift, but occasionally he'd need help in the evenings. Whenever she worked, she'd come home smelling like a bucket of lard. She took a bath as soon as she got off work, trying to rid her body, especially her hair, of the diner's scent. But she loved serving people, and Bill and his wife, Viola, were the perfect bosses for a first job.

"Does Viola still make those delicious cream pies?" Annie asked Lindy.

"Viola has Alzheimer's. When she has a good day, Bill lets her come down and pretend to help out in the kitchen, but he's had to hire an extra cook."

"I'm sorry to hear that," Annie said. "I guess I expected to come back and have everything be the same as it was ten years ago."

"It doesn't change much, not like the young folks would like. I'm one of a handful of single people my age here in town. Believe me, that gets old."

"I don't know—after what I've been through, that sounds pretty attractive right now."

"Bad luck in love, huh?" Lindy asked.

"Or bad choices."

A young waitress brought their food with two glasses of tea. "Bill said he thought you would want tea. Is that okay?"

"Great, thanks!" Lindy said to the waitress, then turned back to Annie. "I hope you stick around. It would be nice to hang out with someone who isn't already married with two kids."

Annie smiled. "At least a couple of months until Grandma recovers from knee surgery."

Bill walked over as he wiped his hands on a rag. "Did that lady rent the stone house from Beulah?"

Annie nodded, her mouth full of sandwich.

"She was turned a little odd, but you know how Northerners can be. I figured with it being a woman, and offering cash up front, it couldn't be too bad." Bill was summoned back to the grill by an employee in a grease-spattered white apron.

"Unless it's counterfeit," Lindy said.

Annie felt like her bite of sandwich turned into gravel as she half-choked it down.

"It's not impossible," Lindy said. "Believe me. I see everything in the court system."

Inside the bank foyer, Annie would like to have admired the marble floors, decorative iron support columns, and walnut teller windows even more, had she not felt a growing sense of anxiety.

Lindy stood with Annie as she handed the teller the twenty one-hundred-dollar bills.

"Into Mrs. Campbell's account?" said the teller. She typed away at a keyboard hidden below the granite and peered into a screen inset behind a hole cut in the stone.

"Yes, please."

"How is Beulah? We heard she had a fall in the garden on Saturday," the teller asked while her fingers clicked on the keyboard.

"She's better, thanks," Annie said, holding her breath and sensing Lindy doing the same thing while the teller counted out the bills and slashed them each with a yellow marker.

The teller put the money in the drawer and printed out a deposit receipt before handing it to Annie.

"So it's real?" Lindy asked.

She laughed. "Were you afraid it wasn't?"

"Actually, we were a little concerned," Annie said.

"You've seen the marker test before, I'm sure," the teller said. "We're also trained to check for microprint on both sides and some tiny lines around Independence Hall. They're nearly impossible for counterfeiters to reproduce. This is good money."

After Annie parted with Lindy, she made a stop at the grocery store, then picked out a tray of petunias from Duncan's Hardware. Might as well do what she could to spruce up the place. This knee operation may be the very thing to persuade her grandmother to sell. If so, she would at least have the place looking good.

"Woody called. He wants to bring a horse over for you to ride," Beulah said, holding the back door open for her.

"A horse? Today?"

"That's what he said." Her grandmother closed the back door behind them.

"Did I say I wanted a horse?"

"I think he's hoping to court you on trail rides."

Her grandmother gave her a knowing grin and turned to go back in the house.

It was midafternoon when she heard a horse whinny outside. Annie was finishing the petunia bed, which now lent a smattering of purple and pinks against the gray stone foundation below the front porch. With a porch swing and a paint job, the house might make a spread in *Country Living*.

She stretched as she stood and gathered up the hand trowel and the plastic trays. Around back, Annie saw Woody in the barn lot, bent over a metal tank with a hose. She set down the trowel and trays on the back porch and walked out to meet him. A brown horse watched Woody's every movement with large brown eyes.

"Woody?" she called.

"Howdy. I knew you were anxious to ride, so I brought over Nutmeg here. I thought I'd go ahead and clean this out for you so you'll be all fixed up."

"I'm sorry you went to all this trouble. I'm really not good on a horse."

"No trouble. We'll turn you into a horsewoman before you can say scat."

Annie felt annoyed at his presumption, but didn't feel like arguing. If he wanted to leave the horse here, she would look after it. She certainly had time on her hands.

"Be done in a jiffy," he said. "Beulah invited me in for pie soon as I finished up here."

Great, Annie thought. Did everybody that came to her grandmother's house have to eat something? Was it possible for people to come and go without food being involved?

She had absently been petting Nutmeg and now the horse wanted more. She nudged her and Annie gave in and rubbed the animal's forehead, feeling her own body relax with the movement. "You have a spot on your lip," she said to the horse.

"That's called a snip. She's a chestnut horse with a snip and two socks," Woody said.

Annie looked down at the horse's feet and sure enough, her two back legs looked like she was wearing socks.

"Gotcha a pair of boots?"

"What for?"

"Better to have 'em in case the horse steps on your toes. It don't feel too good even with boots on, but it's worse in sneakers."

"But Woody, I don't—"

"I'll learn you this first time," he said, his green eyes serious.

Annie wondered how she had gotten herself into this mess. She went upstairs to find a pair of boots while Woody devoured her grandmother's coconut cream pie. She was terrified of horses, always had been, and her grandmother knew it. Annie knew without a doubt it was her grandmother behind this whole horse thing. It was just like her to keep pushing her to get over some deep-seated fear.

Her grandfather kept horses, but they were high-spirited and too dangerous for her, so rarely had she ever even ridden in childhood. There were ponies at the fairgrounds, and once Jake had a horse that he took her for rides on, but that was with him driving, or leading, or whatever you did with a horse.

When she passed through the kitchen, Annie didn't say a word. She glared at her grandmother, feeling all of fifteen again. Her grandmother had the beginnings of a grin pushing at one side of her mouth, but turned to the kitchen sink before Annie could tell for sure.

In the barn lot, Nutmeg stood looking at them with half-shut eyes. She looked sleepy and relaxed—a good sign. The high-strung breeds her grandfather had were jumpy and ready to bolt, the reason Annie had kept her distance with the animals.

Woody eased the saddle onto Nutmeg and pulled straps around the horse's stomach, tugging against the leather.

"She swells up when I put her saddle on to keep me from pulling it too tight. We'll talk a minute while she lets out the air."

"Does it hurt her?" Annie asked.

"Naw, but it'll hurt you when that saddles slips off because it's not tight enough. It happened to me on a trail ride once. I was going down a hill and before I knew it, I was on the ground.

That saddle slipped plumb to her underside."

Woody cleared his throat as if he were about to lecture a college class.

"Okay now, pull back on the reins to stop. Pull on the left rein to go left. Pull on the right one to go right. Let her have her head free to walk. Cluck to pick up the pace and give a light kick in the side to go faster. Always get on and off on the left side and never get too close to the back end in case a horse will kick. Nutmeg doesn't seem to be a kicker, but that goes for any horse. Never trust a horse. Got it?"

She nodded her agreement, but felt a gnawing in the pit of her stomach.

Woody turned back to Nutmeg and pulled hard on the leather straps, then tied them in something that looked like a man's tie knot.

"All right, put your left foot in the stirrup and swing up when you're ready," he said.

Annie tentatively placed her left foot in the stirrup, grabbed the saddle horn with sweaty palms, and pulled herself up. Two hands placed square on her bottom pushed up.

"Good. Now, what you've got there is a Western saddle. I like it better for trail riding, but some prefer an English saddle. It's up to your own likings," Woody said. " 'Round here, we tend towards Tennessee Walkers and most folks ride Western saddles with English reins." He chuckled. "Guess we're mixed up. All right now, cluck when you're ready to take off."

Annie swallowed the fear in her throat and clucked. Nutmeg began to walk, and Annie practiced making her go to the left or right. She followed directions beautifully.

After a few more rounds, Annie felt her confidence grow. "This is actually not bad," she said, more to herself than Woody.

"I'll open the gate, and you can walk her around the pasture," Woody called.

He slowly opened the barn lot gate as Annie guided Nutmeg through the entrance to the pasture. But as she cleared the opening, a clang of metal against wood behind them caused Nutmeg's muscles to lurch forward. Annie was unprepared for the sudden movement and as Nutmeg's front legs pulled hard into a full gallop, Annie felt her body jerk back in the saddle.

What did Woody say? Give Nutmeg her head? No, pull back. The horse jerked as she jumped a small limb, and the right rein fell loose from Annie's hand. *Oh, dear God*, she prayed, *please get me out of this.* She grabbed the horn with both hands and leaned forward. But she felt her balance slipping away as her body tensed. Nutmeg slowed as she reached the fence, but Annie had lost her balance and tumbled off the side.

Her right shoulder took the worst of it before she rolled onto her back. When Annie opened her eyes, she was aware of Nutmeg hovering over her like an anxious mother, her nose within inches of Annie's eyes.

Soon Woody's face crowded Nutmeg's, his eyes wide and his mouth open.

"Annie, you all right?" he asked. Woody's breath smelled of wintergreen tobacco. *Slush.* The word floated through her mind, and she knew it wasn't right. Not slush. *Snush.* No, what was it? She searched for the word in the nostril of the horse. *Snuff.* That was it, his breath felt of snuff. No, smelt of snuff. Wintergreen tobacco crumbled up in a round can that made a faded circle in the back pocket of the high school boys' blue jeans.

"Snuff!" Annie said aloud, proud for finding the word.

"You want some snuff?" Woody asked. "I got some right 'chere!"

Annie shook her head from side-to-side gently. It hurt along with her right shoulder.

"Can you help me get up?" she asked.

"Take it slow now."

She held onto Woody's arm as she rose slowly from the ground. She waited for a few seconds before attempting to stand with Woody holding onto her arm.

"What in heaven's name?" It was her grandmother, limping across the field toward them with her cane.

"That old gate slipped its hinge and spooked Nutmeg. When she saw Annie wasn't in control, she just took her for a ride."

"Are you all right? I looked out the back porch window and

saw you on the ground." Beulah's eyes went to Annie's shoulder where her hand massaged the muscles.

"I don't think anything is broken," Annie said. Annie fixed her eyes on Woody, sorting out what he said. "She was trying to see how much she could take off of me. You mean she did that on purpose?"

"Did you hit your head?" her grandmother asked.

Annie stood and waited for Woody to respond.

"Well, yeah, I'm afraid so. Nutmeg is kind of bad about that. She sensed you weren't in control and took over."

"I can't believe it. Now I'm betrayed by a horse?"

"She might be a little addled," Woody said to her grandmother as if she weren't there.

"Does your head hurt?" Her grandmother looked worried.

"Annie, I sure am sorry about all this. I guess you won't feel like riding for a while. I'll bring the trailer over tomorrow and take Nutmeg back home," Woody said.

"We'll get some Bengay on you, and I'll put the kettle on for tea." Beulah turned to the house.

"Oh, no, I'm keeping her. We have some things to work out."

Annie was done being a victim.

Chapter Sixteen

BEULAH SAT AT the kitchen table, sorting through two drawers and finding things she didn't even know she had, like an old-fashioned cherry pitter and a cheese grater she had never even taken out of the box. Now that she had a date for her surgery, it seemed time was flying by, despite all the things she wanted to get done beforehand.

The operation was set for late June, but the surgeon's office had called and said he'd had a cancellation. Could she come on June 15th instead? She was sure there was something wrong with that surgeon for him to be having cancellations. When she called her family physician, Dr. Bright, to voice concern about the change in dates, he laughed.

"Dr. Wylie is the best for knee replacements in the region," he had said. "We're lucky to have him in Rutherford."

Beulah wondered about that. Maybe Lexington would have been a better choice. But she believed in buying local, and as much as possible that went for her medical needs too.

Beulah wondered if Annie might be laid up in a hospital bed too, after that fall from the horse. She had suggested that Annie go to the doctor, but she would have none of it.

"There's nothing wrong. I got the wind knocked out of me, that's all," she had said that afternoon after Beulah poured several cups of hot tea into her.

Annie was exactly like her: stubborn and hard-headed the girl was, unlike her mother who went any way the wind blew. The only things Annie seemed to get from her mother were her looks, her love for faraway places and her taste in men.

Sure enough, she seemed fine and was back on that horse by the weekend. Determined not to let that animal get the best of her, she finally mastered trotting the old mare around the pasture after first getting the hang of it in the barn lot. Woody was a good teacher, Beulah had to give him that. But he was awful attentive to Annie for more reasons than his love for horses, or so she thought.

Annie had finally gone to church on Sunday morning and Beulah had preened like a rooster at Somerville Baptist, showing her granddaughter off to all the churchgoers. Annie looked real pretty. She wore a red dress that set off her dark hair and brought the color to her face. They sat in their normal place, six rows from the back on the organ side. Even the preacher commented on Annie's presence, right from the pulpit.

They had gotten a lot of attention on Sunday, what with Annie there and Beulah's upcoming surgery. They were already passing around a sign-up list in her Sunday school for folks to bring supper to them the week after she came home from the hospital. It was mighty hard to think about being on the receiving end of charity, but she reckoned it was all right this once.

Sunday dinner had the whole group gathered around Evelyn's table. Annie fell right into the conversation, laughing and talking with Scott, Mary Beth, Lindy and Woody. Even Evelyn commented on Woody being there on such a prime fishing day.

"Went early this morning," Woody had said. The question of why he couldn't do that on other spring Sundays hung in the air, but no one pulled it down.

The days seemed to fly by and here it was Monday. Beulah pulled a garlic smasher out of the drawer and put it in the

Goodwill pile. Rarely did she ever use garlic in her cooking—it didn't sit well on her stomach. She was an old-fashioned cook, and to her all these kitchen gizmos were a waste of time and money. They were bought at these home parties when Beulah felt sorry for some young woman trying to make a little extra money to help out her family. And here they sat in the back of her drawers, most never even used. Who needed fifteen gadgets for chopping when a knife did the trick?

Going through these drawers and cabinets was something she had wanted to do for a long time, but looking at the job made her tired. Annie tackled it with a vengeance, climbing down on the floor and pulling Tupperware bowls out of the dark recesses of the cabinets. With a Clorox mixture, she wiped out the dust and dirt from crevices Beulah hadn't seen in years.

A scream pierced the air making Beulah jump as if she had been shot. The metal gadgets dumped onto the floor.

"Heaven help us! What in the world?" She grabbed her cane and managed to stand and slowly make her way to the back door.

"Snake! Snake!" Annie was outside hopping around like she was stepping on hot coals.

"What in heaven's name?"

"Don't come out! There's a snake right under the door!"

Beulah pushed open the door to see what was causing her granddaughter so much distress. There in the threshold was Booger, her old black snake.

"Calm down. You'll scare him," Beulah said.

"I'll scare *him*?"

"Booger, I thought something happened to you." Beulah glanced up at Annie. "Hush now, he belongs here."

Annie looked at her like she had sprouted another head. "You want a snake next to your back door?" she asked.

"Booger keeps the mice down. Black snakes also eat poisonous snakes, though we usually don't have that kind of trouble around here. This is the first time I've seen him this spring."

Annie was still hopping a bit, like she had to go to the bathroom.

"Now, if I could only bend down, I'd pick him up and get him out of your way. Do you want to get him for me?" Beulah asked, amusing herself.

"No! I'll go around to the front door."

She watched Annie high-step it around the side of the house and chuckled to herself. Beulah could almost hear Fred laugh with her. If he was still living, it was something they would replay to themselves over and over, milking the humor until they had their fill.

Annie picked up the mess Beulah had made when she jumped up at Annie's screaming, then she hightailed it upstairs to go through more closets. *Away from the snake*, Beulah thought, laughing again to herself. Her granddaughter had country in her, but it was going to take peeling off layers to get it out.

Later, the phone rang and Beulah sighed, anticipating the effort to get up out of the chair and answer the wall phone. It stopped ringing and soon she heard Annie coming down the steps, the portable in her hand.

"That was Woody. He's on his way over with the tomato cages you ordered. He said he'd put them on for us," Annie said over an armful of clothes from one of the upstairs closets.

"Good! My old cages were falling apart. I finally sent them off with Joe to the scrap metal place last fall."

"Is Woody always this … available?" Annie asked.

"This is not quite normal, but I'm grateful for it, whatever the reason."

Annie raised her eyebrows and shrugged.

Minutes later, Woody was at the back door.

"I see Booger's back," Woody said.

"Is he still under the door?" asked Annie.

"Naw, he's moved up to sun himself on the old millstone."

"Would you like a sandwich, Woody?" Beulah asked. The peanut butter and grape jelly were still on the counter from their lunch. When Woody nodded, Annie sat down at the table with the bread and fixings. Beulah did not know what she would have done without Annie this last week. She had become her hands and legs, doing everything Beulah's knee kept her from doing.

"Woody, how's your mother doing?"

"She's no different. I reckon she'll be laid up in that nursing home until she draws her last breath. I go see her twice a week, but she don't know me."

"Well, it's good of you to visit her. She may know more than we think," Beulah said.

"That's what I tell myself, but it's awful hard seeing her like that for all these years. Now, I'll just tell ya, thar's things worse than death. Fred did it the right way. He just took out of here quicklike. Made it harder on y'all, but better for him. But a horse kick to the head, now that's not something to be trifled with."

Woody folded his long legs into a chair at the table and wiped his brow with a napkin. To Annie he said, "So you fly around in those airplanes for a job."

"That's right," Annie said, and Beulah watched her spread the generous portion of peanut butter over the bread.

"I wouldn't get on one of those airplanes if my life depended on it." He blew on the palms of his hands as if they were clammy.

"Really? Isn't there somewhere you'd like to go?" Annie asked, setting the sandwich down in front of him.

"Noooo, ma'am! Anywhere I want to go, I can drive." He gulped his sweet tea.

"Don't you want to go to another country, like France or Italy?"

"I don't want to go nowhere the people don't speak English. I like to understand when somebody's talking to me. I don't have no use for vacations. I hear 'em talk all the time about saving up for a trip to Hawaii or a cruise to the Bahamas. They get worked up in a frenzy trying to leave, then they come back all wore out and tellin' about what all went wrong. I did it once and that was enough. I take my vacation every time I get up on my horse."

Beulah saw Woody was getting worked up and decided to change the subject. "Tell Annie about your farm, Woody."

His mouth was full of bread and peanut butter, but he tried talking anyway. "Little bit of everything. I still raise tobacco and a little corn. I've got goats, chickens, cows and I trade horses here and there. Got several kids too."

Beulah watched as peanut butter oozed around his loose bridge, likely the only thing holding it in place. Poor Woody needed a wife to advise him on personal care issues, but as amused as she was with his attention to Annie, she knew that would never work.

"How old are your kids?" Annie asked.

"Well, let me think. I had twins two weeks ago and a set of triplets the week before. Last month it was another set of twins and quadruplets."

Annie's eyes grew wide.

"He's talking about his goats," Beulah said.

Chapter Seventeen

ANNIE RUBBED HER arms, not sure if they were sore from riding the horse, planting more rows of beans and corn, or scrubbing out cupboards, drawers and closets. Either way, the pain reminded her she was making good use of her time here. After sprinkling a generous amount of Dead Sea salts into the water, she eased down into the warm bath and relaxed in the old clawfoot tub.

While her grandmother was in the notion to do it, Annie had gone full force into cleaning and sorting through the stuff in the house. The days had flown by, and it felt good to clean out areas that had not been touched for years.

"This will make things so much easier if you ever decide to move," Annie had said once when they were both working in the kitchen. Her grandmother had not responded. It had to be considered, Annie decided, with the reality of surgery looming.

More than once she came across a small stash of bills. In the guest room, she found five one-hundred-dollar bills stuck between the Old and New Testament of a Bible in a nightstand. In the kitchen, she found two hundred dollars stashed in an envelope marked "tomato seeds" stuffed inside a Mason jar.

"There's money in a vase in the corner cupboard of the dining room and tucked between tablecloths in the linen press," she had said when Annie started working in there. In each case, her grandmother knew about the money and even told Annie where the other hiding places were. And every item Annie pulled out for her to say what to do with it, she knew exactly what it was and where it came from. There was no sign of senility yet, thank goodness.

***

There had been no new updates from Janice, but a call on Sunday from Prema had made her homesick again for Manhattan.

"Annie, we miss you. The three of us are preparing to go out to an art festival and we decided we must call. We know how much you love this kind of thing," Prema had said, and then passed the phone around to Evie and Kate.

Annie could imagine them getting up and having brunch together and then dressing for the outing. Annie did love those first outdoor events after a long winter. There was excitement in the air, anticipation of a summer, and a feeling of goodwill in the Village.

Despite a few bouts of homesickness, she had fallen into a comfortable routine with her grandmother. Annie was queen of the upstairs now that her grandmother was sleeping on the first floor. It seemed an absurd amount of space to loll about in compared to her small apartment in the city.

She reached for the shampoo and massaged some into her hair. Frequent phone calls from Jake had gone long past her grandmother's report, going on to books they had read, recent movies, and current events. Annie was a sounding board for him as he analyzed the options and she liked it not just a little. He told her of Camille's father who wanted to develop a business with him, of the bank's foundation work and what his job might look like, but most of all he talked of farming.

He even talked about grass. Orchard grass, timothy, clover,

fescue, alfalfa, and Johnson grass and the right mix that made the best nutrition for cows and how chickens were good to bring in after cows and how it all worked to make the land produce the way it was designed.

She told him about her travels and experiences, about life in New York and about the men she had dated right up to her relationship with Stuart. Annie had missed him in the two weeks since he went back to Cincinnati. Even that was an odd revelation for her, that she could miss someone after being apart for so many years. But she looked forward to the next weekend when he planned to come down for a meeting with like-minded farmers.

After rinsing her hair, Annie grabbed a towel and stepped out of the tub. She had daydreamed too long in the bath and would not be ready for her dinner in Lexington with Lindy if she didn't get a move on.

Dressed and downstairs just in time for Lindy's arrival, Annie called goodbye to her grandmother and was out the door. A sweet aroma assaulted her and she stood for a moment breathing it in. Catalpa, her grandmother had called the tree. Large, white blooms hung in conelike shapes from the branches. It would only be this way for a week or two and Annie took every outside opportunity to let it fill her senses.

Once in the car and on their way, they talked nonstop while green farmland rolled by. When they were just outside of Lexington Lindy said, "Okay, I've been dying to ask you: Why did you break up with your boyfriend?"

"Well," Annie said, trying to figure out how to sum up her feelings. "He wasn't what I thought he was," she said, waiting for the sensation of a blade twisting in her gut. *It didn't happen this time.*

"The rumor around town is that he worked for the airline and had to fire you, and that's why you broke up with him," Lindy said.

"People are saying that?" Annie asked in an agitated tone.

"It's a small town. People fill in the blanks with what is most interesting," Lindy said. "Don't take it personal."

Annie pictured herself in a romantic entanglement with Bob Vichy and burst out laughing. "That's so ridiculous it's funny," she said, hardly catching her breath.

"You know what they said about me when I came home? I had nowhere to go, so I came back to work with my dad. Annie, I had offers from Chicago and Atlanta, but I never even told anyone. I figured they'd find out soon enough if I could handle it."

"Who are 'they'?"

Lindy adjusted the radio. "Women who married young, green with envy that we got out. Loafers down at Bill's Diner, the old men and women with time on their hands. It's fairly harmless, but annoying just the same. Can I ask you another question." Lindy had a mischievous look in her eye. "Did you ever date Jake Wilder?"

"Jake? No! We're only friends. We used to be like brother and sister growing up. We barely kept in touch the last several years, although I don't know why. I guess life takes you in different directions and you forget how much someone means to you."

"You have to admit, he is a catch," she said.

"It sounds like he's been caught," Annie said.

"Maybe. Evelyn was in the office yesterday, bringing us cinnamon rolls, and said Camille is coming with him next weekend."

They had talked about everything but Camille when Jake called. But of course he would bring her, especially as he was considering moving *home* as one of his options.

The restaurant walls were covered with black and white pictures of local celebrities. Featured prominently were the University of Kentucky basketball and football coaches, and some of the players, both past and present. Even Hollywood stars like Ashley Judd, George Clooney and Johnny Depp were proudly featured Kentuckians. The fare was fine Angus steak, prime cuts and cooked to order, served in an atmosphere of dark paneled walls and white table linens.

After the salads arrived, Annie asked, "So what happened with your mom?"

"I was in my last year of college. She had a brain aneurism and died almost immediately. It was shocking. My older brother was home at the time, quite by accident. He called 9-1-1, but she was basically gone before they got to the hospital."

"I'm so sorry," Annie said.

"You know what it's like. It made that first year of law school way harder, but I also had a determination not to let Dad down after all that. And I realized I had a great mother for a lot longer than some folks."

"It's still painful, no matter when it happens."

"It made me realize none of us are here forever and sometimes when you say goodbye to someone it might be the last time you see them on this earth. I was home the weekend before it happened. I had no idea when I kissed her goodbye on that Sunday that I would never see her again, in this life anyway."

They fell into silence, and Annie pondered Lindy's words. The thought of a life after this was pleasant enough. She was brought up to believe in Heaven and Hell, but were they really true? With her life in New York so full of activity, schedules and events, she had not spent much time thinking about what happened beyond. Really, she had not wanted to, other than to console herself with the belief that her own mother and grandfather were in some better place.

Annie's cell phone vibrated. "Excuse me," she said to Lindy. "It's Evelyn. I better take this." Annie left the booth and walked just outside the front door.

"I was going to leave you a message. I hope I'm not disturbing anything."

"No, it's fine. Is everything okay?"

"Oh yes. I had an idea and wanted to see what you thought. Beulah's been talking about painting her house with that money from your renter. Of course, Fred had always handled that sort of thing for her, and she doesn't realize it won't be nearly enough. I may get in trouble for this, but we've cooked up a way to get your grandmother's house painted while she's in the hospital."

"How?"

"A couple of church members have volunteered to do the

work for free. Now, you know Beulah won't take outright charity, so we'll let her pay for the paint and materials, which will probably be a good chunk of the money she set aside. They can start the morning she has her surgery, and with the few days in the hospital and if the weather holds, they should get a good start on it before she gets home."

"Evelyn, that's wonderful," Annie said. "She'll be thrilled."

"I promised to provide lunch while they're there, so I might need your help and use of the kitchen."

"No problem. I'll do whatever I can."

Back at the booth, she shared Evelyn's idea with Lindy.

"I would love to help!" her friend said. "I think my schedule is a little crazy next week, but any free time I have, I'll come paint."

After the dinner and movie, they stopped for a cappuccino. And this time Annie bought a bean grinder and beans to leave at her grandmother's house. There was still hope she might persuade her grandmother to leave off the cheap stuff.

Chapter Eighteen

BEULAH TIED HER orange apron around her waist, the one given to her by her Aunt Sara years ago. It was still her favorite, despite her having half a dozen now. Soft as a lamb's ear, it felt the best to her and she needed a little comfort today. Slices of country ham sizzled in the iron skillet. A dozen store-bought eggs sat awaiting their turn in the frying pan. They were pale, anemic little things compared to the rich eggs she used to gather from her own chickens. That was one of the many things she had let go of after losing Fred. One by one, the hens died of old age, and she never replaced them.

Tomorrow was her surgery, and she dreaded it. The nurse told Beulah not to eat a thing after midnight, but who in the world ate anything after midnight? Yet somehow, hearing what she couldn't do made her feel deprived. Surgery was not for the weak, but neither was growing old. She flipped the ham slices, breathing in the salty aroma. Well, the Lord knew best, and she had to trust Him. That was all there was to it.

Preparations were made. Every closet and drawer in the house had been organized and cleaned. The garden was growing and beans would be ready for picking soon. She might even be able to help Annie break beans, if the Lord let her live through the surgery.

There, she had pulled the niggling thought out into the open. What if she went to sleep and never woke up? It wasn't that she was afraid to die; no, the Lord had taken care of that for her. It was Annie. Beulah felt the child was in the middle of a great transition and needed her right now. With everyone else in her life abandoning her either by choice or by death, Beulah did not want to leave Annie alone, and especially as their relationship had taken a subtle turnabout.

Beulah's stubborn streak had almost reared and made Annie go back. But Annie's offer to stay and help had touched her in a deep place, and by God's grace, she accepted. Pride. She had struggled with that old sin all her life and reckoned she would until the end.

Beulah poured water on top of the ham. A little boiling made the slices good and tender. Black coffee sat on the counter, ready to make red-eye gravy as soon as the water boiled off and the ham was removed from the pan.

"Lord, your will be done tomorrow. I'm in your hands," she whispered.

"What can I do?" Annie asked. Beulah noticed she had changed out of her church clothes into jeans and a short-sleeved top.

"You can get the biscuits out of the freezer and put them in the oven. When I made them up I froze them in the pan, so they're all ready to go."

Annie did as Beulah asked, then set about dressing the table. "Lindy won't be coming today. Do you know who might be here?"

"Scott can't come this week. Set for five, and we can add to or take away if necessary."

"What happened with Mary Beth's marriage?" Annie asked.

"Her husband took up with a beautician over in Rutherford. Met her through taking his son to little league games. Left Mary Beth and didn't look back."

"Do you think she and Scott will get together?"

"Hard to say. They seem compatible, but he's never been

married before, and it might be hard for him to take on a woman, two children and an ex-husband who will always be in the background. We'll see. Were you interested in Scott?"

Annie smiled, but shook her head firmly. "I'm not interested in anybody. I guess there's a romantic inside me who would like to see people be happy together. How did you and Grandpa meet?" Annie asked, pulling glasses out of the cabinet.

"Oh my goodness, I haven't thought about that in years." Beulah eased into the chair and took a deep breath.

"You know the old stone house is where I grew up. It's also where I met your grandfather." Beulah watched Annie fill the glasses with ice and tea.

"Did you go to school together?"

"Oh, no. Fred's people were from Gravel Switch, over in Boyle County. In September, after World War II ended in August, Daddy hired on two brothers from over there who were just back from fighting. They needed work, and he needed help getting his tobacco in the barn and we had lost my brother Ephraim in the war, you know. He fell in Italy, at Anzio."

Annie sat down and nodded, her eyes wide.

"The first day they worked, Mama had me take a glass jug of water out to them midmorning. That was when I met the brothers, Fred and Pete Campbell. Of course, I'd been eyeing them at a distance from my room upstairs anytime I could slip away from my chores. When Mama asked me to take water out to them, I was so nervous I couldn't even speak. I was used to the boys around home, but these two were strangers."

Beulah could remember the way Fred looked as if it were only hours before. Before he nodded his hello, he wiped the curtain of sweat off his forehead, as if he were making himself presentable to her. Dark hair and sparkling brown eyes under thick eyebrows—that was what she remembered most. Pete had red hair and freckles. They were different as two brothers could be. Both were a little skinny, but the war had taken a toll on most of the boys coming back. It wouldn't take long to get the muscle back on them, Mama had said, but it would take years longer to get the haunted look out of their eyes.

"They were hard workers, getting to the house early and sometimes sleeping in the barn at night if they worked an extra-long day. Fred and me, we started looking at each other all the time. It was like we couldn't help ourselves. But never once did we have a conversation alone." Beulah felt the tears fill her eyes. "I was so sad when that last leaf of tobacco was hung in the barn. I thought I would never see Fred again. I watched them leave from the upstairs window of the house, until they disappeared behind the trees on Gibson Creek Road."

Beulah took a long drink of the tea. "That night at supper, I was so low I had to look up to see a snake's belly. Daddy said, 'Beuly, there's no sense in mopin' around. That boy'll be back around here before the month is out.'" Beulah chuckled. "He was right. Fred came a courtin' the next weekend, all cleaned up and combed so that I barely knew him."

"It was no time at all until we knew we wanted to marry, but I was not quite fifteen and had more schooling left. Daddy said I had to wait until after I graduated from high school. Education was important to him, since he didn't get past the eighth grade. We agreed, but the day after graduation, I was married in the yard of the stone house." Beulah felt a tear slide down her cheek.

"I had no idea the house had all that family history," Annie said.

"Honey, the stone house has been in my family for six generations. This house was part of a tract my Daddy bought when he added this front section. Fred and I moved here when we got married, and after Mama and Daddy passed, we rented out the stone house."

Late that afternoon, Beulah poured hot water into the teapot and called for Annie. Her grandchild was deep into one of Janice Holt Giles's books, a local author who wrote about the Kentucky frontier, long since dead. The back porch had become Annie's favorite reading place when she wasn't busy working around the house or outbuildings.

"I wanted to talk to you before I go in for this surgery tomorrow. Sit down here a minute."

Her granddaughter sat down, a serious look on her face.

"I want to make sure you know how things stand if something happens to me tomorrow," Beulah started.

"Oh, Grandma, nothing is going to happen to you. It'll be fine!"

Beulah covered Annie's hand with her own. "It probably will be, but we need to have this talk anyway. There's a lockbox under my bed behind the shotgun. The key to it is taped inside my medicine cabinet door. A copy of the will and all my account numbers and life insurance policy are in there—everything you need to know when I die to handle all the paperwork."

"Grandma, you're not going to die."

"Maybe not this time, but if we have this conversation now, it will make it easier on you when I do go. It may not be tomorrow, but it will be someday." Beulah took a drink of her tea while Annie sat quietly, waiting.

"I'm leaving ten percent of my estate to the church. There should be more than enough cash in the life insurance policy to handle that. The rest will go to you, including the farm. It's all paid for, and I've squirreled away a nice sum down at the bank. It doesn't provide much cash flow for running the farm, but Joe pays a good amount for the lease in January, and between my social security and interest on the CDs, I've been able to manage. The farm will be yours to do whatever you wish with it." Beulah smoothed out the wrinkles in the orange apron. "Of course, I would love for you to keep the farm and live on it, but I know that's unlikely. If you decide to sell it, it would be my preference that you give Jake a fair price on it and first option. If Jake turns it down, I'd like you to offer it to Joe and Betty next. If neither family wants it, you are free to sell it to whoever you wish at whatever price you wish."

"I had no idea how much history was here. I mean, I've been to the cemetery a hundred times, read the names on the stones, but somehow I never connected it all."

"I'd love to see you keep it, of course. But if you marry a man you meet up North, it's likely he would rather have the cash so you can buy something there. And it's hard to maintain a farm when you're not here to see after it. Joe or Jake might be glad to farm it for you, but it won't be the same as having someone live here."

Annie was quiet the rest of the night, and Beulah was sorry to have laid such heavy talk on her. It had to be done sooner than later, and the surgery tomorrow was a good reason to do it sooner.

Beulah readied herself for bed, pulling on her nightgown and opening up her Bible to read after she pulled the covers around her. After a bit she closed the book, set it on the nightstand, and turned off the bedside lamp.

In the dark, her mind went over a verse she memorized as a child, First Peter 5:7: *Cast all your anxiety on Him, because He cares for you.* Meditating on that sweet thought, she fell asleep.

Chapter Nineteen

THE NIGHT BEFORE her grandmother's surgery, a strange unease permeated Annie's soul. The depth of her own self-centeredness settled full upon her like a heavy storm cloud. Sleep came with disturbing dreams.

There was her grandfather working in the fields. He was hoeing between rows of tobacco, and the sweat rolled off his face and arms in stringing beads that dropped to the ground. On the rich black dirt, the sweat turned to trickling streams of blood filling the furrow between the tobacco plants. It flowed down the hill into Gibson Creek, where it turned back to water, rushing over rocks and around the creek bend until it disappeared beyond sight, beyond the farm.

Then, she was with her grandmother in front of the old stone house. Her mother was there for a moment, but then she left the ground, floating toward heaven like a balloon, her feet dangling. Annie reached for her, grabbing her feet and holding on as hard as she could. Her mother was telling her to let go, pointing to her grandmother who was now leaving the ground. Annie ran to her and held her, and when the alarm went off at four in the morning, she was hugging the pillow tight with both arms.

Annie slid out of the bed and onto her knees beside her nightstand. With a heavy heart, she prayed to the God of her childhood:

Lord, please forgive me. I have gone my own way these many years. Please make me a new person ...

It was still dark outside as Annie helped her grandmother to the car and then slid into the driver's seat. They were silent most of the way, neither of them morning people, before Annie finally broke the silence.

"Grandma, I'm sorry I haven't been around much these last few years."

"Oh, that's all right. When you raise children, you expect them to leave the nest at some point."

"I know, but I could have visited more. I think for a while I was running away from the grief of losing Mom and even Grandpa. I'm sorry I haven't been around for you."

"You're here now, and this is when I need you the most. Let's not dwell on things we can't change."

Annie felt warmth spread over her heart for the second time this morning and knew that all was well. Something was different now, with her grandmother and with God. There would be more visits to her grandmother even when she went back to New York. There was no reason she couldn't hop flights to Lexington anytime she wanted.

"Here we are," she said, pulling up to the hospital.

They spent the next hour filling out paperwork and getting Beulah moved back to the surgery preparation area, where she changed into a hospital-issued gown. Her clothes and personal belongings were put into a plastic bag with her name and room number. A nurse recorded her vital signs and started an IV. They waited in silence under the bright fluorescent light of the pre-op room, tucked behind a flimsy privacy curtain. Annie sat in a molded plastic chair next to the mobile bed Beulah was lying on under blankets and a sheet.

The curtain shifted, and Scott Southerland moved inside the tentlike room.

"Land sakes, what in the world are you doing up here? And

you, not even my own preacher?"

Scott nodded to Annie but made his way over to the other side of the bed where he could reach down and kiss Beulah on the cheek. "I needed to make hospital visits this week, so I figured I might as well come when you're here."

Annie saw her grandmother tear up and clasp his hand. "That was mighty sweet of you, Scott."

"How about a prayer?"

"That's what I was lying here thinking I needed."

She reached out and took Annie's hand and held Scott's in the other.

"Dear Father, we are so thankful for your precious child, Beulah. Please guide the hands of the surgeons and strengthen her during and after this surgery. We ask that you bring Beulah into full recovery and give grace and strength to her caregivers. Amen."

When they opened their eyes, a nurse was waiting.

"It's time to go, Mrs. Campbell," she said.

Scott squeezed her hand and slipped out with a wave to Annie. Annie held on to Beulah's other hand. "See you in a little while."

They wheeled her grandmother out of the pre-op room and down a long, well-lit hall. Annie watched until they turned a corner out of sight, and then she went up a floor where she would wait while the surgery took place.

After settling into a corner of the vast waiting area, Annie prayed for her grandmother and, like Scott had done, even for the doctors doing the surgery. After a few minutes, Evelyn stepped off the elevator with to-go cups of coffee in each hand and handed one to Annie before she sat down.

"Any word yet?"

"They just took her back about thirty minutes ago," Annie said. "Are the men working?"

"They arrived after daybreak and started right away on scraping off the old paint."

The door to the waiting room opened, and a nurse came out and asked for another family. Annie hadn't realized she was holding her breath until she let it out.

Pastor Gillum, in a suit and tie, with his great white head of hair combed back in a wave, stopped by and had another prayer with her and Evelyn. An hour passed. Evelyn went with her to the cafeteria for toast and coffee. Afterward, they settled back in the waiting room, flipped through magazines and watched the news intermittently. The door opened again and a nurse called, "Campbell family."

Annie jumped to her feet. The nurse smiled and said, "Come on back, please."

Annie turned and motioned to Evelyn. "You're family too," she said. Inside the door, the nurse talked to them as they walked down the hall.

"Mrs. Campbell did fine," she said. "She's in recovery. I'm taking you to that waiting room. Someone will come and get you as soon as she is awake."

In a few minutes, she and Evelyn were in the room with a groggy Beulah. Annie thought her grandmother looked so vulnerable, lying there with her leg stretched out and wrapped in bandages.

She smiled at Annie and held out her hand to her. Annie grasped it.

"How are you?" Annie asked.

"I'm still here," she said, letting go of Annie's hand to reach for Evelyn.

"Are you in any pain?" Evelyn asked.

"If I am, I don't know it yet." The corners of her mouth pushed up slightly in an effort to grin. "Did they say when I can go home?"

Annie fought to control a laugh. "They're mostly concerned with getting you into a room right now."

"I reckon."

"The doctor won't be by until tomorrow morning to check on you. Evelyn will come and spend tomorrow afternoon and evening with you. I can stay the rest of today."

"No sense in that."

Evelyn smiled at her. "We can watch soap operas like we

used to."

"I reckon."

Two orderlies entered the room in squeaking tennis shoes, white shirts and pants, with clipboards in hand. "Mrs. Beulah Campbell?" said one of the men, but even though she nodded in answer, he checked her wristband and her chart to make sure.

"We're taking you to room 305."

"Okay," Beulah said. Annie smiled at her still-sleepy grandmother.

Evelyn left to fix lunch for the painters. Annie went on to the room, getting there before Beulah. The squeaking tennis shoes announced her grandmother's arrival as two orderlies wheeled the awkward metal transport bed into the room. With tender, experienced hands, the men transferred her from one bed to another. After they left, she saw that her grandmother was comfortable, had ice water and was settled on the pillow just so.

"Why don't you go on home, Annie? I believe I'd rather you be home seeing after things."

"I don't mind staying here at all. Don't you want the company?" Annie asked.

"I'll be fine. I'll probably sleep most of the day. I think I'd rather you be home. I don't like leaving the house to sit empty. And you've already had a long day." Annie knew the house was anything but empty at the moment, but she didn't want to give the secret away.

"If you're sure ... I'll be back later tonight, anyway."

"Betty Gibson said yesterday she would come by this evening. Pastor said he would be by tonight as well. You stay home and rest. You'll have the full care of me soon enough."

"I'll leave this afternoon, but I'd like to stay for a while." Annie leaned over and kissed her grandmother on the forehead.

After she left the hospital, Annie stopped at a department store and got a few items of clothing she could use on the farm. A grocery store had a selection of organic produce, something missing from the locally owned store in Somerville, and she stocked up on fruits and vegetables. There was a Chinese restaurant in a strip mall out on the bypass, and she picked up a carry-out for supper. She was too tired to fix anything for herself tonight. Funny, she hadn't lifted a finger all day, but waiting in the hospital was exhausting.

It was nearing dusk when Annie passed the grove of walnuts in the driveway. As the house came into view, it looked naked with all the old paint scraped off and the primer not yet on. The men had done good work in one day.

She put away the groceries and then carried the Kung Pao chicken to the front porch, settling herself on the steps as the fading light of evening slipped away. At first it seemed so peaceful and quiet, but as she listened close, there were the bullfrogs croaking in the pond, and in the front yard, a kildeer made a terrible racket as one of the cats got too close to her nest. She feigned injury, trying to lure the cat away, squawking and holding one wing out as if it were broken. The ruse worked, and the cat went after the mama bird, who escaped with a perfectly good set of wings at just the right moment. A hoot owl called from above, adding to the evening cacophony.

Annie was finishing her dinner when a tiny greenish-yellow light floated up from the ground and blinked on and off. Then another and another floated up until the yard was full of hovering yellow beads of light, blinking signals to each other. The lightning bugs put on a mesmerizing show. Annie sat a long time and watched the magical display.

A ringing phone interrupted the wonderment. When she went in to answer it, she closed the door and locked it.

"Are you in for the night?"

"I am," Annie said, happy to hear Jake's voice.

"How's Beulah?"

"Ready to come home, but the doctors are saying Wednesday or Thursday. We'll be lucky to keep her in there long enough for the house to get painted."

"I'll help on Saturday if they are still painting."

"I'm hoping they'll be finished by then. And won't you have Camille here?" Annie asked.

"One of her staff is out sick and she has to help with a convention coming in this weekend. She'll come in Monday and we're both taking vacation next week to be here."

"Good," Annie said. "We'll have time to get to know her."

"She's a great girl, Annie. I think you'll like her."

"If you like her, I know I will," she said.

"Do you mind staying there by yourself? You know you can stay with Mom."

"I'll be fine here. I know where the shotgun is," she said, and laughed.

"But do you know how to use it?" he asked in a serious tone.

"You mean waving it around won't be enough?" she said.

"That's another thing we'll do this summer. You need to know how to use a gun," he said, before wishing her a good night and hanging up.

After turning out the lights and plodding upstairs, Annie washed her face and put on her pajamas. Under the comfort of a frayed quilt, she dropped into a sound sleep.

Chapter Twenty

IT WAS NOT until the morning, with the stillness of a house holding only one spirit, that Annie realized how much she would miss her grandmother if she never came home. The power of the thought forced her to call the hospital room, early as it was, and check on her.

"I'm fine," she said, her voice sounding a little groggy. "Didn't get much sleep last night what with all the vitals, pills and shift changes. I'll rest today."

"Evelyn said she would be there after lunch. If you think of anything you want her to bring you from here, call me."

"I'd love a decent cup of coffee. It's weak as water up here. If she's not coming until afternoon, a strong glass of iced tea might be as good."

"Huh, sounds like you've grown accustomed to my good coffee," Annie said.

"I reckon you've spoiled me."

The quiet morning was soon broken by the arrival of a pickup truck, doors slamming and the screech of metal as a ladder unfolded.

"Would y'all like some coffee?" Annie leaned out the front

door, hearing the painters, but not seeing them.

"We brought a thermos, but thank you just the same," a voice said from above.

After Annie had eaten her breakfast, she went out the front door to see the progress. A man was perched on a ladder, priming the top of the roof gable. The other was painting from the ground, to the right of the porch. The names and faces were familiar, probably from years ago rather than her recent visits, so introductions seemed trivial.

"The back door is open, so help yourselves. There's a fresh pot of coffee and some cold water in the refrigerator. We really appreciate this."

The man painting in the gable turned slightly, his paintbrush suspended in the air. "We're only paying back. Beulah brought me soups and casseroles when my wife was sick."

From under the wide brim of a tobacco warehouse cap, the other man said, "She tended to my mother up till the day she died. We've searched high and low for a way to pay her back. This is the first chance we've had."

A warm feeling of pride spread over her. "She'll be so pleased!"

Once inside the house, Annie set about her work at breakneck speed. There was much to do while her grandmother was gone. She wanted everything to be perfect for her return.

Annie washed curtains, changed sheets and helped Evelyn with lunch, remembering to tell her about Beulah's request for tea. They fed Jim and Elbert, stuffing them full of Evelyn's butter fried chicken and coconut pie.

That afternoon, Annie was cleaning the glass shades on the dining room chandelier when Woody stopped by.

"Better water your garden tonight. We're in a dry spell, and those seeds you planted need some water to grow," Woody said, his bridge wobbling below his upper lip.

"Isn't that a waste of water?"

"Naw, better go ahead and water tonight when the ground holds the moisture. Now, I know that Jake has got some newfangled ideas on farming, but you'd better listen to somebody that's got dried mud on their boots. Wanna go for a ride tomorrow afternoon?" Woody asked.

"Thanks, but I've got some projects to finish before I bring Grandma home. Maybe another time?"

"Oh, okay, sure thing," Woody said. "Maybe a Sunday afternoon trail ride."

He seemed disappointed at her response, and Annie wondered if her grandmother was right after all. Maybe Woody had more in mind than friendship. She'd have to set that straight soon and let him know she was done with dating. Period.

That evening, she attached the water hose to a sprinkler she found in the equipment shed and turned on the water. She left it on while she bathed so it would get a good soaking.

Evelyn called to report Beulah had sent her home early, saying she was fine. "No sense in both of us eating alone. Why don't you come over here? Nothing fancy."

Over pasta and salad, Evelyn shared her excitement about Jake's upcoming visit.

"He'll be home in time for dinner Friday night and is staying for two weeks. Camille will be here for a few days next week, but has to leave on Thursday for a meeting. He's hoping she'll come back for part of the next week as well."

"You'll get to know her much better," Annie said.

"I hope she likes me," Evelyn said in a rare display of vulnerability.

"Evelyn, you would be the best mother-in-law! She'll love you," Annie said. She bit into the pasta and savored the pungent flavors. "Is this pesto sauce?"

"Homemade from my own basil. I freeze it and use it year-round." Evelyn glowed at the compliment.

"I haven't had anything like it since leaving New York. I should add some basil plants to Grandma's garden."

"Better do it before she gets home." Evelyn spoke in a comical stage whisper. "If there's any available space left, she'll want to plant green beans."

Annie laughed. "You're right. We ran out of seeds on the last row, and she fretted about the wasted space."

"I don't know how Beulah has managed it these last few years. She can't seem to scale down her garden, even when she knows she should. It's that Depression-era mentality, feeling the need to store away lots of food and money for hard times. I'll bet if you go down into the cellar, she's got canned goods stored there from several summers ago. We should all probably be more like her."

After they cleared the supper dishes away, Evelyn filled the coffee maker with water and added grounds to the gold filter.

While they waited for it to brew, Annie said, "Do you mind if I use your computer? I'd like to look up a few things."

"Of course, dear. You know we leave the back door unlocked, so anytime you need to use it, come on over. You don't have to ask."

Evelyn had turned the small maid's room just off the kitchen into an office, with a large walnut desk, a computer, printer and filing cabinets. A recent framed picture of Jake sat on the desk. Next to it was a picture of Evelyn, Charlie and Jake taken at Jake's college graduation. Another showed Evelyn with her younger sister, Dixie, a Bohemian opposite of Evelyn.

After deleting all the junk in her e-mail account, she was left with a few updates from friends but no communication from Beverly Enlo. *Chickened out,* Annie figured. After all, Janice delivered the news and the voided rent check was returned. What else could she say?

After logging off her e-mail, she typed "Stella Hawkins" into a search engine. Pages of results came up. After ten pages, she stopped looking. She couldn't find anyone by that name who was an author. Maybe it was a first book, or possibly a pen name. On the other hand, there was no one by that name associated with a criminal record that she could see.

"Coffee's ready if you want some," Evelyn called from the kitchen.

Annie pushed away from the desk with another glance at Jake's picture.

"There's a nice picture of Jake in here. Where was it taken?"

"Camille's father recommended him for a charity board

position and they took professional pictures for their annual report. He would never have a picture like that made on his own, so it was nice when he had a copy sent to me."

"So, how serious is he with Camille?" Annie asked as Evelyn poured the coffee.

"Let's go out on the porch. We can watch the sunset from the back."

The screen door squeaked as Evelyn pushed it open. They settled into two comfortable patio chairs with bright floral cushions.

"Jake has great respect for Camille's dad. Her brother is one of his good friends and Jake's been embraced by her family while he was grieving his own father. Sometimes it's hard to separate those feelings."

"So you think what he feels for Camille is more of a corporate feeling?" Annie took a sip of the rich coffee.

"I guess that's one way to put it. Time will tell. I think bringing her down here will be good for him. He needs to see her in his own environment, especially if he is thinking of moving back."

Evelyn held her cup close to her face and stared at the landscape before her. The sun peaked behind the rolling hills, casting pinks, purples and silver against the horizon.

"I must say, I would love for him to come back," she continued, her eyes filled with unshed tears. "Charlie would have loved it too. But I don't want to say too much. It has to be his decision."

"My sense is that is what he wants, but he is trying to fairly weigh all the options. Either way, I think he wants to spend more time down here even if he stays in Cincinnati," Annie said. "So you'll likely see more of him one way or the other."

Evelyn smiled. "And I hope more of you too."

Annie went to bed early, so when the phone rang at eleven, she thought it was the middle of the night.

"Annie Taylor?"

"Yes," she said breathlessly.

"This is Dr. Wylie. Your grandmother had a small setback this evening. We think everything is fine now, but we've moved her to ICU to keep a close watch."

Annie was wide awake. "ICU? What happened?"

"There was a slight change in the rhythm of her heart. It's likely caused by one of her medications, but as a precaution we want to keep a closer watch for the next twenty-four hours."

"I'll be right there," Annie said, jumping out of bed and looking for her clothes.

"Why don't you wait until morning? She's resting well now but I'm sure she'll want to see you then."

Annie's mind raced. "Are you sure? I can be there in just a few minutes. You're sure she's okay?"

"I think she'll be fine. I wanted to call so that when you do come in the morning, you would understand why we moved her."

Annie couldn't sleep after the phone call, so she got up to make a pot of chamomile tea. After putting on the kettle, she turned on the faucet and washed a dirty glass while her mind worked through the information. She had taken for granted that once Beulah made it through the surgery, all would be fine. But there were no guarantees in life. Her grandmother had said it herself a hundred times.

After turning off the faucet, she still heard water running. In the past few weeks, she had grown used to the sounds of the house, but she didn't remember this one. She turned on the back porch light and went outside to see if the sound was louder. There was a pitter-pattering, as if it were raining. The heavens were clear. The sky was full of stars.

The sprinkler! Annie ran to turn off the spigot, not giving a thought to her bare feet and what might be in the tall grass. With a heavy heart, she surveyed the damage illuminated by the stock barn's security light. Puddles of water stood in every low place in the garden.

I've ruined her garden, she thought. Of all the things she could mess up, it had to be this.

Chapter Twenty-One

BEULAH PUSHED HERSELF up in the bed and tried to get more comfortable without moving her leg. The growling coming from the bed on the other side of the room was near deafening. She was surprised a small, elderly woman could snore loud enough to vibrate the water glass on her tray.

What did hospital people think, calling this type of room "semi-private" when there was no privacy to it? A mere piece of shiny polyester fabric hung between her and this roaring bear with whom she was doomed to share the night.

At least all that ICU rigmarole was behind her. It ended up being a little reaction to her medication, that was all. Just another excuse for the hospital to make a little more money out of the whole deal, is what she thought, or avoid some kind of liability. Anyway, it had all been fine. The worst part was she couldn't get any sleep.

A snort from her roommate's bed caused Beulah to jump nearly out of her skin. There ought to be a noise ordinance in the hospital. It seemed to her there was a competition on who could make the most noise, what with the nurses chattering like magpies at their station, the public address system blaring a lullaby every time a baby was delivered, and equipment rolling in and out of the rooms, banging into beds and carts as they went. They had put her on the old people's floor, that was obvious, and Beulah resented that not a little, what with all the yelping and hollering that went on in the other patient rooms. Beulah couldn't wait to get home.

She never had liked spending a night away from home, even on the few vacations she had taken in her life. How Annie flitted from one hotel to the other in her years of flying, Beulah could never understand. She reckoned you had to get used to it when you were young. Beulah had always been a homebody, and that was a fact. She liked knowing what her bed was going to feel like when she got into it at night, and she liked waking up in her own house.

"Mrs. Campbell, how are you?"

Beulah looked up to see a pretty nurse with a blond ponytail and a belly protruding from under her blue uniform. There was something familiar about the face, the small, upturned nose, and the blue eyes.

"All right, and you?"

"You don't recognize me, do you?" The ponytail swung as the nurse reached over the bed for the blood pressure cuff, attached by a black coil cord to the wall.

"You do look familiar, but I can't place you," Beulah said, studying the girl's face.

"I'm Sandy Sallee, except now I'm a Turner. I cheered with Annie at Somerville High." She wrapped Beulah's arm in the cuff. "I saw your name on the chart up front, and when I saw you were from Somerville, I knew you had to be Annie's grandmother."

"Now I remember. Your daddy is Everett Sallee from over on Cedar Hill." Beulah remembered Sandy. She was one of the pack of girls Annie ran around with after she got her driver's license.

"How's Annie doing? She got any kids yet?" Sandy hit a button and waited.

"No, she's not married." Beulah watched the cuff slowly expand and squeeze her arm.

"You're kidding! I thought she'd have a litter by now. I'm

on my third and due any day!" Sandy rubbed her stomach and turned sideways, giving Beulah the full view of the last days in her third trimester.

"I see," Beulah said, not caring one bit for the younger generation's urge to show their swollen bellies in every conceivable way.

Sandy stuck a thermometer in Beulah's mouth. "I thought Annie would marry Brett, as crazy as they were about each other. I guess you never know." The thermometer beeped and Sandy pulled it out. "Normal, and so was your blood pressure." She threw away the sanitary wrap and put the thermometer back in her pocket. "Give her my best, Mrs. Campbell, and if you need anything, just ask for me. I'm on shift until seven tomorrow morning."

"Thank you, Sandy," Beulah called as the young woman left the room. Well, it helped to know someone. It might get her a quicker trip to the bathroom if necessary.

Of all the things to ponder in the hospital, why did she have to be reminded of Annie's high school boyfriend, Brett Bradshaw. Those Bradshaws were good-looking as Hollywood actors, but a bad lot, heavy into drinking, and some said, drugs. She tried to warn Annie away from him, but Beulah saw right quick Annie wasn't hearing any of it.

When the warnings didn't take, she and Fred talked about it and decided not to say anything else for fear of pushing her in his direction. Looking back on Jo Anne's situation, their dislike for Ed might have made Jo Anne more set on seeing him, but who knew? All they could do was the best they knew how at the time.

Instead, she bit her tongue when Annie talked about Brett and brought him around. She had been pleasant to the boy, fed him meals, soda pop and chips. Annie had dated him until they went to college. He finally broke it off with her in college, and Beulah was never so relieved. Better heartbreak now than later, when she was saddled with little children.

Beulah fiddled with the plastic bracelet on her left hand. Come to think of it, that was about when Annie and Jake quit being so close. When Brett Bradshaw entered the picture, everything between Annie and Jake changed. Jake found a girlfriend after that, and even though the families still got together for special occasions, it wasn't like before when the kids were younger.

It was a disappointment for both her and Fred and the Wilders because Jake's personality suited Annie. It reminded Beulah of how Fred had balanced her out. Annie tended to be high-strung, a little like the thoroughbreds Fred used to trade for from time to time, but Jake was easygoing and cool as a cucumber. Once when the kids were eleven or twelve, Annie flew into the house all in a dither. "Jake's arm, it's broken," she had said, barely able to get the words out. Jake trailed behind, holding his arm and studying the strange angle as if he were looking at it under a microscope. Of course, he might have been in a bit of shock, but that incident had impressed Beulah. He didn't cry or complain one bit, at least as long as he was in her care.

Compatible as two peas in a pod, they had all thought. When they went out to dinner on Saturday nights, as had been their tradition for nigh on twenty years, Fred and Charlie teased that if the kids married, it would join their two farms and make a nice big plantation for Annie and Jake to keep up, but they never went on like that in front of the children. No, the kids never knew how they all felt, and it was better that way, with how things turned out.

Jake had found his way and Annie would too, Beulah was sure. It all worked out good in the end for those who loved the Lord, like that verse in Romans said.

Eleven o'clock. She turned on the television and flipped through the channels to see if anything was worth watching. She found a local channel playing round-the-clock sermons. She listened first to the Baptist who had a tendency to screech. Then there was the Presbyterian who took a whole hour preaching on two verses—"unpacking," he called it. Now, she was in the middle of a breathless preacher laying hands on people right and left. Her knee exercises the nurse was teaching her would go particularly well with the cadence of this preacher. Hold, two, three, four ... "And God said," five, six, seven, eight, "Do not fear!'"

At the end of a sentence, he made a mighty groaning noise, sucking in a lungful of air before he went on to the next sentence. *He ought to have an X-ray*, she thought. Her cousin sounded like that, and he was eaten up with the emphysema.

After that she switched off the television and hoped desperately for sleep. When it did not come, her eyes rested on a sign below the clock. It read, "Dial-A-Prayer."

"Well, now," she said aloud, "I could sure use a prayer right now." She picked up the receiver and dialed the number posted on the sign.

The line was busy.

Chapter Twenty-Two

AFTER THE ICU scare was past, Annie confessed her water fiasco to her grandmother.

"We'll start all over if it is ruined," Beulah said. "I've had to do that before when a late frost took everything I planted one year."

Woody thought most of the garden would be all right, other than one corner that might not survive the drowning. "Nothing to do but wait and see," he said.

As frightened as Annie had been at her grandmother's health scare, the extra days had given the painters more time to work. Another man had shown up on Wednesday to help speed the work along. The priming was finished and they had started the actual painting.

Annie had hoped it would all be done before her grandmother came home over the weekend, but it all depended on the weather, according to Woody, who appointed himself supervisor.

On Friday morning, Annie called Duke at the hardware store and made a request she'd been thinking about all week.

"Sure thing," Duke said. "I'll put your name on it. It'll need a coat of paint, but you should have some left over from the house."

Still in her pajama pants and a long sleeve shirt over a T-shirt, Annie took her coffee to the back porch. Curled in a chair with a throw wrapped around her shoulders for extra warmth against the cool morning, she quietly listened to the birds singing in the trees. It sounded like an enormous orchestra warming up, each playing his or her own song before the conductor approached the podium, and they all quieted in preparation for the musical piece.

Annie tried to remember the last time she heard such a mass of birds singing in New York or even Rome. Had other noise drowned it out or did she not listen? From now on, she vowed, she would listen for the birds no matter where she was in the world.

Nutmeg stood next to the fence, barely moving a muscle. It was as if she were posing for a sculpture. Annie sipped her coffee and watched her for several minutes to see if she would move from the spot, but she didn't. The mare pawed the ground, but remained motionless as if she were waiting for something to happen.

The whole pasture wasn't visible from where she sat on the porch, but she could see maybe a third of it. It was the same section where she fell off Nutmeg, which must be how her grandmother knew what had happened.

When Woody brought Nutmeg over, he said, "Horses can get into anything. Best check them once a day."

Annie looked for Nutmeg once a day, although she didn't exactly know what she was looking for. She figured as long as a horse was upright, it must be okay. And there was Nutmeg standing next to the fence and looking perfectly content. There seemed to be no need to walk all the way out there.

Woody stopped by to check on her, sometimes twice a day and particularly at mealtime. She liked Woody and even felt a little sorry for him. He seemed very devoted to his mother's care and Annie admired him for that; but Annie wondered if she should come right out and tell him she had no interest in dating, now and maybe ever. Being that forthright had always been difficult for her. Janice would come right out and say it: "Woody, I appreciate your help, but if you've got anything else on your mind other than friendship, forget about it."

The contents of her coffee mug empty and the morning wearing on, she went inside and called the hospital number posted next to the phone.

"I'm tolerable well. Ready for better food, that's for sure. You can't imagine what they call sausage and biscuits."

"Be glad you're not on the cardiac diet. I've heard its worse," Annie said, smiling. "Are you sure you don't want me to come today?"

"Law, no. My Sunday school class is coming today. That will keep me entertained. I will be ready to leave in the morning as soon as they sign me out."

"I'll be there by nine. Call if you need me."

Annie had taken over lunch preparations for the painters. Evelyn was busy straightening up her house, preparing the guest room, and "laying up food" as she called it, for the next couple of weeks. Annie prepared fresh hummus dip and baked pita chips as well as a large Greek salad with grilled chicken for each man.

"What is this, if you don't mind me asking?" Jim pointed to the bowl of hummus.

"Garbanzo beans, garlic, olive oil, a little lemon and a touch of sugar," Annie answered.

"Never heard of garbanzo beans," he said.

"They are also called chickpeas," she said, realizing her menu choice might have been a mistake.

"Never heard of that either," said Elbert. "But it don't taste bad," he quickly added.

After the meal, Annie cleaned up the kitchen and made a list of grocery store items before heading out in her grandmother's Marquis. Approaching the hardware store, Annie had a pang of fear at the thought of having to parallel park on Main Street. It had been years and she had never been good at it.

She slowed and searched for two spaces together that she might slide into, but there was only one space. Scanning both sides of the street, Annie saw this was the only spot available.

With a deep breath, she pulled up next to the car in front of the space, wishing all the while her grandmother had traded for something smaller than a Marquis. With her arm over the back of the seat and her body twisted in order to see, she backed up, but soon realized she was too far from the curb.

Turning and putting the car in drive, she pulled forward and tried again. This time she cut too sharp and the front end was sticking out in the middle of Main Street.

The car behind her waited patiently while she pulled forward. She tried again, but was still not close enough to the curb. A group of men in jeans spilled out of the diner. By this time, several people had stopped on the sidewalk, faces curious, to watch her effort. Annie felt her own face flush as she put it in drive once more. Just as she was about to pull forward, a knock on her window made her jump. It was Jake, motioning for her to roll down the window.

"Want some help?" he asked.

Annie hesitated, determined to figure the thing out. But the growing spectacle brought her to her senses. "Please!" she said, and scooted over in the seat.

Jake didn't say a word while he positioned the car, then slid it perfectly into the parking space. When he put it in park, he said, "The space is small. It's no wonder you had trouble."

"Thank you," she said, surprised he didn't tease her.

"Alright, I gotta go. We're headed over to Rutherford to look at a farm," he said, sliding out of the car. "See you later?"

She nodded and he turned to go. Jake was home. Why did that make her feel so happy?

Inside the hardware store, Annie admired the wooden porch swing Duke had set aside for her. "Anything else?" he asked before ringing her up.

"That should do it," Annie said, pleased with her purchase. "Will it fit in the backseat of the Marquis?"

"Oh yeah. That's one advantage of a big car," he said, and winked at her.

After Duke loaded the swing, Annie walked down the street to Wyatt's Drug Store, where ceiling fans hung low from the ancient tin ceilings. A massive wooden soda fountain claimed a section of wall. Round tables with woven iron chairs sat on the hardwood floor near the soda fountain and the film development was in the back, past the dining area and the gift section.

A young woman behind the counter took the pictures after Annie explained the enlargements she wanted. She was nearly out the door when a nostalgic craving for a chocolate milkshake pulled her like a magnet back to the soda fountain. Instead of asking for it to go, she sat at the counter and enjoyed every drop.

"We're almost done," Elbert said after they helped Annie unload the swing and take it to the front porch. "If you don't mind us staying late, we'll try to finish up tonight."

"You've still got hooks up there," Jim said, pointing to the robin's-egg-blue beadboard ceiling. "Want us to hang it for you?"

"Sure," she said, wondering if accepting all this help would serve her well later. Independence was a valuable survival skill in the city.

"I'll grab the ladder," said Elbert.

Jim sorted through the chain and as Elbert held the other end of the swing, he looped a link onto the hook. They did the same on the other side, counting the links so the swing would be level.

"Now, see how high you want that seat. I can raise or lower the chain."

Annie sat down and thought the swing was a few inches high, especially for her grandmother, who would want to sit easily.

"Maybe down a few inches," she said. "Yes, that looks about right."

"We can put a coat of paint on it before we go," Elbert offered.

"No, no. I can do it while you all finish the house," Annie said.

Jim and Elbert left the porch to go around back where the last bit of painting needed to be done. Before Annie started on the swing, she decided to sit again just to make sure the height was right. She sat and swung for a bit, enjoying the feel of it and imagining how pleased her grandmother would be when she saw it.

Just then, a crack sounded above and before she knew it, her side of the swing thumped to the concrete floor and pitched her headlong into the boxwood bush.

Annie rolled and scrambled to stand up as footsteps approached from the side of the house. She did not want to be the center of attention yet again today.

"We should have checked those old hooks," Elbert said, reaching for the loose chain.

Annie fought back the urge to cry, what with the sudden dump into the bush on top of her mortification at parallel parking. Instead, she brushed herself off.

"Who would have thought," she said.

Chapter Twenty-Three

EVELYN HAD INVITED Annie to eat dinner with her and Jake when he arrived Friday night. Annie had been tempted, but she wanted everything ready for her grandmother's return.

"How about a movie after dinner?" Jake asked her when he called to check on Beulah. She had agreed and suggested including Lindy.

While Annie waited outside for Jake, she saw Nutmeg in her favorite spot and staring at her with wide and questioning eyes. Annie started to walk over and give her a rub on the nose, but the crunch of gravel signaled Jake's arrival.

When she scooted into the seat, he said, "How's Beulah?"

"Ready to come home! I can pick her up tomorrow morning. And thanks for bailing me out today. I was horrified to see half the town watching."

"I liked it," he said. "And the single guys I was with wanted to know who you were. I told them not to bother, you were way too good for them," he teased.

"Good. I'm not interested anyway. What was the meeting about?"

"The plan for a processing facility outside Rutherford. We

want to start a butcher shop to sell only meat grown locally and handled humanely, with access to pasture and no hormones or antibiotics. They need growers and I would need a place to process the meat."

"It sounds like the farming stuff is coming together," she said.

"It is. I feel confident enough to give the bank my notice. The more I dig into the foundation work, I realize it's not my passion. That narrows my options down to farming or going into business with Cam's dad. Either way, a partnership with these guys is important. I've been thinking that if I go the hotel route with Cam's dad, it should focus on a small boutique hotel with sound environmental practices and a restaurant with an emphasis on local food: a farm-to-table concept. This next couple of weeks of working through the business plans and having Cam here to weigh in on everything is critical."

Annie felt a slight pang of envy at his reference to Cam. Annie had grown used to being Jake's adviser, especially during a time when Cam seemed busy with work and unavailable.

"Grandma wants to have you, Cam and Evelyn over for dinner. She said she would help slice and dice if I could put it all together. My cooking has improved in the few weeks I've been here."

He laughed. "I remember you making us donuts one time and catching the kitchen on fire!"

She giggled. "We made them out of biscuit dough and tried frying them in the iron skillet. They weren't bad until I dropped several in at one time and the grease caught the dish towel on fire!"

"You ran screaming, and I dumped the whole jar of Beulah's flour on it."

"And you looked like a ghost! Even Grandma laughed after she gave us both a tongue-lashing," Annie said, trying to catch her breath from laughing.

He stopped the car in front of Lindy's office and apartment and turned to look at her. The fading sunlight cast a warm glow on his face.

"Annie, thanks for listening to me through this whole process. It's been good to have somebody who understands."

Annie had never before noticed the tiny white specks that made his blue eyes look crystalline.

"Well," she said, breaking the spell, "I have something for you." She reached into her purse and pulled out the framed picture.

He looked at her with raised eyebrows then tore the tissue off.

"What is this ...?" His words trailed off and he smiled at the picture. "This is great. I'll put this in my office."

Annie watched his face as he looked at the photo. "Look at you in your overalls," he said.

"And you in those highwater pants," she said, and they both laughed.

"Thanks!" He moved slightly in his seat, as if he was going to hug her, but instead he grasped her hand tightly. "I really like it."

"I better go get Lindy, or we'll be late," she said, sliding out of the car.

Rutherford was by no means a large town, but it was four times the size of Somerville's population of four thousand and boasted a stadium-seating movie theater, more stores and a coffee shop. It was a college town, and with that came the advantages of a bookstore, an arts league and theater. Only twenty minutes on a nice, new four-lane road, the drive was easy, and for rural Somervillians, it saved a long trip to Lexington.

After the movie, Annie checked her cell phone to make sure Beulah had not called. No one wanted the night to end, so they finished out the evening in a bustling coffee house near the college that boasted of fair trade practices and homemade desserts. Their discussion of the movie about the struggles of a single parent continued over the coffee.

"Do you realize all three of us only have one parent? Wouldn't you say most people still have both parents by the time they hit their early thirties?" Lindy asked.

"Probably," Jake said, "but I try to remind myself I had a

great dad for as long as I had him. He had me doing chores from the time I was three. He taught me to drive a tractor when I was eight, how to fix machinery, how to build, how to handle cows. It's almost like he knew our time wouldn't last forever so he got everything in early."

"What about your dad, Annie? Do you see him?" Lindy asked.

"My dad left when I was a baby. He called occasionally and sent birthday cards with a little money, but I didn't know him until after I moved to New York."

"Why then?" Lindy said.

"My father is a wanderer. He has lived the world over, ironically living the life my mother would have loved to have had with him. When I could finally travel to see him, he was happy to have me come. He is the kind of man who is proud to be a father, but never wanted to raise children."

Annie stirred her coffee before taking a drink. "When I finally understood that, I expected so much less of him and our relationship improved dramatically. We get along fine today, although we don't see each other very often. When we do, it's good."

"Was it difficult for you to relate to men, not having a father around?"

"Lindy, you really do need to get a counseling degree. I think you have a knack for it!" Annie smiled at her.

"I know!" Lindy threw her head down on the table in mock discouragement. "I can't help myself. I love to know how people think."

"Was it? Difficult to relate to men?" It was Jake this time, serious and waiting for her answer.

"You too?" Annie punched his arm. "I don't know. I've made my share of relationship mistakes. Hopefully, I'll get it right if there is a next time."

"With Woody?" Lindy asked, her eyes dancing with mischief.

"Woody who?" Jake asked.

"Maybe. He might be the one," Annie said, teasing back.

"Woody Patterson?" Jake said.

Annie shrugged her shoulders and raised her eyebrows, enjoying the look of alarm plastered all over Jake's face.

***

Annie hit the snooze button twice before finally throwing the blankets off. Stretching, she felt her sore muscles again. Maybe it was the fall off the front porch that did it this time, but it seemed every day a new set of muscles complained wildly that life had changed for her.

She was pouring her first cup of coffee when the phone rang. Betty Gibson started talking as soon as Annie answered.

"Missy's high school graduation was yesterday. Can you believe she'll be the first Gibson to go to college this fall? Anyway, up we went to Lexington for the ceremony, and it seemed like every high school in the city was having ceremonies. You couldn't stir 'em with a stick. After the pomp and circumstance, we said we'd take her to eat wherever she wanted to go. Law-zee! That was a mistake. Where do you think she took us?"

"I have no idea," Annie said, knowing Betty didn't really want a guess.

"Indian! And I'm not talking Shawnee. I've never seen such colorful food. Bright yellows and red, and spicy as all get-out. Don't you know, Joe gobbled it up! Missy ordered him something with potatoes in it, and he ate like a pig. I think he was puttin' on for Missy, but he swore to me he wasn't. I liked it real well myself, but I was afraid all those foreign spices would tear me up and sure enough, they did. I was up all night with the hiatal. And that's what I called to tell you this morning. I don't usually take to sitting out on the porch at one in the morning, but there I was, not able to sleep and burping up some spice grown a half a world away."

"Yes ...," Annie said.

"I saw headlights come down May Hollow Road. From the security light out by the garage, I could tell it was a small car, kind of silverylike, but I'm not sure of the exact color. It stopped in front of your driveway, and a woman got out. She carried something to Beulah's mailbox and put it inside. Then she got back in the car and drove real slow to Gibson's Creek. I know it's a federal offense to go messin' with another person's mailbox, but I checked to see what she put in there, afraid it was some sort of bomb and I might need to call the ATF. But all it turned out to be was an empty casserole dish and a pie plate." Betty sounded disappointed.

"Thanks for telling me," Annie said. "I'll get them out before the mail runs."

Odd time to return dishes, she thought, but the woman seemed to want her privacy, so Annie shrugged it off and returned to her morning ritual of taking her cereal and coffee out to the back porch. It had become one of her favorite parts of the day. Since her grandmother had been gone, she used that time to pray. It was a nice place to eat breakfast or supper with the back of the house facing south. There was enough room for a table and chairs, even with the old pump and leaving space for the dinner bell. If her grandmother agreed, maybe she would purchase a set since they both enjoyed the outdoor space.

In the meantime, Annie slid onto one of the cold metal chairs, content to eat her cereal amidst the freshness of the morning. She prayed for her grandmother to continue healing and for Jake as he was about to make such a drastic change. When she finished, she looked for Booger, who usually didn't appear until later in the day. Then she watched as two cardinals chased each other in the mating dance, the male, bright red with a pointed head that almost looked like a lodge hat of some sort, and the female with brown feathers not nearly as majestic as the male's.

She pushed a strand of hair out of her mouth and tipped the cereal bowl up to drink the last of the milk. As she did, one of the barn cats grapevined in and out of her legs, meowing and purring, asking for leftover milk. She stopped drinking with a spoonful of milk still in the bowl and poured it out on the concrete. The cat lapped it up.

Watching the cat reminded her of Stuart's orange tabby. Was Chester snuggling in Beverly's lap like he did with her? Had Stuart told her he came from a client, or had he told her the truth? Maybe Beverly was the kind of person he wouldn't have to lie to. The thought of Stuart didn't make her sad now—sorry she had been so vulnerable, sorry she hadn't been wiser, but not sad. It had been a hard lesson learned, but one that had changed her for the better.

The cardinals had flown away, but now a squirrel chattered in the maple tree next to the porch. Annie watched it ease down to the lowest branch, its beady eyes on the cat. The cat looked up once and blinked slowly. The squirrel turned, climbed a branch and disappeared in the leaves.

Annie's years in New York had been so exciting, yet she had drifted away from old friends, her faith and her family. It would be different when she went back. Living in Somerville the past month had shown her how important it was to have a community of people who cared.

Bathed and dressed for the trip to the hospital, Annie remembered at the last minute to check on Nutmeg. From the back porch, she could see the horse standing in the exact same position as yesterday. Annie started to get in the car, but something told her to go out to the pasture. After all, with a large field, why would the horse be in the same place for an entire day and night?

Nutmeg whinnied when she saw Annie coming to her. She stomped a hoof into a freshly made dirt spot. A pile of manure behind her tail told Annie the horse couldn't move for some reason. Something was wrong.

"Nutmeg, can't you move?" Annie grabbed the halter and looked at Nutmeg's head, examining it from her ears to the whiskers on her chin. There were no abrasions. The animal's large eyes followed her movements, assuring her she could see.

"Never trust a horse," Woody had said. His words reminded Annie to take care in the examination. Gently, she worked her hands slowly down the front of her chest, and then her legs. She lifted up each front foot, as Woody taught her to do, and checked for something caught in her hoof. Both feet looked clean.

Tenderly, her hands felt over the back, side and underbelly of the horse. Crossing in front of the horse, she went 'round to the other side and repeated the same move. Next she felt over the back haunches and down each back leg. The horse was standing too close to the fence for her to pick up the back hooves. She patted Nutmeg's behind to try and move her out a foot or so. The horse stepped forward, and it was then that Annie saw the problem.

A section of Nutmeg's tail was caught in a deep fissure in the fence post. It was wedged so tight Annie was forced to climb the fence in order to pry it out from above. It would not budge. Nutmeg's pulling against it had firmly embedded the hair deep into the crack.

"Be right back, girl. Hold on!"

Annie hopped off the fence and ran to the house. Since they had recently cleaned out the kitchen drawers, Annie knew right where to look for the scissors. A minute later, she was gnawing through the tough horse hair. Finally, the last strand was cut. She slapped Nutmeg again on the haunches, and the horse took off in a gallop, straight for the water tank.

Annie watched the horse run, a sick feeling churning in her stomach. It was June, and the heat and humidity were not bad, but if this had happened a month later, it could have been a disaster. The horse might have died of dehydration right there, within sight of the house.

Annie had feared Nutmeg at first, a powerful and unpredictable animal. But day after day, she spent time with the horse, brushing her down, giving her carrots, and in the process they had formed a trust of sorts. Horses operated out of fear, she had read in one of the books in her grandmother's library. She worked to show Nutmeg her intentions were good. Eventually, Nutmeg allowed Annie to lead her and Annie's direction became more confident, her body more relaxed. But even this beautiful and strong horse was completely dependent on the care of the humans around her.

Standing there in the field and watching Nutmeg drink, Annie saw this one incident as representative of everything about living on a farm: *It's interdependent with the humans who care for it. We need what it gives us and the farm needs us.*

Grandma was right, she thought. You needed to live on a farm or have someone living on it. There were too many things that could go wrong.

***

"Would you look at *that*?"

Annie watched her grandmother's face light up as her eyes took in the paint job.

"Who did this?"

"Evelyn orchestrated it. Jim, Elbert and Ronnie from your church volunteered the labor. They just finished this morning."

"Land sakes, how nice. And what is this?" Beulah caught sight of the porch swing and the petunias.

"Do you like it?"

"The old swing broke around the time Fred died. I never got around to putting up another."

"We'll drive around to the back where there's only that one step." Annie stopped the car in front of the step up to the back porch.

"You don't know how good it is to be home. I don't care if I never spend another night away."

Annie laughed. "You weren't exactly staying at the Ritz."

Annie remembered the instructions the nurse gave her at the hospital about how to support her grandmother and let her walk the few steps into the house with the walker.

Inside, her grandmother stopped to look around.

"If I could bend over, I would kiss the linoleum. This looks like heaven to me."

Annie let her stand there and look around as long as she wanted to. She could see joy splashed all over her grandmother's face.

"I guess I better rest a bit," she said, and Annie followed her, holding onto her as her grandmother took small, slow steps toward her bedroom.

"And look at this picture by my bed. I don't know what to say." Her grandmother's voice choked, and Annie could feel her own throat tighten.

Neither spoke as Annie settled her grandmother into bed. When she finished, Annie stepped back and put her hands on her hips.

"As someone I know would say, 'You look as snug as a bug in a rug!' "

Her grandmother laughed, but Annie could see the effort had drained her. "Why don't you get some rest this afternoon? Here's your new cordless phone. If you need me, press these two keys and it will automatically dial my cell phone." She showed her grandmother how to press the 1 followed by the star button. "That way, wherever I am on the farm, I can be reached."

"One and star. I've got it," her grandmother said and leaned back on the pillow.

"Here's the remote if you want to watch television. I'll get you a glass of water in case you get thirsty."

"Do we have any tea?" her grandmother asked, perking up a bit.

"We do, although I made it, so it won't be as good as yours."

Annie brought the sweet tea, and her grandmother took a drink of it before lying back again on the pillow.

"It's good!" she said.

Annie smiled at the compliment. "You rest, and I'll make you sausage and biscuits for supper."

Her grandma's eyes were closed, but Annie was sure she saw a faint smile push up at the corners of her mouth before her face relaxed into sleep.

Chapter Twenty-Four

AFTER VANILLA ICE cream with caramel topping and a final game of Rook where she and Joe barely beat Betty and Jake, Annie helped her grandmother to bed before joining Jake in the dark on the back porch.

"I haven't played Rook in years," she said, sitting down next to him in the other metal chair. "I'm glad you suggested it."

"I used to play when I lived in Atlanta, but everybody in Cincinnati plays Euchre."

"Everybody in New York plays poker, according to Stuart," Annie said, folding her legs up to her chest and hugging them.

"I tried it a time or two, but I don't like losing money."

"Neither do I! But with Stuart, everything was easy come, easy go."

"Did you ever visualize yourself growing old with him?" he asked.

The question surprised her and she thought about the answer before responding. "I guess I never actually let my mind go that far. I thought love was enough to handle anything in the future. But now I know that sometimes what appears to be love for a person might really be love for an idea. I loved the idea of who I thought Stuart could be, not who he really was."

She turned to see his face, but he was looking up at the night sky, his profile lit by the moon and the faint light from the barn lot.

"What about you," she said gently.

"With knowing Camille's parents so well, it's easy to think we'll be like them. I like how they treat each other after almost forty years of marriage."

"We can't always be judged by our parents, good or bad," Annie said.

"True. And that's why it's important for me to have her down here before we take the next step. I want to make sure I'm seeing who she is and not who I think." He looked at her and grinned.

"Perspective. Maybe that's what has changed with me. I don't know if it's being out of the city or having more time on my hands, but I see things differently."

"Maybe you should stay," he said, turning back to her and studying her face.

"Stay here? Permanently?" Annie laughed. "I don't know what I would do for a living."

"You could do lots of things. You're great with people. You're smart, kind and responsible. You could do something with your artwork or something in hospitality. Anything."

"I never thought of it as an option. And I haven't done anything with art in a long time." They were quiet for a moment, both watching as a sliver of cloud passed in front of the moon. Then she said, "It might be like one of those glass jars with the pretty scenery on the inside. You shake it up, and with the snow flying around, it's magical. But when all the stuff settles down, it's not that pretty. I'm in the magical place right now, but when things settle down and go back to normal, I'm afraid the magic will wear off."

"Maybe so, but the magic is still there. You just have to look harder for it. And sometimes it takes shaking things up."

Annie laughed. "Whatever it is, it came at just the right time, thanks partly to you," she said, and then reached over and touched him on the arm. When she did, it was as if a spark of electricity passed from his body to hers. Annie looked at Jake, startled by the sensation, to see if he felt it too.

Without looking at her, he said, "Feels like an electrical storm might be coming."

Annie was amazed at how creative she felt. She woke up the next day wanting to sketch everything in sight. Even sitting up in bed that morning, she had pulled her sketch pad on top of the covers and drawn the outside view from her bed with the old maple tree framed by her bedroom window. She hadn't felt like this in years, since she first moved to New York and everything was so new and exciting.

After making breakfast for her grandmother and herself, and making sure Beulah was comfortable, she packed a small knapsack with her art supplies, her camera and phone, and some water. The stone house beckoned, and the walk out there would be a good opportunity for time alone in nature for prayer.

A storm had blown through in the night and the grass was wet, but she didn't mind. After years of being so protected from nature, having her feet get wet from the rain was actually welcome. It made her feel alive.

Annie settled against a tree and studied the house from many yards away. *What a shame to be surrounded by all this beauty and not allow it in the house. It seems a writer would take inspiration from nature, not keep it out.*

"She's not a writer," Annie voiced the thought aloud. But why lie? And that was where she was stuck. They had no basis to enter the house, she hadn't broken any laws and there was no evidence of wrongdoing, but in her gut, she knew something wasn't right with Stella's story.

Forcing her mind from the mystery inside the house to the outside, Annie began to sketch, slowly at first and then with more purpose until she fell into a rhythm. Three times she flipped the page over and began again, but the last time felt right. With birds calling to one another among the rustling leaves in the trees above and next to the trickling water beside her, the outline of the old stone house slowly took shape.

It would be the perfect present for her grandmother before she left for New York. She would work on the sketch until it was right. With her digital camera, she took two pictures, one with her zoom and one without, so she could continue working back at the farmhouse.

Annie gathered her things into the knapsack, a good feeling of accomplishment washing over her. As she stuffed the camera in, she remembered the cord and software to print pictures were still in New York. She would ask Janice to send it to her along with some other items she needed.

Her cell phone rang just as she dropped it into the sack and she quickly fished it out, thinking it might be her grandmother.

"Annie? It's Vichy."

"Bob, what's up?" Annie was surprised to hear from her boss and hoped it was not more bad news.

"I worked a miracle and got you back in a week," he spit out the words.

"A week!" Annie leaned hard against a tree.

"Monday, nine a.m. You have to go through Patriot's orientation, like any other new employee, but after training, you'll be in the skies again."

Annie felt her chest tighten as if she were wrapped in a rubber band from the waist up.

"Bob, I can't start that soon. My grandmother just had surgery. She needs me here." Annie braced during the brief silence and waited for the eruption.

"Don't give me that! You don't know how hard I had to fight for you! How am I going to say that you want the job, but want to pick when you start? Do you know how many girls are standing in line behind you?"

Annie could almost feel the spray of saliva come through the phone.

"Bob, I appreciate it. You know I do. But you told me it would be three months and maybe longer. I've committed to helping my grandmother for another few weeks until she can take care of herself again. Can't you please get me an extension? I'll take whatever flights are available. Please give me more time."

"Why do I bother to stick my neck out for you?" he grumbled.

"Because you're a kind and caring boss. Please, see if you can get me an extension."

He exhaled a deep breath. "I'll try, but I'm not in charge, so don't get your hopes up! You'll be lucky to keep the job."

Annie turned her phone off and put it in her bag. It was the worst possible timing. Weeks of gardening and canning were ahead. The tomatoes were tiny and green. More beans were coming and the corn hadn't even tasseled. It was too soon. If Bob didn't come through with an extension, Annie would have to disappoint her grandmother yet again.

Chapter Twenty-Five

ANOTHER STORM HAD blown in Monday around noon and the hard rain hitting the roof told Beulah there would be no gardening done this afternoon. Even if you could stand the mud and wet plants, messing in a garden while it was still muddy could spread disease, she had always heard.

The rain had made her nap soundly and there had been no need for any pain pills. In fact, she had a notion to quit the stuff anyway, them being a magnet for dopeheads intent on a home invasion.

Annie had gone out to see what the garden looked like while Beulah made her way to the kitchen to look at the rain gauge positioned on the plank fence beyond the kitchen window. Joe had already called and reported eight-tenths of an inch. Evelyn said they got nearly nine-tenths. They were all hungry for the rain after such a dry spell.

Reaching the sink, she held on to it and looked at the gauge. A good eight-tenths. She called Joe to report, and then Evelyn. It never ceased to amaze them how one farm might get a substantial amount of rain, while another connecting piece of land might only get a drop.

Annie came in the back door from inspecting the garden, looking mighty disappointed.

"You might be able to get in it tomorrow if we get sun and a little wind," Beulah said.

"I was hoping to start canning beans tonight," Annie answered, washing her hands out in the sink.

"That's farm life. Everything around here depends on the weather, and we're not in charge of that."

Annie went back upstairs, and Beulah debated on another cup of coffee, even though it was midafternoon. *Why not?* she thought. She poured another cup and slowly moved to the back porch to enjoy her coffee outside, where the sun was making an appearance.

Finally, she decided there was no more putting off those exercises. Her therapist was coming this evening and she would ask Beulah if she had done her exercises, and Beulah didn't want to tell her no. Sitting down on the side of her bed, she looked at the sheet and went through them one by one.

The phone rang when she was nearly done, but she was glad for the interruption.

"Camille got lost! Jake left to pick her up." Evelyn sounded exasperated.

"What happened?"

"I don't know. His directions were clear as a bell, but when she got off the interstate, somehow she took a wrong road and ended up in Renfro Valley. She called Jake, and he tried to talk her through the directions, but she was tired and upset, so he said he would go and get her."

"Bless her heart," Beulah said.

"Now they'll have to see if they can find a place to leave her car over in Mount Vernon, or maybe she'll follow him here."

"Well, I'll be," Beulah said. "Can we do anything to help?"

"No, I just thought I'd let you know."

After her exercises, Beulah turned on the five o' clock news, a habit she was quickly falling into, since there was little else she could do during the day.

"There is late-breaking news coming from Lincoln County,

south of Lexington."

Beulah leaned forward.

Could it be Jake and Camille, a wreck maybe? She prayed that whatever it was, it was no one she knew. But was that right to pray for? Whoever it might be was loved by someone. Finally, the anchor came back on to fill in the details.

"Several people were arrested in a drug ring this morning in the Poplar Grove community of Lincoln County." The camera spanned over to a group of men and women in handcuffs, herded into the state police vans like livestock.

"They are charged with making and distributing methamphetamine, a highly addictive drug. Meth is known to be flammable and dangerous while being made. There have been three explosions in the state of Kentucky alone this past spring from meth laboratories."

The camera showed the inside of the house, where pots and pans were set about to make the drug.

"Two children were removed from the scene by police with potential burns from the chemicals. Chemicals used to make meth are household items, but when combined they make a drug that is so powerful, a onetime user can become an addict."

The camera showed the outside of the house. Beulah didn't recognize the site, but Poplar Grove was clear on the other side of the county.

"Drug makers attempt to hide their activities by covering the windows." A close shot of a window showed a sheet draped in front of it. "Kentuckians should report any suspicious activity to the state police. From Lincoln County, this is Buzz Adcock reporting live."

"Thanks, Buzz. In Bourbon County today, a freak accident left a man hanging upside down in his car from a tree. The man was released without serious injury, and a crane is now attempting to dislodge the car."

"In national news, a missing persons report out of Chicago shows ..." Beulah clicked off the television and stared unseeing at the gray screen, her mind racing.

Stella Hawkins had covered the windows of the stone house.

Could she be involved in something so terrible as making drugs? Beulah hated to even think such a thing of another human being, but she hadn't fallen off the turnip truck yesterday.

With her walker, she hobbled over to the phone number list stuck between two out-of-date phone books and searched for Jeb Harris. He had given her his number a year ago and told her to call if she ever had need. What would be the harm of asking the young detective simply to drive by?

Trying not to sound overly concerned, she told him about the blankets over the windows and the electronic eye at the bridge that let Stella know who was coming in or going out. Jeb was such a nice boy, he said he would drive by this afternoon and check it out. She felt better now, knowing it was in the hands of the police.

"Who was that?" Annie asked, coming into the room dressed in shorts and sneakers.

Beulah told Annie about the news story and her conversation with the detective.

"Did he seem concerned?"

"Oh, I don't know. It's hard to tell with people like that who are used to dealing with so much. He said he would check on it."

"I'm glad you called." Annie stood on one foot and bent the other leg back behind her—stretching, she called it. "I'll take another look around tomorrow."

"Well, don't go snooping around. Let the police handle it."

"I want to see the old cemetery anyway. I haven't been there since I've been home. And then, I hope it will be dry enough to pick beans," Annie said.

"Don't forget the groceries. I'm nearly out of butter."

"I'm headed there now," Annie said, gathering up her purse.

Chapter Twenty-Six

HUGGING THE FENCE line between the Wilder and Campbell farms, Annie swung her arms back and forth to the rhythm of her steps. The rain left the air pure and clean, the lines of color between the green hills and the blue sky crisp with contrast. The rock wall that provided the fence between the two farms also served as the back wall of the family cemetery, another half-mile beyond the crossover place.

When she reached the rock steps on the stone fence, she sat down to take in the beauty of the morning. For a moment, she wished for her sketch pad, but it was nice letting her arms swing freely. Annie was enjoying these walks back on the farm, so much so that she had given up her running to hike over the uneven farmland, up and down the gently rolling hills.

When she got to the wall crossing, she paused for a moment. This spot would always represent Jake to her, since it had been their meeting place for so many years. They had fallen into an easy intimacy that had evaded them in the later years of high school and into college. Different friends and interests had pulled them in separate directions. There had never been a fight. It had just happened. To be able to pick back up now, years later, was such a gift. It was as if the distance after childhood never happened; yet the relationship had grown mature, supportive.

"It's an opportunity," he had said during one of their early talks about her breakup and the layoff. She was starting to believe he was right. It had already afforded her this priceless chance to come home and reconnect with people who loved her and whom she loved.

She leaned back and held her face up to the sun, enjoying the warmth on her skin and the light that, even through her closed eyes, seemed to fill her soul. Stuart had been so little in her thoughts lately that she almost felt guilty. By staying next to the fence, Annie avoided the stone house, only catching glimpses of it from the wooded hillside where the fence led through a stand of locust, maple and oak trees. From the crossover place, she followed the fence up and over one hill covered with hardwood trees, then up the side of another wooded hill. At the top of that hill lay the May family cemetery.

The cemetery was marked off by a dry-laid stone fence with a rusty iron gate that was never locked. It creaked and groaned when she pushed it open. The area inside was neatly mowed and trimmed. The older stones were in the back, the newer ones in the front. In the front row, the larger granite stones stood straight and even, whereas the older, smaller stones cocked slightly to the left or right, the result of the ground settling over decades.

Her mother's grave was the first she came to. Kneeling on the soft grass, Annie touched the cold granite and wished for the hundredth time she could feel her mother's arms around her. Lavender drifted through her senses as if she smelled a bouquet. It was what her mother had grown in their back yard, and it had scented the stone house, sitting in bouquets in the kitchen, dried and crumbled in sachets for their clothing drawers. If she ever had a house with yard, she would grow lavender, like her mother.

Next to her mother's grave was her grandfather's, its grass still not even with the rest, his only two years old.

Grandpa's silent but gentle ways included secret winks he

shared with Annie when he was teasing her grandmother and extra dollars he slipped her for a movie or music, on top of the money she earned by doing extra chores. He worked long hours in the field, in the barn, in the garage, but he was home every night. Other than games of Rook with the Gibsons and church functions, he had no interests that took him away from his family and the farm.

On the other side of her mother's stone was the small grave of her grandmother's newborn son, Jacob. He would have been older than her mother, had he lived. She had always known about Jacob, but now she imagined the pain that must have caused her grandparents to lose an infant child, with so much promise and so many hopes left unfulfilled. And then to later lose a daughter.

In the next row were her great-grandparents, Lilah and William May, and her grandmother's brother, Ephraim May, who was killed in Italy in World War II. There was a military stone at the foot of the grave. Annie read the words aloud: "Ephraim May, PVT US Army, World War II, December 14, 1923-February 1, 1944."

Annie looked at the cemetery with her grandmother's eyes. Her parents were gone, of course, but she had also lost her brother at a young age, then her newborn baby, her daughter and her husband. Annie was all Beulah had left.

The reality stunned her. She had never thought of the losses from her grandmother's point of view, only from her own. And yet, she had run from home as soon as she could get out. Hadn't that been another grief for her grandmother?

Though no one was around to see, Annie felt a hot flush in her face, ashamed yet again at her self-centeredness. But she had dealt with her own pain for some of those years, and how could she have done differently? Her need to get out and away from the loss had propelled her like a jet engine.

Annie moved to the back and read the names on each stone in the cemetery. They were all relatives going as far back as the pioneer days of Boone, Logan, Whitley and Shelby. Each represented heartbreak for those left behind and, for some, heartaches multiplied.

Annie sat down next to her mother's grave and allowed understanding, like a photographer's sepia tone, wash over her. She could do nothing for the dead, only the living. Out of the whole family lying under the hillside, only she and Beulah were left, the last of the May family. She knew why Beulah couldn't let go. It wasn't merely land to be traded whenever the right opportunity came along. It was their heritage.

The wrought-iron gate creaked again as she shut it. Coming off the hillside, Annie was lost in her own thoughts as she walked along the rock fence toward home; but when she heard a man's voice, and then a woman laughing, she edged closer. Annie could see the clearing, the crossover place, and Jake holding a woman in an embrace.

His back was to her, but Annie knew Camille had arrived. She stepped behind a tree and watched, feeling like a voyeur, yet wanting to see this woman before making her presence known.

The young woman had straight, blond hair pulled back into a ponytail, which swung from side-to-side when she moved her head. Smiling at him with full lips and an upturned nose, she reminded Annie of a petite Barbie doll.

Size two or maybe zero, Annie thought, judging the girl's fitted jeans. *Not good child-bearing hips,* she could almost hear her grandmother saying. Camille had on a crisp, white long-sleeved shirt, the collar open and loose around her neck.

Camille had her arms around Jake's waist. He held her and listened to her talk, and then he laughed at something she said. Camille lifted her chin as if waiting for a kiss. Annie turned then, not wanting to see anymore. Unexpected anger flashed through her. Why did he bring Camille to the crossover place of all the places on the farm?

Annie started back up the hill at a near jog. It was shrouded by shrubs and trees, obscured from view by the lovers in the clearing below. Why did it matter to her, she wondered, the anger adrenaline fading. She shouldn't have been watching. What was it to her where he romanced his girlfriend?

From here, she could either take the longer route back by

the cemetery and take the lane out to Gibson Creek Road, or she could take the shortcut by the old stone house below and stay near the creek until she was close to the horse pasture. An urge to be home as soon as possible settled the decision.

The hillside led down into the extended backyard of the stone house. She was on the outside of the plank fence, which encircled the yard itself. Sheets covered the back windows, and Annie shivered at the thought of living in darkness.

With the windows covered, no one could see her, she mused. She might not have another opportunity like this. On an impulse, Annie moved close to the back door. When she did, she heard a long, low moan. She moved even closer and listened.

"Ooooohhhhh," the voice cried from inside the house.

Chills ran down Annie's back. She knocked on the door. "Hello, do you need help?" The moaning stopped immediately.

Silence. "Stella, do you need help?" She knocked on the back door, louder this time. Silence, and then a voice, close to the door, yelled back, "Leave me alone!"

Annie drew back. "Sorry, I just thought you were hurt!" Her hands trembled as she pushed her hair back off her face, elbows suspended, waiting. When no response came, she turned and left.

Chapter Twenty-Seven

WHEN SHE REACHED home, Annie called Lindy and told her about the exchange with Stella Hawkins. "Something strange is going on inside that house!"

"Do you have a solid reason to think she's involved in something illegal?"

"No, but she's acting very odd and what with the windows covered, it seems like something is going on. Grandma thinks she might be involved in some kind of drug lab."

"You need 'reasonable basis' to go in without her consent. Suspicion of illegal activity would certainly qualify, but you would need some basis for the suspicion in case she filed a lawsuit," Lindy said.

"You're right. We don't know anything. But if you could have heard that cry ... something is wrong, I just don't know what."

Annie made hot tea before going to bed that night. She poured two cups and carried them into her grandmother's makeshift bedroom.

"How about some tea?" Annie said, setting a cup down on the nightstand. Her grandmother was propped up in bed, reading her Bible.

"That would be real nice," she said, closing the book and reaching for the cup.

"Grandma, when I went to the cemetery today, I saw things in a way I had never seen before. I realized how much you have lost over the years. I want you to know things will be different from now on. I'll come here more often and maybe you can come to New York for a few days. We are all we have, and I won't let that slip away." Annie felt tears well up in her eyes and her throat close on the last words.

"Now, now," her grandmother said, patting her hand. "I've done my share of making things hard between us too. I will come to New York if you promise not to make me ride on that subway."

Annie laughed. "I promise! But there's something else I want to say. I will do everything I can to hold onto this farm. I understand what it means to you, to our family, and I'll do my best."

"Annie, that's the best gift you could give me. The reason I'm so frugal is so I can leave you fixed to where you can keep all this." Her grandmother's face glowed with approval.

The next morning, Annie dressed feeling there was much to do. The beans her grandmother had planted before she arrived were ready to pick, break and can. And they were expecting Evelyn, Jake and Camille for dinner. Annie had thought Jake might bring Camille over yesterday to meet her, but they had probably enjoyed their time alone together. A seed of jealousy tried to settle in her heart, but she pushed it away, glad for reasons to keep busy.

"While you're in the garden, I'll put a couple of pies together if you'll put all the ingredients for me on the table," her grandmother said. "I thought we'd pull out that chicken casserole I froze before the surgery and some of the biscuits. You'll have us a mess of green beans, and that ought to be enough for supper tonight."

"Do you want me to make up more sweet tea?" Annie asked.

"That's fine, but add a little more sugar than you did the last time. It wasn't quite sweet enough."

Annie smiled to herself and headed out to the garden. She had put nearly a cup of sugar in the last gallon of tea. Sweeter was better, but she would just as soon not know how much sugar went into it.

Time in the garden was the best for thinking. And after all the talks with Jake, she was beginning to look at the work as life giving. It made her feel good to think she was growing her own food for once, that she knew where it came from and that it only traveled a few feet from her garden to the kitchen.

Perched on a small stool in between two rows of green bush beans, she worked her way down, plucking the pods from plants on both sides and dropping them in the basket. She picked the visible beans first, and then lifted the vines to find the beans hidden underneath. Her mind drifted to conflicting emotions that tumbled like a pile of clothes in a dryer. If only she could take each one out as if it were a piece of clothing and separate it from the rest, then she might get to the heart of the issue.

There was the impending deadline of work on Monday, unless Bob could get her an extension. She prayed for more time, but he hadn't called yet and Annie felt like that might be bad news. Hopefully Evelyn would know some ladies who could help Beulah until Annie could come back.

Then there was Stella Hawkins. The wail she had heard at the stone house had haunted her in some deep place. Something was wrong, but with no clear evidence of anything criminal, there was nothing to do but watch and wait.

And what was up with this crazy feeling of jealousy with Jake? The hardest thing to figure out was her anger at him for sharing the crossover place with Camille. It was the perfect place to pause for conversation or a kiss. Even she and Jake had shared a kiss there once when they were in middle school to see what all the fuss was over. But Annie had felt like she was kissing a relative. Jake agreed, and that was the last time they tried it.

So why, all of a sudden, was she thinking of him in a different way? Was she being needy or selfish at losing Jake's attention? Or threatened by Camille who was everything Annie was not? Or, and this was the most disturbing thought, was there something truly growing between them, some tiny seedling that had sprouted in the last few weeks?

Annie stood and carried the two full baskets of beans into the kitchen. An aroma of baking desserts overwhelmed her when she opened the door.

"Chess?" Annie said, admiring the pies fresh from the oven.

"One chess and one lemon chess," her grandmother said. "I didn't know which Camille would like better, so I made one of each. Look at those beans! We have enough for supper and one canning. Let's break them on the back porch."

Annie carried the bowls and the beans out while her grandmother eased out with the help of her walker. With a bowl between them for the ends and strings and a large bowl for the broken beans, they settled in to work.

Out of the corner of her eye, Annie saw the black snake stretched out on the millstone and soaking in the afternoon sun. She started a little at first, then relaxed.

"How long has Booger been around?"

"Only a couple of years. Since he's been here, my mice problem has gone away. This is a new spot. Last year, he liked the spot there around the pump. I always worried somebody would step on him there. I'm glad he's got a new place."

"I never thought I'd be keeping company with a snake," Annie said.

Beulah chuckled. "We're always keeping company with snakes. We just don't always see them." After a few minutes of work, Beulah spoke again. "How did the cemetery look? I want to get up there and put flowers down as soon as I'm able. I hated I missed Decoration Day."

"What's Decoration Day?"

"Memorial Day is what it's called now, but it used to be Decoration Day."

"The cemetery is beautiful and so peaceful," Annie reached into the basket for another handful of beans. "Grandma, do you remember much about your brother?"

"Oh yes. Ephraim was older than me by seven years. In fact, mother always said I was a welcome surprise when I came along. I was only ten when he went into the Army. He was a good brother, looked after me and played with me."

"I always wanted a brother like that. I guess that's partly why Jake and I were so close."

"It was a wonderful thing to have. I guess our age difference was enough that he paid even more attention to me than if I had been closer to him in age. He played games with me, brought me a piece of candy when he went into town, and rode me around on his back, acting like a horse. He was sweet on Bessie Sprinkle, and she became like an older sister." Beulah sighed. "But then Pearl Harbor came, and our world changed. Ephraim enlisted immediately. Daddy was proud of him, doing his duty, but we were all so sad to see him go, wondering if he would come back to us. But we'd been attacked, you see, and there was no going back.

"For a while, letters came with foreign stamps, and we heard the updates both on the radio and on the movie newsreels. When we heard the news from Anzio, everything changed. The letters with foreign stamps stopped coming and Bessie Sprinkle, the girl he was sweet on, married another boy."

Beulah sighed and leaned back in the chair, lifting her chin and closing her eyes in memory. Annie thought what a strong face it was: solid jawline, giving her the look of someone who knew what she was doing and where she was going; a straight nose; and few wrinkles. She wasn't pretty, but she had a beauty of her own that came from inner character and dependability. Her eyes could be intense and straightforward, or kind and gentle, depending on the subject. Annie was surprised to see a small bead of water make its way slowly down her cheek from the outside corner of her eye. When she spoke, her voice was steady. If Annie hadn't seen the tear, she would not have known Beulah felt any emotion.

"Thousands of our boys died there. Most families couldn't afford to bring them home, and so they were buried there in an American cemetery. The government paid for the burial if you let them stay. I've seen pictures of the cemetery on the news. They did a special on it one night, and it showed rows and rows of white stones, under these pretty Italian trees that looked like big green umbrellas. I thought I'd like to go there someday, for

Ephraim's sake, and look up the boys he talked about in all those letters. I don't know if they lived or died."

"We brought him home," Annie said, surprising herself with how closely identified she felt with a great uncle she never knew.

"Yes. It was expensive, but Daddy wanted him buried on the farm where he belonged."

"As many times as I've been to Italy, I had no idea my great uncle fought a battle and died there."

They were both silent for a few minutes, than Annie voiced the idea forming in her mind.

"I could take you there, Grandma. The area is familiar to me. I have friends who could help us find it."

Beulah chuckled. "I can't even get around my own home right now."

"After you get well, you'll be able to move around better than before. It would give us something to work toward," Annie said, growing excited about the idea.

"We'll see. I've never been much to travel, but it might be time I did a little of it. Evelyn might want to go. She said she's always wanted to go to Italy."

"We could make it a girls' trip!"

Sterilized jars sat empty on the kitchen counter, a teaspoon of salt in each. A large canner was on the stove, a quart of water and a tablespoon of vinegar in the bottom.

"Now, I used to can the old-fashioned way, by cooking the beans and ladling them into jars, but I like this method much better. Seems like I get more done," Beulah said from her seat at the kitchen table. "Now that the beans are clean and broken, fill each jar up to the top, stuffing in as many as you can. You don't want them so high they poke into the lid, so keep it below that."

Annie did as she was told, pushing the rubbery beans in and making room for more.

"Now, ladle the hot water into each jar until it's about an inch below the top."

Annie poured steaming water into each jar and watched it fill around the shape of the beans. "Okay, that's done."

"Take a paper towel and wipe all the water off the surface of the jar lid. A drop of water will keep the lid from sealing."

Annie wiped each off carefully, pulling off a new towel when she needed it. "Done."

"All right then. Now do the same with the sterilized lids and bands. Make sure to get every drop of water off."

That took a little longer, since she wanted to be sure and get all the water. "Now, I put the lids and bands on each jar, right?"

"That's right. Place them in the canner. Seven jars will fit, then lock the top in place."

Annie did as she was told.

"Now put the pressure cap on fifteen and turn the burner on high."

"Got it," Annie said.

"When it starts jiggling, set the timer and turn the heat down. When the time is up, turn off the heat. When the canner cools down, we'll take the jars out and wait for the lids to seal. Tomorrow we can take them to the basement after we mark the year on the top."

Annie was writing everything her grandmother said on paper even as she did it. "I want to make sure I get this right. Now, will this be the same way for the tomatoes?"

"No, a little different pressure and length of canning time. There's a book in there if you're ever in doubt. It'll tell you what to do."

"And you're sure this won't blow up or something?" Annie said, cleaning the used paper towels off the counter.

Beulah laughed. "I've never had one blow up, although that was a common tale years ago when things were done a little differently. They have safety features, but you still have to pay attention."

"Why don't you get some rest before supper? There's not much left to do, and I can handle it."

"That sounds like a good idea," Beulah said, pushing herself up to the walker.

While Beulah rested, Annie set the table and cut some of the honeysuckle for a centerpiece. *Help me to be nothing but happy and supportive for Jake,* she prayed silently. She knew it was how he would be for her.

Annie had judged Camille to be someone with whom she couldn't be friends just because she looked like a Hollywood actress and made Annie's size six feel like a size sixteen. Jake had called her Cam, but to Annie she looked like a Camille.

With the supper preparations finished, she went upstairs to change clothes. She settled on black pants and a cool blue top with a V-neck and three-quarter-length sleeves. In her jewelry box, she looked for something simple to wear. She put on a pair of small silver loop earrings, and then looked for a silver necklace to go with them. Nothing satisfied her. She opened the drawer to her dressing table to see if there was anything in the old jewelry box inside.

She found old earrings and necklaces from high school. A silver chain gleamed from the bottom of the intertwined jewelry. Annie pulled it out gently, untwisting it as she worked it free. The silver chain held a small cross, the one Jake had given her when she was sixteen.

Jake had called and told her to meet him at the crossover place. When she got there, he was already waiting, a long, thin box in his hand. When she opened it, the silver cross and chain lay inside the Chaney's jewelry box. He blushed when she hugged him and kissed his cheek. "I thought you should have something special on your sixteenth. Mom helped me pick it out."

"I love it," she told him and put it on immediately. She had worn it constantly after that, until she started dating Brett that fall. Then it wasn't cool anymore because none of the girls he hung out with wore crosses, so she had put it away in this box and forgotten, until now. Looking back, Annie wished she hadn't cared so much what her new friends thought.

Annie held it up to the lamp light and watched the silver reflect the light against the mirror. It went perfectly with the earrings and the blue top. She would wear it tonight.

"Annie, they're here!" Beulah called.

She reached for the necklace and touched it, taking comfort from it.

Chapter Twenty-Eight

THERE WAS NO sense in putting on airs, and as much as Beulah might like her guests to come to the front door, it rarely happened. The back door was her front, and there were no two ways about it. She was about to open the screen door when a scream ripped through the air and nearly knocked Beulah off her walker.

When Beulah opened the door, she saw Camille, or so Beulah assumed since they had not properly met yet, running to the car, Jake right behind her, and Evelyn looking at Beulah with an apology on her face.

"What's happened?" Beulah asked.

Evelyn reached for a tobacco stick that stood next to the back door.

"It's the black snake," Evelyn said. "We forgot to warn Camille about him."

"Booger's out here this late? That's unusual," she said as she watched Evelyn scoot him off the porch with the stick until he slithered into an opening in the concrete below the porch. It was still daylight, but he liked the millstone for his sunbath and when the sun moved on, so did he.

"It's all right, he's gone." Jake had his arm around the young woman and walked toward them. Strands of golden hair fell over the girl's face, like the flax Beulah's grandfather grew, ready for the harvest. She wiped her eyes and pushed the strands back off her face, and gave Beulah an embarrassed smile.

"I'm sorry. It's quite a way to make an entrance," Camille said and extended her hand.

Beulah shook her small hand, smooth and free of calluses. "It's our fault. We forgot about him," Beulah said. "Do come in."

She stood back as the group moved into the back room. Camille reminded her of a lovely, rare bird. Her teeth were as white as any Beulah had ever seen, and her skin looked like the porcelain on her old china doll.

"Is everything okay?" Annie asked, coming from the kitchen.

"We forgot to warn Camille about the snake," Evelyn said.

Camille smiled tentatively. "I'm terrified of them," she said.

"This is Annie," Jake said, and Beulah sensed pride in his voice as he introduced the two women.

"I'm barely used to him myself," Annie said in a consoling tone as she extended her hand. Camille smiled warmly back at Annie.

The only mar to Camille's beauty was a black smudge of mascara under her left eye from the excitement. This child needed a minute to collect her wits, Beulah thought. "If you would like to use the restroom, it is right there," she said, and pointed the way to the downstairs bath.

"Oh yes, that would be wonderful. Thank you," Camille said as she turned to go.

"I'm so sorry," Beulah said. "I never thought to check on Booger this time of day."

"Don't worry," Jake said. "She might as well get a taste of country life sooner rather than later."

"Annie, did you do this canning?" Evelyn asked, pointing to the jars of beans on the counter.

Beulah watched as Annie's face shone with pride. "I did! Grandma told me what to do, but I think I can do it on my own now. It was fun!" she said.

"I'm impressed," Jake said. "You'll make a good farmer's wife," he teased.

Camille appeared, much more composed, and Beulah moved them into the living room for a visit before dinner. No sense in rushing into the meal when everything was fine to sit for a minute. While Annie brought glasses of tea, Beulah said, "Camille, how long will you be here?"

"A few days, I hope. It depends on the hotel. We're wrapping up our spring conference season, so it depends on how many problems happen while I'm gone." Her accent was Northern, Beulah noticed, but of course it would be living up in Cincinnati.

Annie handed a glass of tea to Jake and with one in her hand, sat down. "Tell us about your job," Annie asked.

Cam's eyes lit up. "I'm the director of sales for my father's largest hotel. We book the conventions and meetings. I love it!"

"It's a lot of responsibility, I suppose," Evelyn said.

"Yes, but it doesn't feel like work. It's kind of like putting on a big show every week."

They were quiet for a moment and Beulah watched Camille lift the tea and sniff it before taking a sip. She hoped Jake or Evelyn might jump in with something to keep the talk moving.

"Your house is beautiful," Camille said, looking at Beulah. "It's very quaint and farmy."

"Thank you," Beulah said, wondering what "farmy" meant. Had someone tracked in manure?

"Camille was telling me on the way over she wouldn't mind riding while she's here. What about Nutmeg?" Jake directed the question to Annie.

"Sure, anytime," Annie said.

Camille's dimples deepened. "When I was a child, my father took me for lessons in Northern Kentucky twice a week for a couple of years. I have several trophies and blue ribbons from horse shows. It's been a long time, but I would love to ride again."

"You can probably teach me a thing or two," Annie said, standing. "I'll get dinner on the table, family style, then ya'll can come."

When Annie left the room, Evelyn said, "Beulah, Annie is

talking Southern again. Have you noticed?"

Beulah chuckled. "I'm glad. She'll be easier for me to understand."

Jake laughed, but Camille seemed lost at the joke.

Annie seated Jake at the head of the table with Camille on one side and Evelyn next to Camille. Beulah was instructed to sit next to Jake and Annie took the seat next to her and closest to the kitchen.

Jake offered the blessing and after he said "Amen," something Annie was wearing caught Jake's attention when he opened his eyes. He stared for a moment and looked back again as he passed the casserole. Camille noticed his attention on Annie and Beulah thought she saw a faint twitch of irritation on the girl's face. Annie seemed oblivious as she handed the casserole to Beulah.

"Jake said you live in New York," Camille said, directing the question to Annie. "Where do you live?"

"I had an apartment in Greenwich Village with three other flight attendants. Fortunately, there were usually only two of us there at a time, so we made it work."

"I love Manhattan. My dad takes our whole family every year in December. It's been a tradition since we were small. We stay at the Waldorf, see the Rockettes and the latest Broadway shows, shop and eat at the best restaurants. I told Jake he has a lot to live up to," she said, looking up at him with large brown eyes through the longest eyelashes Beulah had ever seen.

"I can't argue with that," he said. "Cam's dad is a great guy. He's been a business mentor to me."

Beulah noticed Camille's plate had a small amount of food on it, a sampling instead of a portion. What's more, Beulah noticed, she delicately sniffed each bite of food before putting it in her mouth. It was ever so subtle, one might mistake it for just a pause, but Beulah detected a slight flaring of her nostrils before the food went in. She felt a tickle rising up inside her, but chastised herself immediately. *For goodness sakes*, she thought. *You're an old woman acting like a child!* Thank God Fred wasn't here to egg her on.

The rest of the dinner conversation flowed like milk. The

awkwardness of the snake scare had worn off and everyone was putting in to make it a nice evening. Beulah didn't know about fashion, but Camille was put together as neat as you please, like a Christmas gift wrapped with a large bow from one of the old department stores up in Lexington. Beulah could see why Jake was taken with her. She was a beauty and smart as a whip.

At times, the dinner had the feeling of an interview, as much as Beulah thought everyone didn't want it to feel that way, but there was no way to get to know people without asking questions. Camille was the center of attention, except when Jake was casting sideways glances at Annie. But Camille was a sharp girl and she seemed to know when Jake's eyes were off her and looking toward Annie for what reason, Beulah did not know. Annie seemed unaware and paid full attention to Camille, but Jake looked to have a question he couldn't ask.

They finished up supper, and Evelyn helped Annie clear the dishes away. It was one of those times Beulah wished she could get up and do it herself. After all, it was her house, and here she sat like a queen, letting everybody wait on her.

Annie brought out the chess pies, and Beulah explained which pie was lemon and which was plain. Annie poured decaffeinated coffee for everyone, set out the cream and sugar, and took a seat while Beulah cut pieces of pie.

"Beulah, you made my favorite," Jake said, scooping up a large slice of the plain chess.

Cam refused dessert at first, but Jake finally persuaded her to take a small slice of the lemon.

Beulah couldn't help herself but to watch Camille sniff the small bite of pie before she ate it. Never in her life had she seen such. She had heard of folks smelling their food before eating it, but every bite?

"Have you shown Camille around town?" Annie asked.

"Yeah, we spent part of the day there," Jake said.

"Jake bought me a bracelet at the jewelry store downtown," Camille said and held up her arm to show off the gold circle.

"Chaney's is a treasure," Beulah said. "We're so glad to have a local jewelry store."

Cam set her fork down. "His inventory isn't very large, but Jake wanted me to find something and this worked nicely with what I already have."

"I think it's wonderful that you're trying to do business with Mr. Chaney. All the big stores are pushing businesses like his out, until every community in America looks all the same," Annie said.

"That's exactly how I feel." Jake's blue eyes flashed with intensity. "We can't keep running to the big stores every time the small independent stores don't have exactly what we want or need."

"But it's so limiting," Cam said. "America is all about freedom of choice."

Jake leaned in to make his point. "What happens to the American dream when a person can't have their own business and be their own boss because the big stores make it too difficult to compete with their massive buying from China? We need to buy local and support each other."

"I agree," Annie said. "I can't tell you how many cities I've been in and literally wondered where I was, because they all look exactly alike when you get out of the downtown area. Same stores, same restaurants, same gas stations."

Jake started to say something, but Cam interrupted. "What a treat," she said and folded her napkin. "Thank you both so much for a lovely dinner."

Jake took the hint. "Yes, we better go. Can we help you clean up first?"

Evelyn said, "I can stay and help you clean up, Annie, if you don't mind running me home afterwards."

Beulah thought Annie would refuse Evelyn's help, but she surprised her by saying, "That would be great, thanks." Then Annie turned to Camille. "Cam, anytime you would like to ride Nutmeg, come on over. I'm not good at saddling her up yet, but you probably know how to do that anyway."

"Thank you! I'd love to ride before I leave."

"Maybe you two could have lunch together this week. I'd like for you to get to know each other better," Jake said.

"Great idea," Annie said. "I'll call and set it up."

With Jake and Cam out the door, Evelyn and Annie sat back down at the table, forgetting the dishes.

"What do you think, girls?" Evelyn asked.

Beulah sighed. "Looks like a doll and smart enough," she said.

"Puts on shows for a living," Annie said.

"Adores Jake," Evelyn said.

They sat in silence for a few seconds.

"Evelyn, honey, do you think he could marry her?" Beulah laid it on the table.

Evelyn sighed and shook her head. "I don't know. I think this visit is crucial to see how she likes it around here."

"We can pray for wisdom," Beulah said.

"Yes, that's the only thing to do. She might be exactly who he should marry," Evelyn said.

"Guess we need to try harder," Annie said. She fingered the cross around her neck and stared at the pantry door as if it held the secret to a mystery. That necklace was what Jake was staring at, but Beulah still couldn't figure out why.

Evelyn reached across the table and grabbed Annie's hand. "Thank you. I need to try harder to do the same."

"Does 'trying' mean not scaring her to death?" Beulah asked, looking at Annie.

"Grandma, I didn't know Booger would still be there."

"Annie, you devil!" Evelyn pointed her finger and then broke out with laughter.

Annie gave herself away with the hint of a grin. "Old Tom drug up a half-dead mouse, and I tossed it over to Booger this afternoon to finish off. I guess he decided to let his meal digest before going back to the smokehouse."

Beulah cut a sharp glance at her granddaughter before allowing herself to laugh too. "Well, I swan. You can almost set your clock by that snake's habits. I couldn't figure out what happened."

They laughed and talked some more with Beulah drying the dishes while Annie and Evelyn washed and put them away. That was something she could do easily enough sitting down, as long as someone set the dishes in front of her and put them up. The twisting and turning in the kitchen was the hardest for her to do. That would come later when she was all healed.

While Annie drove Evelyn home, Beulah put on her nightgown. She heard a car creep back up the driveway. Beulah went to the window, looking out over the back porch to make sure it was Annie. Her granddaughter had gotten out of the car and was leaning against it, looking up at the waxing moon.

There was something to that necklace she had worn. There was an unspoken communication going on between Annie and Jake that no one else was meant to understand.

Chapter Twenty-Nine

ANNIE PULLED A weed next to a bean plant, then another. The invading plants threatened the health of her green beans and there was something therapeutic about jerking them out of the ground. There was a feeling of accomplishment as she went down the row, a mark of where she had been. The sun warmed her back as she tossed the weeds into a brown paper bag and then scooted her stool to the next section.

In the morning light, she was ashamed of herself for her churlishness toward Camille the night before. The cross necklace was one thing, dragging out something from her past with Jake as if to lay claim on some prior connection. Although he never said a word, couldn't of course, he had recognized it. She knew from the way his eyes lingered on hers with a question.

And then Booger ... Annie stifled a grin even now. She hadn't known he would stay to digest the mouse, but she thought it might work. What she did didn't bother her as much as why. Was it a need to feel superior over Camille while she was on her turf? Or to help Jake see Camille wasn't right for him?

"Kitty," her grandmother called from the back porch. Annie looked up to see her grandmother pour a small amount of milk into a bowl by the back porch door. When she looked toward the garden, Annie waved to her.

"I'll be in to fix lunch in a minute," she called to her.

It had been two days since Annie had talked to Bob Vichy. She had waited to tell her grandmother in the event he might quickly get her an extension. Annie was so full of hope, she had called Janice and requested her camera accessories, a swimsuit and a couple of summer blouses she missed. All would be an entire waste of Janice's time if Annie was heading back to New York herself on Sunday.

When the brown truck groaned in the driveway earlier and the gum-chewing delivery man left the overnight package from Janice, Annie realized even Janice wasn't as hopeful, or else she wouldn't have spent the extra money on overnight service.

With no word from Bob, Annie knew she had to tell her grandmother. When she thought about going back this soon, her chest tightened. There was so much left undone. She had wanted to finish the garden, to see it through from planting to canning, and finally to putting the goods on shelves in the cellar.

And who would keep an eye on the renter, Stella Hawkins? Her grandmother had alerted the police, but even Jeb Harris admitted they were understaffed.

"Ouch," she said after grabbing a weed with tiny thorns on it, pricking her fingers. After a while, she learned how to recognize the thorny weed and grab it from the base, avoiding the stickers. Worries were like weeds, she thought. *Best to grab them by the root and yank them up. But sometimes they cause pain. And if you don't deal with them, they multiply and choke out the good things.*

At the end of the row, Annie stood and stretched. She had dealt with enough weeds for the day. It was time to confront a worry.

Annie went into the kitchen and pulled a chair out and sat. Her grandmother had heated leftovers for lunch.

"Grandma, my boss called two days ago and asked me to come back this Monday for work. I told him I couldn't come Monday and asked for an extension. I don't know if I'll get it,

Grandma. When all this happened, he told me it would be at least three months, possibly six, and it's been less than two. I'm sorry."

"Now, there's nothing to be sorry for. You have your job back. That's a blessing, not something to be sad about." Her grandmother reached across and lightly laid her hand on Annie's before pulling away. "Besides, I'll make out fine. Evelyn already said she would help me if I need her. You got me through the worst part of it, and look what all you've done around here! This place doesn't even look the same."

"I can hire some extra help for the garden if you know somebody who could use the work," Annie said.

"I'll manage fine. Having you here these last few weeks has been wonderful. I'll miss that. But I want you to live your life."

"I'm still hoping for the extension. Even without it, I'll fly back on days off this summer and help with the garden as much as I can. I'll come so often you'll be tired of seeing me." Annie stood and kissed her grandmother on the cheek.

"Now, I better get to my exercises," Beulah said as she pushed herself up from the table.

"I think I'm going to run over to Evelyn's and use her computer. I tried calling, but no one's home." Annie grabbed the camera accessories and stuffed them in her pocket for the walk over.

Despite all her words to comfort her grandmother, Annie felt a hollow in her own chest on the walk to the neighboring farm. Using the crossover place in the rock fence and coming up behind the dairy barn, she tried shaking the heaviness by enjoying the beauty of the warm day and Evelyn's flower garden as she passed through it to the back door.

The driveway and garage were empty, other than the old farm truck parked in the open-door garage. No one was home. All she needed was to print out the old stone house pictures so she could finish her drawing. It was even more important to her now that little time remained. Annie wanted to leave it with her grandmother before she left.

The back door was unlocked, just as Evelyn had said. Annie

called before entering, but when no one answered, she made her way to the office. Annie uploaded the pictures and in a few seconds, they were on the screen. She enlarged them to get a better view. While they were printing, she checked her e-mail, which included one lengthy note from a friend in Rome. She was in the middle of a reply to an e-mail from Prema when she heard the back door open. Before she could call out, Annie heard voices in the kitchen.

She logged off and gathered up her pictures.

"Jake, don't you think it's possible to do a little farming on the side and still partner with my dad? Wouldn't that be a way to do it all?" Annie recognized Camille's voice and heard what sounded like a purse tossed onto the kitchen table.

"Sure, it's a possibility. But if I go into business with your dad, it would be creating a new concept from scratch and you know how much time and energy that would take. The farming would get very little time. So it really comes down to a choice between the two, if I want to make a success of either one."

"Why not save farming for later, when you want to slow down. Who says you can't do both at different times in your life?"

"So you're not too excited about this option," he said.

"Oh, Jake," her voice turned to syrup. Annie wanted to gag. "I understand hotels and I can help you. We would be a team. But I don't understand farming. To be honest, when you talk about grasses and cows and chickens, my eyes glaze over."

"I didn't realize I was boring you," he said. His voice had an edge.

She let out an exaggerated sigh. "You are so good with people. You know how to lead a company. Do you realize what a rare gift that is? Why would you want to throw away all your talent on this farming thing?"

Camille had stepped in it now, Annie thought. The silence before Jake's response stretched and Annie could feel the tension thick as a hazy and humid July afternoon.

When he spoke, his voice was controlled. "This farming thing feeds people. Not processed junk from halfway across the world, but real, nutritious food that allows people to live healthy lives while also caring for the environment. I can't think of many things more important than that."

She sighed. "I'm sorry Jake. You're so different here than back home. I guess I'm missing the old Jake. Maybe it's not so bad. I do like horses," she said with a lilt at the end of her sentence. Annie could imagine her dimpled face, upturned and waiting for a kiss to make it all better.

Annie hoped they wouldn't launch into a make-up and make-out session. She wanted to get out of there as soon as possible without being seen!

"Let's talk about this later. You need to do some more thinking and so do I. Right now, I need to return some phone calls."

A cabinet door opened and then she heard running water. If Camille responded, Annie didn't hear it, and soon the voices faded as they moved down the hall.

Annie slipped quietly out the front door and down the driveway to make sure she wasn't seen from the back window. Annie wouldn't tell her grandmother about hearing Jake and Camille argue. It was a private matter she shouldn't have heard anyway, and her grandmother would remind her of that if she told her.

Annie had almost forgotten the pictures on her walk back and now they were crumpled. Once inside her grandmother's kitchen, she smoothed them out on the kitchen table. The house filled the paper, giving her architectural details for the drawing. She craved her charcoals now, seeking the escape an hour or two of drawing would provide.

"Annie?" Beulah called from the kitchen. Annie was upstairs, changing into her work clothes.

"Coming!"

Annie pulled on her old tennis shoes and tied them, then pulled her hair back in a short ponytail. Her grandmother was seated at the kitchen table.

"Did you look at these pictures?"

"I glanced at them. I thought I could use them to finish my sketch."

"You can almost see the license number on her car. If we had that, we could give it to Detective Harris. I'd like the comfort of knowing she's not some criminal."

"You're right. I could enlarge that section or just walk back and write the numbers down."

That afternoon, Annie intended to walk back to the stone house, but the threat of overnight showers forced her back into the garden to collect more ripe beans. The beans she had already picked had produced again, and now the new rows were bearing their first offerings.

With two full baskets between them, Annie and Beulah broke the beans, tossing the ends into a brown grocery bag and plunking the beans into a large metal pan. The sun cast long end-of-the-day shadows on the yard. Booger was stretched out on the millstone, and a barn cat sat on the smokehouse step and watched with curious eyes.

"Believe I'll go to prayer meeting tonight," Beulah said. "Evelyn said she could drive me into town if you want to stay here."

"I'll drive you tonight," Annie said. "But I might go to Lindy's church this Sunday if you don't mind."

"No, that's fine. I wouldn't mind visiting there myself one Sunday, but it would be the talk of town. I better wait for some special event when our church isn't meeting."

"Does Evelyn's church meet on Wednesdays?"

"Not usually. When I talked to her earlier, she said Cam and Jake were going to dinner in Lexington. They had invited her, but she decided to give them a little time alone."

"Good. I might run over and see her after we get back."

Prayer meeting lasted only an hour and was exactly what it was called. Church members sang, offered up prayer requests and prayed silently then out loud under the direction of Pastor Gillum. After they were dismissed, Annie dropped Beulah off at the house, seeing her inside, then drove over to Evelyn's, since it was getting close to dusk.

"Come in," Evelyn said, happy to see her.

"Is this a good time?" Annie asked.

"Of course! Jake and Cam are in Lexington and probably won't be home for a couple more hours."

"I came by the other day," Annie said. "No one was home, so I used your computer to print out these pictures." She handed them to Evelyn. "I need to enlarge one to see if we can make out the license plate letters. I could walk over tomorrow, but Stella Hawkins is coiled like a snake and I'm afraid the third time she might strike."

"Of course. Anytime," Evelyn said, reaching for the pictures in Annie's hand while Annie booted up the computer. "Looks like she's taken the curtains down in two of the windows. Beulah said she had them all covered before."

Annie pulled the picture up on the computer screen. "I didn't notice that before. Maybe it's some kind of signal related to selling drugs."

"You think its drug related? Why?" Evelyn took off her glasses and sat down.

"She's put up some kind of sensor on the old oak next to the bridge. She was out of it when we took food, like she was high on something. And then the other day I went by the house on the way home from the cemetery, and I heard wailing coming from inside the house. I knocked on the door and the crying stopped. The second time I knocked she yelled for me to leave her alone." Annie shrugged. "I don't know what to think."

"Now, let's see if we can get that license number." She adjusted the picture so the license number was in the center, and then enlarged until the letter and number combination was readable. "CJX 478. It's an Illinois plate." She pressed print.

"Can you stay for a cup of hot tea?" Evelyn asked. Annie was tired and wanted to go to bed, but she could tell Evelyn wanted to talk.

"Sure," Annie said and sat down at the table.

Evelyn set the kettle on the gas burner and brought out cups and saucers while the water heated.

"Jake's been different since Camille got here," Evelyn said. "Have you noticed it?"

"Not really, but I haven't spent any time with him. What do

you mean?"

"Oh, maybe I'm just imagining things. But he's on eggshells," Evelyn said. "I wonder if I should I say anything? Try to offer some counsel?" Evelyn poured hot water in the teapot.

Annie thought back to that sunny afternoon in Rome, when Janice told her the story about her sister and the diamond earrings. It had upset her, and at the time she didn't appreciate it, but it had planted a seed of doubt in her mind, and when the truth was revealed through that unexpected conversation with a woman on the airplane, she was ready to receive it. It had all worked to keep her from continuing a dead-end relationship.

After reflecting on her own experience, Annie answered Evelyn's question: "Maybe. But you have to be careful. If he thinks you have doubts about Camille and they end up married, it could be a source of division."

"That's what I'm worried about. I wish Charlie were here. Men can talk about things differently. They can speak plainer to each other."

"Jake respects your opinions. When the right time comes, you'll know what to say, if anything."

Chapter Thirty

JAKE WAS OUTSIDE, talking on his cell phone, when Annie pulled into the Wilders' driveway. He smiled when he saw her, disconnected the phone and leaned in her window.

"Cam will be right out. I think it takes her longer to dress for girl outings than it does for a date with me." He leaned in close to her. "Thanks for doing this. I was hoping you two could spend some time together."

Annie shielded her eyes from the sun. "Aren't you afraid I'll tell her about all your secrets?"

Jake's slow smile crept wide across his face. "I'm hoping you do."

"Lindy is meeting us at the diner."

"Good."

"Hello!" Camille waved from the porch, bracelets jangling. Her light-blond hair rested against a black shirt with a scalloped neckline and jeans. Annie and Jake watched her as she came down the stairs as graceful as a cat, her bracelets clanging like bells.

Annie felt like a middle-aged frump next to Camille. What had happened to her fashion sense? Shopping was not her favorite pastime, and the ability to wear a uniform to work had allowed her to go for a long time without updating her wardrobe.

"You two girls have a good time!" Jake hit the hood with his hand and waved as Annie backed around.

"Bye, honey!" Camille called out the window, her arm waving and bracelets singing a goodbye tune. Annie wanted desperately to roll her eyes, but she fought the urge, chastising herself once again for her immaturity.

Lindy had been buried in work with a case this past week, and Annie had barely had reason to hope she could peel away for lunch. When she called to check and Lindy said she could meet them, it had given her a tremendous sense of relief. For once, she felt at a loss for making conversation. Having Lindy there would keep things going.

"What's that growing over there?" Camille asked, pointing to a leafy green crop. "It's so pretty."

"Tobacco."

"People still grow it?" Camille asked, looking as if she smelled sulfur.

"Some do. I asked my grandma that a couple of weeks ago. She said the buyout took out most of it, but a few people still plant and sell directly to the buyers."

"That's terrible. I think it should be banned altogether," Cam said. "Whoever grows that stuff should be tried as criminals."

Annie felt a bubble of anger rise. "Well, you'll have to try the members of mine and Jake's family, plus every neighbor and friend on our road."

Cam looked at her, stricken. "You mean Jake's family grew tobacco?"

"Of course. We all did, among other things, until the buyout. It's all our farming families have known for generations. We depended on it for survival long before anyone realized tobacco caused cancer."

"But as soon as people realized how bad it was, they should have stopped!"

"It's complicated. You can't stop farming one crop without something to take its place. Farmers have made substitutions but it's not that easy. There has to be a market for the crops that will make it worthwhile.... Here we are," Annie said, parking next to the diner, and vowing to keep the conversation light and pleasant for the remainder of the lunch, fifty-nine minutes and counting.

As soon as they were out of the car, she saw Lindy coming from across the street. Annie wanted to hug her friend, she was so relieved. She made the introductions before they moved into the diner. Lindy and Camille went through the door while Annie hung back to look at the chalkboard sign on the sidewalk. It read: *Locally Grown Heirloom Tomatoes Served Here.*

Annie smiled to herself. Even Bill was making an effort to serve local food, although she suspected the tomatoes were the only local produce offered on the grease soaked menus.

Inside, they found a corner booth. The waitress reminded Annie of herself when she worked at the diner. She was probably on break from college and starting her summer job. She asked for their drink order.

"Do you have any sparkling waters?" Cam asked.

"Huh?" the waitress said, clearly confused.

"San Pelligrino or Perrier?"

Compassion for the waitress compelled Annie to intervene. "It's just tap. They don't offer any kind of bottled water."

"Okay, plain water is fine. Is it filtered?" Cam asked as the waitress marked on her pad. "I've been reading about all the chemicals," Cam said to Annie and Lindy.

"No, it comes right out of the faucet in the back," the waitress said. "If I was you, I'd get a Diet Pepsi."

"That's okay, I'll take my chances with the water, but no ice please and lots of lemon." Cam smiled sweetly at the waitress as if to apologize for the trouble.

Out of the corner of her eye, Annie could see Lindy's raised eyebrows, but she forced herself not to look, afraid of what might happen if they made eye contact. When the waitress finished with their drink orders, Annie said, "Lindy is working on a big case. How's it coming?"

"Good. I just had a deposition down the street. It's probably going to go to trial, so it'll be my first one. I'm excited and nervous."

"Oh, what kind of case is it?" Cam asked.

"I'm prosecuting a guy who took pornographic pictures of his foster daughter and sold them on the Internet. That's all I can say for now, but it's going to be a big trial for us," Lindy said. "So what do you do in Cincinnati?"

Annie mentally patted herself on the back again for thinking to invite Lindy.

"I'm in hotel sales. I book meetings and conventions," Camille said. "It's a blast, but I'm dying to get out of Cincinnati and go to a bigger market."

The waitress brought Cam a water, Annie a sweet tea, and Lindy a Diet Pepsi. "Know what you want yet?"

"Cheeseburger and fries for me," Lindy said.

"I'll take the BLT," Annie said, "with one of those locally grown tomatoes." She smiled at the waitress.

"What kind of salads do you have?" Cam asked.

"Just one kind. You can get it with or without fried chicken," the waitress answered.

"Oh, okay. Definitely without the fried chicken. What kind of lettuce is it?"

"Just plain old lettuce," the waitress said, her brow crinkled.

"It's Iceberg," Annie said.

"Any fat-free dressings?"

"We have a light Italian. That's it."

"That's fine," Cam said, closing her menu and turning back to the girls. "Actually ..." Camille's eyes took on a mischievous glint. "This is top secret, just between us girls, okay? My dad called this morning and has secured an option to buy into a large hotel in New York City. It will be a great opportunity for Jake if the deal goes through."

"Oh, has Jake decided to do the hotel business?" Lindy looked at Annie then Camille.

"He's almost there," Cam said. "He'll drop everything when he hears about the deal in New York. This would be the chance of a lifetime." Camille smiled like a cat with a belly full of mouse.

"Why don't you tell Jake now?" Annie asked, sipping her iced tea through a straw. "Wouldn't your dad want Jake to weigh in on the deal before he takes such a big step?"

"Dad wants to wait until we know we have it. The owners are coming in for negotiations this weekend. That's why I have to leave on Saturday. Jake thinks I have a sales meeting, but if it goes through, he'll know all about it soon enough."

The waitress brought their food with a clatter and some of Camille's lettuce fell onto the table. Camille looked at the waitress sharply but held her tongue.

"That's very generous of your father," Lindy said. "But are you sure that's what Jake wants to do?"

"Jake will come around eventually. He'll see the benefit of us working together as a family. That's how it is with us—we all work together."

"I don't know if I would want to work with my husband all day, but with the guy I'm hung up on, that wouldn't be a problem," Lindy said, wiping her mouth. She peered at Camille as if she just spotted a bedbug. "Are you sniffing your food?"

Annie nearly spit out her tea and instead started choking.

"Are you okay?" Lindy asked. Camille frowned at Annie with a slight look of disgust. Annie threw up her hand and choked out the words, "Fine, wrong pipe."

"So what's up with the sniffing?" Lindy asked again, just in case Camille forgot the question.

"It's a technique I learned in college. If you take the time to sniff each bite, you eat less. It's kinda like tricking your brain into thinking you're full. It really works!"

"No kidding!" Lindy said. "I'll have to try that."

Annie fought hard against her eye-rolling urge.

"Now about this love interest. What is keeping you from going for it?" Camille asked.

"Mainly, he stays out West to climb rocks. He's a free spirit and I'm traditional. Maybe one day," Lindy said.

"Don't wait. You should go for it. Decide what you want and grab it," Camille said.

Advice to the lovelorn, Annie thought. She should write a

column.

"What do you think, Annie?" Lindy asked.

"I think you should." *Before he goes falling in love with someone else,* she thought.

***

Annie checked on Nutmeg when she got home. She put her arms around her neck, drinking in the smell and letting it calm her. Horses had a distinct scent unlike any other animal she had known. It was a rich, musky relaxant, better than a glass of wine. While she brushed Nutmeg, she went over the lunch with Camille, replaying the conversation.

Was Camille so used to getting her way that she thought this New York opportunity would change Jake's mind? Did she really think money bought people? New York would make even weekend farming impossible. But that was probably what Camille wanted—to get him away from the farm.

"You don't know Jake Wilder," she said out loud. Nutmeg turned her head in question at Annie's voice. "Not you."

Annie tossed the brush back in the tack room and patted Nutmeg on a hindquarter.

In the house, she picked up her cell phone to call Lindy and mull over the strange lunch. She was distracted by the sight of a voice mail and checked it first.

"Annie, Bob Vichy. Call me."

She sighed. What would she do if he said she had to leave on Monday with so many things up in the air? She dialed the number, her stomach tense, waiting for the punch.

"It's Annie. What did you find out?"

"Two weeks from Monday or you lose your job. That was the best I could do, and I was lucky to get it."

She let out her breath, relief washing over her like an ocean wave. "Great! I really appreciate it, Bob."

Two weeks. It wasn't enough time, but it was better than having to leave on Monday.

With a deep sigh, she said, "Thank you, God." It was an

answer to her prayer.

"Grandma, you all right?" she called, wanting her grandmother's company. Annie realized her accent was creeping back into her speech. Her "I" was sliding to the right a bit, as if it were lazy and having trouble standing up straight.

When she didn't answer, Annie poked her head into her grandmother's downstairs bedroom. Beulah was asleep in the recliner, with a book lying open and facedown on her lap.

Annie left her and went back to the kitchen, the heart and soul of the house. She sat down and mulled over the reprieve. Two weeks. There was still the problem of where to live. She could bunk with Prema and the girls, but it was already crowded with four people. Janice had no room to spare with a mother-in-law even though she said she could stay there. "Don't worry," Janice had said this morning. "It's on the bulletin board in the crew lounge. Something will open up."

What if ... no, it was crazy. It was the only work she had known, her only security. A good paycheck and benefits, a retirement account, several days off at one time, and the ability to hop flights to anywhere in the world if seats were available. If she didn't show up two weeks from Monday, all that would be gone. If she ever wanted to go back, she would have to start all over with no seniority, taking whatever flights the other attendants didn't want.

Wouldn't it be odd, she thought, if she ended up coming back here while Camille tried to convince Jake to move to New York? Should she talk to Jake about his girlfriend's manipulations? Jake couldn't possibly want to spend the rest of his life with someone like that, could he?

The many questions swirling around in her brain made her tired. She took the stairs up to her bedroom and stretched across her bed, falling sound asleep.

Chapter Thirty-One

BEULAH OPENED THE *Farmer's Almanac* and checked the dates for when Annie planted most of the garden. It was best for the moon to be waxing for the above ground vegetables, but it wasn't always possible. Beulah didn't go in for all that astrology business that predicted the future. She knew for certain it was straight from the Devil. But there was something to the moon's effect on things, and she'd seen too much evidence of it herself to believe differently. When Fred was alive, he castrated his steers by the moon's placement in the sky. It made a difference in how much they bled and how quickly they healed. He weaned his calves by it, and when most people suffered three days of cows mooing and lowing in the fields for their lost babies, a day passed and all was quiet. Jo Anne was weaned by the moon and had done real well.

Beulah grabbed her walker and used it to lift herself up from the recliner. It was high time she walked by herself to the garden. Annie took her out last week after she had weeded it and seeing that rich black dirt turn made her want to get her hands in it. There would be none of that right now, not yet. All she could do was sit in a chair and admire it.

The doctor thought she was healing up fine, or so he said during her appointment yesterday in Rutherford. "A little more walking won't hurt a thing. It'll be good for you," he had said. He gave her some new exercises to do to help her get her movement back. It was a gradual progress. She hadn't been upstairs since the surgery, but the doctor recommended she take it slow and use the stairs. In a month, she should be able to move back to her bedroom. It was something to work toward. Beulah took small, slow steps around the smokehouse and to the garden beyond. Annie was out in the paddock, brushing down Nutmeg. It seemed to be one of her favorite things to do. Nearly every day, she went out to tend to that horse.

The garden was as pretty as Beulah had ever seen it. There were nice straight rows, and the last plantings showed little curls of bean sprouts pushing above the surface. Delicate leaves of corn waved in the breeze, looking like a row of tiny flags. Easing down in the chair, she watched as Annie took the halter off Nutmeg and patted the horse on the rump. Her granddaughter disappeared into the barn and returned without the halter. She called out, "How did I do?"

"Prettiest garden west of the Alleghenies. You tilled it up nice. I couldn't have done any better." Beulah meant it. "By the way, Jeb Harris called. He'll be here before noon."

"Good. I hope he can find something out with the license plate. Maybe we're making a big deal out of nothing." Annie sat down on the grass beside her. "But Joe's phone call this morning makes me think even more that she is up to something," Annie said, twisting a blade of grass.

Indeed, Beulah thought. Joe had spotted the woman with the flyaway hair out in the middle of the creek, twice this week before daybreak, pouring something out of a five-gallon bucket. With his cows drinking out of that creek, they couldn't afford some poisonous ingredient from her drug making being tossed into the water, if that was what she was up to.

"Let's hope it is nothing. And if so, then no harm's been done."

They sat in silence for a few moments, listening to the birds sing. Annie reached out and picked a dandelion.

"Grandma, what would you do if you thought someone you loved was making a mistake? Would you tell that person?"

Beulah thought for a minute before she answered. "Proverbs says a wise man seeks counsel."

"But what if the man hasn't exactly asked?"

"Maybe he has. If you're talking about Jake, I think that's why he brought Camille here. To see what she thinks of us and what we think of her."

Annie pulled her knees up under her chin. "I worry about him," she said.

Beulah leaned back, considering her words carefully. The sun's warmth felt life giving to her, as if she could soak up that energy and have more of her own. How could she tell Annie what she saw in Jake's face? Both of them were too frightened to recognize it because of what it might mean. Providence guided Annie back here just when Jake was about to make the biggest decision of his life. It was no accident. But it was not for her to uncover it. *What will be, will be.*

"Time will tell," Beulah said, closing the subject. The sound of gravel crunching in the distance grew louder. "I believe Jeb is here."

Beulah held Annie's arm so she could walk a little faster over the uneven ground. The policeman parked his gray car next to the gate.

"Jeb Harris, you're looking more and more like your daddy every day!" Beulah exclaimed.

"Mrs. Campbell, I take that as a compliment, although my hairline is receding a little faster than his. I think it's the job."

Beulah could hear the pride in her own voice when she said, "This is my granddaughter, Annie Taylor."

"Nice to meet you." Harris stuck out his hand.

"Come on in, Jeb. We've got some coffee or iced tea."

"Coffee sounds good." He held the door while she managed the step into the house with Annie's help.

"I heard you had a knee operation. You doing better now?"

"Little better every day. Annie's been staying with me before

she goes back to New York. Annie, if you'll get the coffee, I'll
show Jeb the picture."

"I just got your voice mail this morning. I've been down in
Eastern Kentucky with a big operation. It's taking a lot of our
manpower."

Jeb looked at the picture and took out a small notepad from
his shirt pocket. He wrote down the license plate numbers.

"I'll drive by on my way out. What makes you suspicious?"

Annie placed a mug full of coffee on the table next to Jeb.
"We think there's something very strange about her story. Her
name is Stella Hawkins but she's vague about her background.
She paid Grandma in cash up front, so there's no bank account
that we know of, and we noticed a sensor at the entrance to her
driveway. One day when we dropped off food, she seemed high
on something. She keeps her windows covered and she's made
it clear she wants no one around," Annie said.

"And," Beulah interrupted, "Joe Gibson has spotted her out
in the creek twice before daylight, dumping something out of a
five-gallon bucket. We're wondering if she's making drugs and
using the creek to get rid of the evidence. We don't want our
cows poisoned."

Annie studied his face, unsure if he thought they were crazy
or if there might be something to be concerned about.

"It's possible. There have been reports of animals being
poisoned from meth ingredients being dumped. We'll try
running the plates first and see if anything comes up. Have you
noticed more traffic on your road lately?"

Annie looked at Beulah for an answer. "Not really, but we're
usually in bed by nine-thirty."

Jeb nodded. "We'll see what we find out, but I have to be
honest. We're pretty shorthanded right now. But if you notice
anything else, give me a call."

Chapter Thirty-Two

ANNIE SAT ON the polyester couch, her legs comfortably stretched across it, a sketch pad in her lap. With the pictures, she was working on another drawing. There were a few details she wanted to get right. The work relaxed her. It was as if all her troubles floated away while she created, making something out of nothing and then changing it after it was formed. The more she practiced, the better she would be, she thought, studying her work from the mantel where she perched it for viewing a few feet away.

She heard a car in the driveway. When she got to the back door, Jake was stepping onto the porch.

"It's you," she said through the screen door.

"It is me," he teased. "Were you expecting someone else?"

"No one, I heard a car …" Her voice fell away. Why did she feel like an adolescent all of a sudden?

"Can I come in?" he asked, his eyes wide in question.

"Oh, sure, I wasn't thinking," Annie said, pushing the screen door open.

"Have you had supper?" he asked.

"No, I haven't even thought about it."

"Why don't we run up to Lexington and eat? Call Lindy and see if she wants to go with us. There's a new Italian place on the south side that's doing farm-to-table. One of the guys here in town told me about it last week."

"Sure, but Lindy is holed up working on a case. I talked to her earlier today."

"Then we'll go by ourselves."

"I need to change." Annie started to go, but Jake gently held her arm.

"You look great now."

Annie had a vision of Camille in her designer clothing, clean and starched, bright whites and dark blacks. Annie looked down at her T-shirt and pointed to the coffee stain.

"Okay. But nothing fancy."

She cut him a sharp look. "Do I ever get fancy?" He grinned, and she heard him mumbling something as she dashed to the stairs.

In her closet she pulled out a recently purchased red blouse with a V-neckline. It was a good color for her and was by far the most updated and fashionable item she owned. She put on the cross necklace, then took it off again. A pair of jeans, a squirt of perfume, a quick brush through her shoulder-length hair, powder for her nose, and a coat of lip gloss for her lips, and she was ready. She was at the top of the stairs, but hesitated and went back for the cross necklace. It belonged with this outfit.

"Wow," Jake said. There was genuine admiration in his eyes. His eyes froze when his appraising look saw the necklace.

"Annie, isn't that ...?"

"It's the one you gave me when I turned sixteen. I found it in my jewelry box the night we had Camille over."

"I noticed it."

"I don't know why I left it here all these years."

"I can't believe you still have it," Jake said, opening the car door for her.

When they were both inside the car, Annie asked, "When is Camille coming back?"

"Sunday or Monday. She has stuff at work tomorrow."

Annie watched the pastureland roll by, fighting the urge to tell Jake the truth. For a brief moment, she played with the idea, but in the end, she decided it was not her secret to tell.

"Annie, you've always been honest with me. What do you think about Camille?"

The direct question startled her. She needed to walk very carefully through this minefield, yet also be honest.

"I think she is beautiful and obviously very smart. I can see why you were attracted to her, especially if she has such a great family," Annie said. "But if you choose to follow your farm dreams, she will have a big adjustment to make."

Should she say more? His brow creased and he stared at the road ahead. He *did* ask for it.

"I know it's not any of my business, but I hope you decide to come back. I think it's exactly what we need around here."

"We?" he said, the tension draining from his face like water out of a clawfoot tub.

"I mean, the community."

"Sounds like you consider yourself part of it now."

"I am. Something's changed for me these last few weeks. I think I'll come back home much more often. I've read a couple of the books you dropped off for me about sustainable agriculture. It all makes so much sense."

He looked at her sharply. "You've been drinking the Kool-Aid," he said, grinning.

Annie shrugged her shoulders. "I think it's in the water around here," she said.

"In that case, I need to get Camille off that bottled stuff. Remember this?" he said, turning up the radio volume.

It was a song by Genesis, a band Jake had turned her onto when they were teenagers, along with a string of other classic rock performers. Annie knew the song well, and for the next few minutes, Jake played drums on the dashboard and steering wheel while Annie accompanied him on air guitar. They both sang at the top of their lungs before collapsing in laughter by the end of the song.

"Okay, see if you can read my notes on how to get to the

restaurant." He laid his open hand on the seat and Annie saw words written on the inside of it.

"You wrote the directions on your palm?"

"Sure," Jake said. "It's my palm pilot. See if you can make it out. I think we turn right up here at Brannon's Road."

Annie picked up his hand, aware of its size compared to her own, and its warmth. Pushing back his relaxed fingers, she tried to make out the words. "It's a little smudged, but I think it says, right at Brannon's Road, left into first lot, first building on right?"

"Yep, sounds right," he said.

The restaurant was cozy and surprisingly Italian for a place in the suburbs of a Southern town. Annie scooted into a leather booth and relaxed in the dim lighting. The waiter handed a menu to Annie and then Jake and left after taking the drink order.

Each item on the menu listed the farm name where the meat or product originated. Long Shadow Pork, Rolling Hills Eggplant, Turtle Hollow Herbs, Sweetbriar Beef. Each name made the menu listing more enticing.

"Do you know any of these folks?" Annie asked.

Jake looked up from the menu and smiled. "Oh yeah," he said. "The guy at Long Shadow Farm is a partner in the processing plant over in Rutherford. I've been talking to him a lot lately. I also know the folks at Sweetbriar."

When they placed an order the waiter was sure they would love, Jake said, "Any news from Jeb Harris on the identity of your mystery renter?"

"I'm not sure he thinks there's anything wrong. He'll run the plates just to make Grandma feel good about it, but it sounded like they have other priorities. Did you know Joe saw her dumping something into the creek two mornings at dawn?"

"Yeah, he told me. Even if she's not dumping something poisonous into the creek, I need to get those cows out of there. Their runoff is not good for the creek."

The waiter brought their salads and a loaf of warm bread with a slab of butter on a small white plate. She felt her stomach growl and realized she was hungry.

"How's Joe taking the changes?" Annie asked.

"He's fine," Jake said. "He's done a good job these last few years after we sold off the dairy herd and went partners with him on Angus. He does a lot of the right stuff already and when we talk about the things I want to change, he's open."

"It has to be a little hard to make changes after all these years of doing things a certain way."

"Yeah, but Joe is different. He remembers the way his grandfather ran his farm and how the new stuff is really like the old ways, so he's cool with it."

Annie took a bite of bread, a slab of butter melting on the warm crust. "This is amazing," she said.

"It's real butter. We'll have to make it sometime. Just need some fresh cream."

"I wish I didn't have to leave in a couple of weeks," Annie said. "I feel like there is so much I've left undone."

"You're leaving in two weeks?" Jake asked, his butter knife suspended in midair.

"I just heard. I actually thought it might be Monday, so I was relieved to have more time," Annie said.

"I thought you had all summer," Jake said, putting down the knife to concentrate on her words.

"I did too, but my boss worked hard to get me hired back, which is what I wanted in the beginning, but now I wish I had more time," Annie said, feeling her own appetite diminish.

"That's too bad," Jake said.

"It will be different this time," Annie said. "I'll be coming home a lot more. I needed this grounding. It was unexpected, and unwanted, but it's been the best thing that ever happened to me." She paused. "But I'm sorry I can't finish out the plans for the summer, mainly seeing Grandma through the rest of her recovery."

The waiter removed their salad plates and set down pasta alla carbonara for Jake and pasta primavera for Annie.

"They make the pasta here," Jake said. "I wanted you to see this to catch a vision of what Bill's Diner could be like."

"Is Bill going Italian?" Annie asked.

"Not Italian, but we're talking about changing it into a farm-to-table breakfast and lunch spot. It would be a great way to showcase the local foods. We just need to recruit a chef who has the same vision." He turned his fork until he had several strands of pasta wrapped around it, then lifted it to his mouth.

Annie dropped her fork and sat back against the leather. "Does Bill have a say in this?" she asked, feeling heat rush to her face.

Jake frowned and then slowly, he began to grin.

"What?" Annie said, feeling the anger dissipate as fast as it boiled up.

"I forgot to tell you that detail. It was his idea to sell."

"Why?"

"Viola," he said.

"The Alzheimer's," Annie said, understanding now.

"He approached me when he heard I was plugged into the local food stuff. He wants it to stay a restaurant. It's been the heartbeat of town for so long. We'd all like to keep it going, just in another form."

Annie was quiet a moment, trying to discern her emotions. Another change among so many.

Jake put his fork down and leaned in. "Do you think it's a bad idea?"

Annie sighed. "It's not that. It just makes me sad to think about Bill's Diner not being around anymore. I guess I'm feeling nostalgic now that I'm back. I want things to be how they were when I was young."

"You're still young, Annie. And if Bill wants to sell, at least we can make something good come out of it."

"Sometimes I feel a hundred years old," she said. "But you're right, it sounds like a good solution."

They talked the rest of the way through dinner, catching up on old friends and talking about the books he gave her to read. On the way home, there was finally a quiet moment and Annie let her mind drift.

"Sometimes I wonder," she said aloud.

"About what?" Jake asked.

"What it would be like if I didn't go back to New York," Annie said, running her fingers through her hair. "I have no idea how I would make a living."

"Do you have debt?" he asked, sounding like the banker he was.

"None. And I have savings, but that won't last forever."

"How much of a living would you need? You have a place to live. You can grow your own food."

"True, but I would need some kind of car, and enough to help with utilities, taxes, insurance, all that. But I see your point. It wouldn't have to be a lot, especially compared to what I'm used to in New York."

"Annie, you could do this. You would have no trouble finding some kind of work around here," Jake said, his voice growing passionate.

"I have been happier here, more at peace in the past weeks than I've been in years. But I'm afraid ..." She wanted to tell him more, that the memories of what might have been would be too much, that she couldn't bear to live near him and Camille if they ended up living here as a married couple.

"What are you afraid of?" Jake asked.

Annie searched for the words, but knew she could not tell him the truth.

"What, Annie May?" It was what he used to call her all the time, but that was before tenth grade, before things had changed between them.

"Of the unknown," she said, and that was truth enough.

Chapter Thirty-Three

ANNIE HATED HOLDING back from Jake, but what else could she do? He sensed her hesitation but she had tried to stop the probing. It was not a surprise to her when he called first thing the next morning. It was his way of making sure everything was okay between them.

"I'm going to teach you how to handle a firearm before you go back," Jake said when she answered the phone.

"I don't think I need it now that I'm going back in two weeks," she said.

"You probably need it worse in New York," he said, and she could hear the grin in his voice.

"Where are you?" she asked.

"On my way to Mt. Vernon. Camille's decided she missed me and is coming down tonight, but can't seem to navigate the country roads past there," Jake said.

"She'll have to do better than that if she wants to go to New York," Annie said and realized her slip immediately.

"What do you mean?" he asked.

"Nothing. Be safe. We'll talk later." Annie hung up before he could ask more questions. She was not going to lie for Camille.

On Monday morning, Annie wrapped herself in a towel and took each step slowly, walking as if she were bowlegged.

"Grandma?" she called.

"In the kitchen." Annie found her grandmother looking over the coupon inserts from the newspaper.

"Something is wrong. I have a terrible pain in my backside, near my tailbone. It hurts like heck. It's bigger than a quarter and burns. It's almost like I've been branded with a hot iron."

Beulah chuckled. "Sounds like a saddle sore. After riding for three hours, it's no wonder. There's some Gold Bond powder in the medicine cabinet down here. It'll sting a little. "

Annie found the powder and doctored her sore. It tingled and burned. She waddled back into the kitchen and refilled her coffee cup.

"I can't ride with Camille today. I'll call Woody and tell him not to bring another horse."

"Can she ride by herself?" Beulah asked, looking up from her coupons.

"Sounds like she's a champion rider from all the trophies she's won, or so she says. Nutmeg will be a sorry horse for her if she's as good as all that."

"That was when she was a child," Beulah said.

"I guess it's the same as riding a bike. It will all come back to her. Anyway, she's the one so determined to ride. It doesn't matter to me if she does or doesn't."

Her grandmother looked at her over her glasses, and Annie felt chastised for something, but she wasn't quite sure what.

Cam drove Jake's SUV over from the Wilders'. Annie felt a pang of jealousy at seeing her in the driver's seat, as if it belonged to her. She smiled when she got out and waved, no jangling bracelets this time. At least she had the sense enough to leave them off. As spooky as Nutmeg was, the bracelets might send her running into the next county.

She wore a yellow oxford shirt, with an open collar and a small diamond pendant. Her blond hair was pulled into a ponytail at the nape of her neck, and she had on dark sunglasses. The blue jeans fit nicely around her slim legs. They were tucked into decorative cowboy boots. Annie took in the whole picture in a split second.

Be sweet, she told herself.

"You look nice!"

"Thanks. I'm meeting Jake later, but comfy clothes might have been better," she said, nodding at Annie's attire.

It was true. Annie had on loose jeans, partially because of her saddle sore, and a cotton T-shirt. Annie gave her one of her best smiles, the one she reserved for customers who were red-faced and irritated at the delay in taking off or the kind of meal they were served.

"Cam, I can't ride with you today. I went on a long trail ride yesterday and got a saddle sore."

Camille laughed. "Saddle sore? I thought that was something from a Western."

"No, actually, it's very real, I can tell you." Annie said, ready to change the subject. "Anyway, Nutmeg is all saddled up and ready for you. There's a whole pasture you can ride in."

Camille took off her sunglasses. "Annie, Jake said you two went to dinner on Saturday. I am so sorry you are having such a hard time right now. Jake is so full of compassion for those who are down and out. That's what I love about him."

The insinuation that Jake's attention to Annie was out of pity cut like a knife, just as Camille intended. Annie fought the urge to lash back. She would not stoop to this woman's level, would not let her see that she had cut her to the quick.

In her moment of hesitation, Camille's eyes softened. "I really like you, Annie. I want us to be good friends. And when we get to New York, I'm hoping you'll show us around, help us get settled."

I'm not going back to New York, she thought. And in that moment, Annie knew it was true. She wasn't going back to live. Visit often, yes, she would do that, but she was not going back. Even if it meant dealing with her own ghosts and grief-filled memories, she would do whatever it took to stay in the place she loved. Even if it meant facing her own mistakes and missed opportunities every day of her life, she was not going back.

"Thanks, Camille. I would love to tell you where to go ... in New York," Annie said, mumbling the last part of the sentence. "Nutmeg is over here."

Annie led the way to the horse, which looked docile and innocent next to the fence. Annie tightened the saddle like Woody taught her, using her frustration to pull it tight.

Astride Nutmeg, Camille looked every bit the champion rider she claimed to be. Her back was straight; she held her arms out, holding the reins with enough give in them for the horse to feel some control, and her head pointed forward. Annie could envision her in the riding garb, boots and top hat, and she imagined Camille would make quite an impression on the judges.

"This walking horse gait is nice, but I would love to get her in a trot," Camille called from the other side of the barn.

Annie barely knew how to get on a horse, much less change gaits. She watched Camille go first one way around the lot, and then the other way.

"She hits a trot, but I can't get her to stay there," Camille said, speaking to no one in particular.

From the other side of the lot, she called to Annie: "Open the gate and let me take her in the pasture. I'll try her canter."

"She usually spooks when the gate is opened," Annie called back. It was fair warning, but Camille's response was to kick the horse up in a canter.

"I guess she doesn't care," Annie said to herself. Annie unlatched the gate and debated whether to gently open it, which wouldn't startle Nutmeg. Then she thought of Camille's veiled warning, her deception with Jake over the New York hotel, and her size zero jeans. She unlatched the gate from outside the fence and pushed it wide open, allowing it to hit the fence with a bang.

Camille was slowing Nutmeg back into a walk when the gate hit. In one instant, Nutmeg's ears went back and her eyes grew large. She lurched forward, and Camille was unprepared for the horse's sudden energy. The motion threw Camille back almost flat on the saddle, loosening her boots from the stirrups. When she managed to upright herself, her legs were pointed straight out to the sides of the horse. Her left boot hit the gatepost as Nutmeg flew through the opening, the impact enough to throw her from the horse. Annie's heart flew up in her throat as Camille fell in a crumpled heap next to the post.

"Dear God, please," she prayed as she ran to her. "Let her be okay."

Annie fell on her knees beside Cam, who was moving and stretching out her legs. "Are you all right?" Annie asked, trying to check out Camille's position to see if anything was broken.

"Don't touch me!" Camille spat the words with venom. "You did that on purpose."

Annie reached to help her but Camille pushed Annie's hands away. "Cam, please, you might be hurt," Annie said.

Camille dusted off her boots and jeans before she pushed herself up. "I'm fine, but thanks to you, I've ruined a pair of thousand dollar boots." Blond hair bounced as Annie chased her to the pasture gate.

"Please, let me drive you to Jake's."

"You stay away from me. And stay away from Jake!" Camille was in Jake's car and had the door shut before Annie could say anything else.

"I'm sorry!" she said through the closed door.

Camille did not look at her when she put the car in reverse and spurted gravel from under the tires.

Annie stood, her hands on her hips, and watched Camille drive off. "I guess that means we won't be friends," Annie said out loud. "I'll sure miss showing you and Jake around New York!" she yelled.

Her grandmother poked her head out the door. "What's wrong?!" she asked.

Annie threw up her hands. "Camille fell off Nutmeg. I pushed the gate open, and it spooked the horse."

"Good heavens. Is she hurt?"

"She was well enough to get in her car and drive back to the Wilders'."

"Did you do it on purpose?" her grandmother asked in her usual way of getting right to the point.

"No! I mean, yes, but I thought she could handle her. I didn't want her to get hurt. I didn't even think she would fall off, but I thought it might take her down a notch or two. Ahhhh!" Annie pressed her hands against her head. "Why am I acting as if I were in junior high school? What has come over me?"

"Better see to that horse before she gets tangled in the reins."

Annie had forgotten about Nutmeg. She found her standing near the entrance to the pasture, perplexed as to what had happened. The reins hung loosely to the ground. Annie went to the horse, buried her face in her neck and let the tears flow. She breathed in the animal's rich, leathery scent and wiped the tears from her eyes with Nutmeg's shiny mane.

Annie led the horse back to the barn lot and shut the pasture gate. Removing the saddle, saddle blanket, and girth, she carried them to the tack room, leaving her bridle for last. Nutmeg stood still when Annie changed out the bridle for the halter, then brushed her down after her brief exercise. Annie's adrenaline was flowing and she felt like she could crawl out of her skin.

"Annie, what happened?" The calm, deep voice startled her.

"Is Camille okay?" Annie asked, turning to face Jake. He must have walked over, coming through the crossover on the stone fence.

"She's not hurt. What happened?"

"Camille fell off Nutmeg and ruined her expensive boots. That's what happened."

"She says you pushed the gate open to spook the horse. I didn't believe her."

Annie laughed. "Jake, there are things about Camille not to believe, but that happens to be one thing that is true."

"What is it between you two? It took some persuading to get her back down here again and now she's packing to go back home."

"Jake, she has no intentions of living here. That was settled long before she came over here to ride today."

"What do you mean?"

Maybe it was her business after all. She seemed to be right in the thick of it. "She wants to go to New York. Her father has it all worked out. Your future, if you plan on staying with her, is all planned, whether you like it or not. And ask her about her meeting last weekend. It had nothing to do with sales, believe me."

His face was flushed with anger, but Annie couldn't stop now. There was nothing to lose. It had to be said.

"Jake, she is all wrong for you! You will be making the biggest mistake of your life if you stay with her. I'm sorry, but it's true."

She turned and started away.

"How do you know she's wrong for me?" his voice called after her. "You haven't been around me for years!"

She wheeled around. "That's right, Jake. And why is that?"

He walked closer. "You know why," he said, and grabbed her shoulders with firm hands. "You knew how I felt, what the necklace meant. That's when you chose Brett Bradshaw and went your own way. You've been going your own way ever since." He almost spit the words out.

"I don't know what you're talking about," she said, but the tremble in her voice betrayed her.

He released her shoulders and said, "Forget it. It's in the past." Annie watched him walk across the barn lot, his body taut with anger. What could change if she ran after him? He was angry, and she deserved it. How she had managed to screw up every good thing in her life was beyond comprehension.

Chapter Thirty-Four

BEULAH ADMIRED THE four arrangements of fresh flowers in the trunk of Evelyn's car. Three were the same size; the fourth was smaller. They were all made with vibrant spring colors, a feast for the eyes.

"Those are real nice. The florist did a good job."

Evelyn agreed. "I put a fresh one on Charlie's grave for Father's Day."

"This is the first year I've missed getting flowers out on Decoration Day. Did Dixie take care of your people this year?" Beulah knew this was always a tender subject. Evelyn's sister was ten years her junior and not the most reliable person. Twice divorced, Dixie managed to float through life on one drama after the other.

"No. But when she called this morning and I told her about taking flowers to Charlie's grave for Father's Day, she thought that was a wonderful idea. She said she would plant a morning glory on Father's grave and let it twine around the tombstone."

Beulah chuckled. "One round with the caretaker's weed eater and that will be the end of that," she said.

"Of course, but what Dixie says and what she does are two

different things. I dared not say anything to her. I was glad she was thinking about it. Need help with the door?" Evelyn asked.

"I believe I can get it." Beulah opened it and eased herself in the seat, taking care not to twist her knee. "I appreciate you driving me up there, Evelyn. I planned for Annie to take me, but about thirty minutes after Camille left, she ran upstairs to her bedroom and slammed the door."

A look of understanding flooded Evelyn's face. "That must be where Jake went, flying out of the house after Cam got back. I was upstairs in the sewing room and I heard her pull in. They talked out in the parking lot for a few minutes, and then I saw Jake take off through the field."

"So the fight was with Jake, not Cam," Beulah mused.

"I'm guessing Cam is at the center of it," Evelyn said.

"And Jake said they were leaving?" Beulah asked.

"He had to take her to her car anyway, so he said he would go on home with her and try to come back later in the week."

The two old friends traded glances with each other that a multitude of words could never describe. Beulah sighed deeply. What would become of this mess?

When they eased past the way to the stone house, Beulah glimpsed the house through the trees and noticed there was only one window covered up now. Maybe whatever the woman was doing was over. Or maybe she wasn't seeing right. It was time to get a new set of glasses, but she had put it off until after the knee surgery.

The May family cemetery looked peaceful in the speckled sunlight that came through the tree branches. She took her time getting out of the car, for that was the hardest part. Evelyn already had one of the arrangements out of the trunk by the time she stood up.

"Where would you like this one?" Evelyn held an arrangement with red and blue ribbons.

"That looks patriotic. Let's put it on Ephraim's grave." She watched as Evelyn carried it over and placed the arrangement in a Mason jar, then filled it with water from a plastic jug.

"That's nice," Evelyn said.

Beulah looked in the trunk and pointed to one with pink and yellow flowers. "How about that one for Mama and Daddy's grave?" Evelyn picked it up. "This one to Jo Anne, and this small one to Jacob." Beulah supposed it sounded as if she were speaking of them in the flesh, rather than a tombstone, but Evelyn understood.

"I'll get the flowers. You grab my arm with your free hand." Evelyn offered her arm. "The ground is a little uneven."

One small step at a time, Beulah made it into the cemetery, but Evelyn had to lean down and put the arrangements in the jars and pour the water. While Evelyn worked, she looked at each grave and the loss it represented.

Mama and Daddy lived way up into their eighties, a good long life by any standard, but she felt the loss of them even now, deep in her soul. How they grieved for Ephraim, especially her Mama. Beulah still had the flag the government gave them after he died, and the Purple Heart.

And her own little Jacob, born premature and living only three days, was another grief that seared even deeper than the others. Often she had wondered if he would have survived nowadays with the technology for early babies. She heard tell of babies living who were born much earlier than Jacob, but it wasn't meant to be, and she trusted the Lord's judgment in that and the other pains in her life.

And of course there was her beloved Fred. She missed him terribly. During the days, she could pretend he was still out working in the fields, but the nights and mornings made it painfully obvious he was gone. Still, she would see him again, all of them, thanks to the Lord who provided a way. The older she got, the sooner it would be.

Evelyn and Beulah stood back to admire the newly adorned tombstones. It was unlikely anyone else would, it being such a small and private cemetery, but Beulah knew her duty. It was right to remember the dead.

On the way back, Beulah and Evelyn were quiet. Cemeteries had a way of doing that. They made you think about your life and how much time you might or might not have left. If there was any regret Beulah could say she had, it was being too reserved in her emotions. When she looked back at the many times she could have said more to Fred, Jo Anne, even to her parents and Ephraim, she wished now she had told them more how she felt, how much she loved them.

Those opportunities were lost, but she had today, this living, breathing moment.

"Evelyn, you are my dearest friend," Beulah said. "And in case I've never told you, I love you like a sister, even though twenty years separate us."

Evelyn's eyebrows flew up, and Beulah saw tears in her eyes. "Oh, Beulah, you know you've been family to me." Evelyn reached across and grabbed her hand. "Thank you for telling me that. I needed to hear that today."

Back at the house, Beulah called upstairs, "Annie, do you want some supper?" She wished she could manage the steps and check on her granddaughter.

In a moment, the door opened and Annie came out. Her eyes were heavy and swollen, her hair messed up.

"I don't, but I'll fix you something."

"No sense in that. I put on another mess of green beans to cook before we went to the cemetery, and they're almost ready."

"Oh, Grandma, I forgot you wanted to go. I'm sorry."

Beulah noticed her voice was low and hoarse as she plodded down the wooden stairs in her sock feet.

"Now, don't worry about that. You had other things on your mind. These last few hours in the kitchen have done me more good than anything."

"I fell asleep after Cam came over." Annie sat in a chair, her shoulders sagging as if she carried a fifty-pound feed sack on her back. Beulah knew she had done more than sleep by the looks of her red eyes, but that could go unsaid.

"Couldn't patch things up with her?" Beulah asked, her back to Annie while she dished out two bowls of green beans and new potatoes.

"You saw her tear out of here. Jake came over right after that and said they're going back to Cincinnati," Annie said, her face resting on her closed fist, elbow on the table.

Beulah carefully carried the beans to the table. Annie jumped up. "I'll get drinks."

"Silverware too, please."

Annie set the two glasses of iced tea on the table and went back for the silverware.

"I don't feel like I know who I am anymore. I'm acting like a crazy person, but Jake is about to make the biggest mistake of his life. Evelyn knows it, you know it, I know it, but Jake doesn't know it. And he's the only one that counts."

The beans were delicious, salty and seasoned with fatback. There was nothing like fresh green beans. Beulah ate slowly, savoring every bite.

"Are you worked up over Jake's potential mistake or do you think it might go a little deeper than that?"

Annie looked at her grandmother and her eyes filled with tears. "I've made a terrible mess of things. I have no right to make it worse."

Beulah nodded. "I believe it will all work out in the end."

"How can you be so confident?" Annie asked her, finally eating her beans.

"Because I'm praying and trusting God to work it out," Beulah said.

Chapter Thirty-Five

ANNIE FINISHED CLEANING the sink, locked the doors downstairs and went up to her bedroom. She rubbed the back of her neck, trying to work out the knotted muscles. *Jake wanted to be her boyfriend in high school.* Is that what he was telling her?

She sat looking at herself in the mirror of her dressing table, her face washed and her hair pulled back in a headband. Jake had said, "When you chose Brett Bradshaw."

Her eyes fell on the silver cross lying in her jewelry box. She reached for it and the cross felt cold in her hands, the silver chain soft and delicate. Annie held it up and let it shimmer in the reflection of her ceiling light.

Jake gave it to her the night of her sixteenth birthday. Her grandmother had made a cake with butter cream icing and pink writing that she squirted out of an aerosol can. It was a family dinner that included Evelyn, Charlie and Jake. Her grandfather gave her a hundred dollar bill, with his chuckle. Her grandmother had looked at her sternly and advised that she use it for clothes and not music. Her grandfather had said, "Now, Beulah, it's her birthday—and she can spend it however she wants." His eyes twinkled. Annie hugged him, feeling his whiskers scrape the side of her face and smelling the tobacco from his pipe.

Later, she and Jake met at the crossover. It was nearly dark, the April days not as long as the days of summer. When she opened the package from Chaney's Jewelry store, she held her hair up and let Jake clasp the chain around her neck.

"It's beautiful. I love it." Annie reached over and hugged Jake as tightly as she could. "Jake, will we always be best friends, even when we're older?"

"More than best friends," he said, smiling at first and then getting a serious look on his face. "Do you want to go to the homecoming dance with me?"

"Sure. Who else would I go with?"

But two weeks later, Brett Bradshaw started hanging around her locker between classes. He was on the football team, and she had thought he was cute since the seventh grade when she saw him in the library. Never would he have looked her way, she thought, but making the cheerleading squad had changed everything. It was as if a whole new world was opened up to her with the cool kids. She was invited to their parties and included in their circles before school, at lunch and after school.

When Brett asked her to homecoming, she had to calm her voice before saying yes so she didn't squeak it out like a rusty hinge. She was still smiling when Jake came by a few minutes later. Jake wouldn't mind, she told herself. He didn't even like dances; he'd told her that.

But he had seemed to mind. When she told Jake about Brett, he seemed disappointed in her. She thought it was because he didn't like Brett very well and he was being protective. Now she knew it was more, and in truth, she had known it even then.

Annie lay in bed, unable to sleep. Like letters unread for years, she kept turning memories over in her mind, each one a new revelation in light of what Jake had said.

Their friendship had changed after she started dating Brett. Never before had she realized when the rift started. She'd never really thought about it.

Jake started hanging around the baseball players and a girl

named Emily. He became a standout on the baseball team and earned a scholarship to college. In his free time, he worked on the farm with his dad.

Annie hung around a different group in high school where her social life was filled with late-night field parties after the football games. Bourbon mixed with Coke and hooch flowed freely, and everybody felt young and invincible. Her grandmother only let her spend the night with a couple of girls, screening the parents as one can only do in a small town where everybody knows everybody's relatives and they knew who watched their kids or not.

But they had their tricks and learned how to sneak out of the house without a soul knowing it. For some like Annie, there was a tree near an upstairs window, a creaky window pushed up earlier in the day, a car waiting on the country road.

Jake and Annie saw each other on breaks during college, caught up on what they were doing and news of mutual friends, but that had been the extent of it. Jake had always been an important connection to her past, but never did she think he could be part of her future. Their lives had long ago taken different roads.

***

"Who called this morning?" Annie set the risen dough in a bowl in front of Beulah. The phone had rung early while she was still in bed.

"Joe saw that woman out by the creek again. He said she was sitting there staring into the water as if she were half-asleep. He watched her for nigh about half an hour before he had to go check the cows," Beulah said, turning out the dough on the biscuit board.

"I'm calling Jeb again. How hard can it be to run plates? It should take seconds."

The call went immediately to voice mail. Annie left a message and then decided to call the sheriff. The sheriff was on vacation and his deputy was reticent to get involved since the state police were already on it.

"They're not exactly on it," Annie explained. "Jeb is a friend who agreed to help us, but he's too busy with another case. We just need somebody to run plates."

"I'm sorry," the deputy said. "We'll have to talk to Jeb first. We'll contact you as soon as we talk to him."

Annie hung up the phone. "Good grief," she said aloud. All roads ended with Jeb Harris and he was down in some hollow in Eastern Kentucky.

Annie took baskets out to the garden and worked row by row picking beans, and even zucchini and squash. The garden was coming in earlier this year, her grandmother had said, partly because she had planted earlier and partly because there had been good hot days and plenty of rain.

Beulah was seated at the kitchen table when she came in, ready to start breaking beans, her coffee cup full beside her.

"That's a nice mess," she said. "At least two cannings."

Annie was amazed at how her grandmother could judge by looking at the pile of raw vegetables. Sure enough, a few hours later, fourteen quarts of beans sat on the counter, the heat emanating from the jars. As they cooled, the lids would start popping, which was music to Annie's ears. It meant the canning took, but would need another several hours of cooling before she moved them to the cellar.

The phone rang as Annie was drying the canner. She handed the phone to her grandmother before going back to the sink.

Annie took the empty baskets to the back room so they would be handy for the next harvesting. It would be awhile longer on the next round of green beans, but peppers, onions, squash and zucchini would keep her busy. Sweet corn and tomatoes would be ready for picking soon. And now, Annie could be here to see it all come in if she would only make that phone call to Bob Vichy. But somehow, her courage faded when she picked up the phone. There was no way to go back once she placed that call. She had made so many mistakes in her life. She was afraid of making another.

That night, Annie tossed and turned, twisting the bedcovers

into knots. By midnight, she gave up fighting the covers and went downstairs for a cup of hot tea. She put on a kettle of water and set a pot of chamomile to steep. She sat with her robe pulled tightly around her, waiting on the tea and anxious for the steaming comfort of the warm brew.

Jake was never far from her thoughts. The few weeks of recaptured friendship had been such an unexpected gift. How could she have known this friend from her childhood could turn into this kind of man ...? But she was in a long line of women and men who had learned that lesson the hard way.

It wasn't meant to be. She had to hope he would forgive her immature actions with Camille, hope they could have some sort of relationship as neighbors, if not friends. She would tell him how wrong she was and that she would do everything in her power to make Camille welcome. God would give her the strength to do it and to even grow to love Camille. Who knew, they might be as close as her grandmother and Evelyn someday. Weren't all things possible?

Finally Annie felt she might be able to sleep. She washed out her cup and emptied the tea kettle. She was about to turn off the kitchen light when the shrill sound of the wall phone cut through the night's stillness.

"Hello?"

"Annie? It's Betty Gibson. The old stone house is on fire! Joe was out with Jake pulling a calf on Evelyn's farm when they saw flames in the second-floor window. He called the fire department and they're on their way over there right now."

"Oh no!" Annie said. "I'll wake Grandma."

Chapter Thirty-Six

ANNIE PULLED ON a pair of jeans and a shirt and grabbed her tennis shoes to put on downstairs. She flipped the light on in her grandmother's bedroom. Her grandmother sat up, her face frightened and alarmed.

"Who was on the phone?" she asked.

"Betty Gibson. The stone house is on fire! Do you want to go with me?" Annie knew the answer, but she asked it anyway.

"Good heavens, where's my housedress?"

Annie reached for one her grandmother had worn that day and helped her change.

"Be careful, we'll go slow. There's nothing we can do anyway," Annie said.

They heard sirens wail, slowing for the turn on Gibson Creek Road. Annie was afraid that in their excitement, her grandmother would wrench her knee. She told herself to calm down and walk slowly with her to the car.

On the car ride over, Beulah prayed aloud, "Dear God, please keep everyone safe."

Annie prepared herself to see the house in a smoldering pile of stones, but when they arrived, she could see the flames were contained in the second-floor room.

"It might be saved," her grandmother said, telling Annie she had prepared herself for the same thing.

A water truck was parked in front of the house with two hoses attached. Men were pulling the hoses off the side of the truck to position them according to the directions of one of the firefighters. Annie's heart skipped a beat when she saw Jake, in jeans and a T-shirt, his muscles glistening with sweat from the heat. He worked alongside the men holding the hose as water surged in an arc to the fiery hole in the roof. Joe was there too, helping to feed the hose so they could move in any direction needed.

Annie could feel the intensity of the flames, even from the safe distance where they parked. The men were much closer, taking the brunt of the heat. Steam rose from the house as water doused the wood rafters. Annie watched, mesmerized. The roof over the second-floor room was completely gone, giving it an eerie look under the bright spotlights. Was Stella inside?

Betty met them at the car.

"Joe saw it just as it started," Betty said, her white teeth glowing in the firelight and a bead of sweat on her nose. "He was faced toward the house while Jake was pulling the calf."

"Tell Beulah what you saw, Joe," Betty said as Joe joined them.

"We were near the fence between you and Evelyn when I noticed flames licking up inside the upstairs window."

"And you didn't see Ms. Hawkins?" her grandmother asked, her voice getting hoarse.

"Her car is gone," Annie said.

"Looks like they're about to get in. Then we can see what's what," Joe said.

"Joe Gibson, don't you go in there," Betty called after him.

"Lord Jesus, please let every living thing be out of that inferno," Beulah prayed aloud.

"Amen," said Betty.

A state police car pulled up. Detective Jeb Harris got out. "Everybody all right?" he asked.

"Jeb, we're all white-eyed!" Betty said.

He addressed Beulah. "When I heard it was your place, I called in to see if anything came up on those plates. One of the boys ran them while I waited. The car is registered to Stella Hawkins, Chicago, Illinois. She's a missing person."

"What do you mean?" Annie said. "Did she do something wrong?"

"We don't know yet. We have a call into the Chicago PD to get more details. First and foremost, we want to make sure she's not in the house. Let me talk to the chief over here and see how things are coming," Jeb said, making his way over to an older man in a fire hat and large coat.

The men were making headway with the fire, and in a few minutes, they had it out. A spotlight shone on the house from the fire truck, lighting the way for the men as they worked. In the place of licking flames up to the heavens, a smoldering billow of smoke drifted upward and the stench of water-soaked burned wood filled the air. The house would survive this night, but not without significant damage.

A generator powered two spotlights that shone on the site and when Annie saw Jake go into the house with two other men, her heart lurched, feeling the same fear Betty expressed. Was it safe? Even though the fire was in the upstairs room, couldn't timbers fall and hurt someone downstairs? Annie chewed on her lip until she saw Jake follow another man out the door a minute later. Across the span of the yard, their eyes met. He turned to one of the men and said something, then walked toward them. Annie noticed his shirt was soaked through with sweat, soot smeared his forehead and his dark hair curled around his temples.

"Jake, did they find anybody?" Betty spit out the question on all their minds.

Jake took a deep breath. "Nothing yet, but it's too soon to tell. They're going to put a guard out here and leave it until morning."

"We'll go on back to the house and put on some coffee. Tell the men to come by as soon as they finish," Beulah said.

"I'm sure they'll appreciate that," Jake said. He nodded at Annie and turned back to the house. Her legs felt like butter and she sunk back into the driver's seat of the car.

Back at the house, Betty put on a kettle for tea and made two pots of coffee. Jake came in with two of the firemen and it took everything Annie had not to go to him. Instead, she filled his coffee cup, black as she knew he liked it, and handed it to him without a word.

The conversation went on in subdued tones with her grandmother sitting at the kitchen table, her leg stretched out on an empty chair.

"Too hot tonight ...."

"Good sign we didn't find anything so far ...."

It was well into the night, but they were all too wound up to go to bed. Annie missed Evelyn's soothing words in the group, but she was in Lexington taking care of her sister Dixie, who broke her arm.

The unspoken questions hovered over the group. Had someone been in the upstairs? Would they find a body tomorrow morning? The thought nauseated Annie, the stench of fire and wet wood still strong in her nose.

When the phone rang, Annie grabbed it and handed it to her grandmother.

"This is Beulah," she said.

There was a long pause. Annie tried to read the look on her grandmother's face, but as in so many other times when Annie had watched her under stress, her facial expression betrayed nothing.

"Thank you." She handed the phone back to Annie to hang up.

"It was Jeb. He said no evidence of a body so far, but they still haven't found Stella. They think the fire might have started from a candle."

Jake nodded and stood. "I'm going on home. Call if you need me." He looked at Beulah when he said the words but his eyes didn't seek hers.

"We better all get to bed. I'm as weak as a kitten." Betty stood and put the coffee cups in the sink.

"I'll get that tomorrow morning," Annie said. "Thank you all for coming over and sitting with us."

"And for calling the fire department. Evelyn's cow knew when to calve, didn't she?" Beulah said.

"She's a fine little Jersey heifer. Annie, you might want her for a milk cow. You could call her Firebug," Joe said.

It felt good to laugh after the intensity of the night. "I might," Annie teased back.

From the back door, Annie watched the Gibsons walk to their truck, and she felt an overwhelming exhaustion press down on her.

"You need anything before I go upstairs?" she asked her grandmother.

"Nothing. I'm glad you were here with me, Annie. With Evelyn gone, I would've been up a creek with this knee not quite right yet."

Chapter Thirty-Seven

THE NEXT MORNING, Detective Jeb Harris sat in the living room. Beulah was full of a hundred questions, but she sat as patient as she could be and waited on him to set the pace.

"We found Stella Hawkins last night," Jeb said.

"She was in the house?" Annie asked.

"No, she had gone to Rutherford to get groceries. When she turned down your road and saw the fire, she panicked and tried to leave the county. One of the deputies spotted the car and pulled her over. We brought her in for questioning and identification as the missing person."

Beulah exhaled, not even realizing she'd been holding her breath. "Why was she a missing person?"

"Yeah, did she do something wrong?"

"Nothing illegal. She drove down from Chicago in a distressed state, planning to end her life at some point on the journey, but she can tell you about all that. As for her legal troubles, it will depend on how you all feel about her leaving a candle unattended and damaging your property."

"But what was she dumping in the creek?" Annie asked, her forehead creased like the folds in a quilt.

"Nothing. She was using the bucket to sit by the creek, then decided to try scooping up minnows, then pour them back out. She was ... playing, for lack of a better word."

Beulah rubbed her forehead, wishing she could remove the dull ache that gripped her head like a vice. "Jeb Harris, you're telling me this woman walked out of her life up North, came down here planning to kill herself, and ended up playing in our creek?"

Beulah didn't know quite what he found so funny, but Jeb burst out in laughter.

"There's more to it, but she wants to tell you herself. I'll bring her out as soon as we're finished."

He started out the door and hesitated. "You might have reporters and TV crews bothering you about the fire and Stella's ordeal. If you get phone calls, tell them you're cooperating with the police. If you want, we can block off the end of your driveway for the day if it would give you some peace and quiet."

"Yes, that would be real nice. Of course, we don't mind our good friends and neighbors stopping by."

"I've got an intern right now who would be perfect. We'll put him down there for the day."

After Jeb left, Annie went upstairs to rest. There seemed to be nothing to say until they heard Stella's side of the story.

Beulah was too keyed up, so she called Evelyn and told her all about the goings-on.

"Jake said it was awful to think somebody might be in that house. Call me when you know more," Evelyn said, her voice full of sympathy.

"How's Dixie?" she asked.

"Feisty as ever, but loving my attention. There's a single doctor in charge of her care, and I suspect she'll tire of me soon enough."

The phone started ringing as soon as she hung up with Evelyn. The first call was Betty Gibson.

"Beulah, the Lexington news vans are lined up along the road in front of your house. They'll be here until after the five o' clock broadcast and maybe until eleven! When I went into town for the pie ingredients, I picked up two fryers for you. I thought you might want them if you can't leave for a couple of days."

"Betty, that's wonderful. Can you make it through the reporters?"

"Joe's got it all figured out. He'll drive his old farm truck through the gate between you and Evelyn and act like he's going to check cows. I'll scrunch down in the seat with the chickens. We'll be there in two shakes of a lamb's tail."

The phone rang continuously after Betty called and Beulah tired of saying, "The police are handling the investigation," like Jeb instructed her to do with reporter calls. Finally, she turned off the ringer, glad for the silence.

The Gibsons delivered the chickens. After they left, Beulah eased back on her bed and rested her knee and her mind. Rarely before had she ever relaxed in the afternoon, but the knee surgery had changed that. It was as if her whole body was helping the knee to heal and forced her to save her energy.

When she woke up, there was one thing on her mind. Beulah wanted to cook, and cook up a storm. She would be very careful about any quick movements. But if she took it slow, it could be done.

Annie could help her by getting pots and pans and fetching things from the cabinets and refrigerator, but Annie was sleeping and Beulah didn't want to disturb her.

While Annie needed rest, Beulah needed to shake off the troubles of the night and morning by feeling flour between her fingers, throwing in salt and pepper, and frying up chickens. Beulah wanted to knead dough until her hands hurt, to release pent-up tension and anxiety. She wanted to whip up eggs, sugar and butter for chess pies or beat the meringue for a coconut pie. Getting lost in mixing, frying and baking was her therapy. It might only be her and Annie for supper, but she would cook enough for an army.

But it wasn't just Beulah and Annie for supper. Stella Hawkins joined them with the help of Jeb Harris, who must have realized they needed him more than that sting operation down in the mountains of Eastern Kentucky.

Arms crossed and shoulders hunched, Beulah felt immediate compassion for the woman with the flyaway red hair. She was pale as a ghost, except for two rosy circles on her cheeks. Her eyes barely looked up from the ground when Jeb led her into the living room.

Annie settled herself into a chair and they all waited for someone to speak.

Jeb nodded at Stella when she looked his way. She pushed her glasses back on her nose and cleared her throat.

"First, I just want to say I am very sorry about the fire. I left a candle burning accidentally when I went to get groceries. I didn't mean for that to happen." Stella met Beulah's eyes and then looked at Annie.

She took a deep breath and continued, one hand gripping the tail of her sweater and twisting it. "Things got real bad for me this past year. My job at the library doesn't pay much and I got into trouble with my finances, too much credit card debt and all. I sold the only thing of value I had other than my car. It was an antique Jackson Press that my foster mother gave me when I left home. I got three thousand dollars for it, but it wouldn't make a dent in my debt, what with the high interest rate, so I just put it in my savings until I could figure out what to do." She let go of the twisted sweater tail, and rubbed her palm on her pants.

"A few weeks ago I got word my foster mother passed away, down in Georgia. The worst thing was, her real kids didn't even tell me. I found out from a neighbor when I called her." Stella's chin quivered and she nervously glanced at Beulah, who nodded for her to go on.

"She was dead and buried and I didn't even get to say goodbye. I felt like things were caving in. My doctor gave me something to help with the stress but I never could feel any better. Then, one day, I just decided that if this was all there was to life, I didn't want anymore of it." Stella picked up the sweater tail again and twisted it.

"I took out the money, put a few things in a suitcase, my bottle of pills, and headed south on Highway 27. I planned to drive to Georgia, leave the money at the church where my foster mother used to take me, and end it there in the church parking lot with that bottle of pills."

A half-smile played at the corner of her mouth and she met Beulah's and Annie's eyes.

"It was a good plan, I thought. But by the time I got to Kentucky, I was so tired. I pulled off in Somerville to eat breakfast after driving most of the night. While I was sitting there, I thought to myself, 'You made it across the Ohio River. You are in the South now, and maybe this place is as good as Georgia.' I was just too tired to go on. But the longer I sat, I thought maybe I should wait a week or two. Maybe I should find a place to stay just long enough for me to think through things a little more before I … you know."

"And that's when you came to us," Beulah said, "to rent the stone house."

"That's right," Stella said. "I covered the windows, stayed in the darkness, and was convinced it was time. I took two of my pills and was in the process of taking the rest when you knocked on the door." Stella looked at Annie. "With food."

Annie nodded, her eyes wide with understanding.

"It happened another time not long after. I was just ready to finish off the whole bottle when you heard me crying and knocked on the back door. I'm sorry about being so rude. I just can't tell you how much pain I was in," Stella said, letting go of the sweater tail and pulling the cardigan close around her, visibly shivering over the memory of it.

"It's okay," Annie said. "I'm glad I disturbed you now."

Stella smiled. "After that second time, I thought God might be trying to tell me something. I started taking some of the coverings off the windows, letting more light in. I was going after midnight to get groceries when I needed them and many times I would stay up until dawn, so I could sit by the creek without anyone seeing me. One morning when I was out there, I saw a beautiful flower growing by the house. I don't know what kind it was, but it reminded me of a song I learned years ago at that church in Georgia. *Remember the lilies of the field, for Solomon dressed in royal robes has not the worth of them.* It has more verses than that, but that one line was all I could remember. But it made me think that if God dresses lilies like that, then doesn't He care for me? Something changed inside me then, and I knew He did."

Stella took a deep breath. "I felt like I had a new direction, but then I went to get groceries and forgot the burning candle. And when I saw the fire, I felt like I had messed up big this time. I didn't know what to do but run away." Stella rubbed both palms on her pants. "I am terribly sorry for how I treated you both, especially after your kindness. And I don't know how long it will take, but I will work to pay you back for all the repairs to the house."

"Stella, you don't owe us anything," Beulah said. "There'll be insurance for that. We're so glad you came to us."

"You are?" Stella's eyes widened behind the glasses.

"Of course," Annie said, reaching over to clasp Stella's hand. "It was meant to be."

Jeb stood. "I guess I better get Stella to her hotel and leave you ladies to rest."

"What? With fried chicken ready to put on the table?" Beulah said.

He looked at Stella. "It's up to you, Stella, but if you've never had Beulah's fried chicken, it would be a big mistake to leave now after that invitation."

Stella smiled for the first time and Beulah thought she looked like a hundred-pound weight had been lifted from her shoulders.

Beulah heard the back door open and loud footsteps pound through the kitchen. Woody appeared in the doorway.

"I was dropping off a few more tomato cages and I smelled chicken," he said, his eyes scanning the room. He saw Stella and something in his expression changed.

"Well, how do?" Woody offered her his hand.

Stella stood and extended her hand too. For a moment, it seemed as if they were the only people in the room.

Chapter Thirty-Eight

ANNIE COULDN'T BELIEVE how wrong she was about Stella. And to think she had simply walked away when Stella was about to end her life inside that stone house. Thank God nothing happened.

She stared up at the ceiling of her room, plaster peeled in the corner and the old Victorian light fixture hung just as it had when she was a teenager. Time and time again, she had rested on this very bed and stared at that same light fixture, the gold shade decorated with pink flowers and the ornate brass curlicues holding the lightbulb under the shade.

She had always walked away. It was how she handled the difficult things of life.

Like walking away from Jake those many years ago ... he was right. Deep down, she had known he wanted more, but it had scared her. She was afraid it would keep her from leaving this place, and she had to get out and see the world. Brett was never someone she could have married, not like Jake. Marriage and a baby had kept her mother here, and she had died before ever seeing a single thing outside of Kentucky. Annie had walked away so she could get away.

But for every action, there is a consequence. *Doesn't the Bible say something about reaping what you sow?* There was a price to be paid for freedom, and now it was time to pay. As her grandfather always said, "If you make your bed, you have to lay in it."

Annie knew in her soul she didn't want to walk away anymore. Courage mounted and she pulled out her cell phone and made the call.

Annie had to hold the phone away from her ear while Bob Vichy let out a tirade of curses.

"I'm sorry, Bob. But remember, the airline fired me."

"I know, but you don't know what I've gone through to get you back on!" He screamed the words in her ear.

"Calm down, Bob, you're going to have a heart attack. Listen, you find a week when you can bring your wife down here, and we'll treat you to some home cooking and a soft bed. I promise I'll make it up to you."

"Boy, I need it, but if I keep having to deal with people like you, I don't know when I'll get a week off!" He was softening, she could tell.

"You've got my number, and the invitation stands. Call whenever you're ready." She hung up the phone, feeling a smile spread across her face. Free! She was free! She threw her hands in the air and shouted, "Hallelujah!"

Two more phone calls.

"Annie, where've you been?"

Annie spent the next thirty minutes filling Janice in on the play-by-play.

Finally, she told her the news. "I'm staying here, Janice, for good. I wonder if you would mind having a moving service pick up my stuff from the storage building. I'll pay you for your time."

"What? You're not coming back at all? Annie, are you sure?"

"I've never been surer of a thing. It's where I want to be. But you have to promise to come for a visit, and bring Jimmy and the kids and even Mrs. DeVechio if she wants to come. She will love my grandmother. We'll stick them both in the kitchen and see what comes out!" Annie laughed at the picture of her grandmother and Janice's 'pasta mama' fighting for control of the kitchen.

"That could start World War Three," Janice laughed with her. "But we'll come. I promise! The kids would love to spend time on a real farm."

Annie dialed Prema's number, hoping she wasn't traveling today. When she answered, it was the same as with Janice. Prema wanted to hear every detail of the story.

"I'm so happy for you!" Prema said. "You should be home with your grandmother. That is as it should be."

Annie took a deep breath, relief spreading over her like a healing balm now that the decision was made. She had one last piece of business and then she would tell her grandmother.

Taking out pen and paper, she wrote:

Jake,

I am deeply sorry for how I treated Camille. The truth is, I was jealous. You were right. I did walk away from you all those years ago because I was afraid of never getting out of Somerville. I did know you cared for me. I cared for you, but I was afraid of staying here for the rest of my life, of not seeing what was out there, not experiencing the world. I didn't realize what I gave up all those years ago until these last several weeks.

It came as a surprise to me, these feelings for you, and I took it all out on Camille. I'm staying home. It's where I need to be. But I promise, if you decide to come back as well, I will be the best friend and neighbor to you both and will never speak of this again.

Annie

Annie went downstairs to tell her grandmother the news and to deliver the letter. Her grandmother's voice was coming from the kitchen.

"Evelyn, that is wonderful news! A wedding at your house will be beautiful."

Annie stopped on the stairs and listened.

"October is such a pretty time with your mums in full bloom.

Who will marry them? I see. Won't that be lovely?"

The feeling of lightness left her, floating away like a helium balloon. A heavy dread replaced it; the thing she had feared was actually happening. Now it was more important than ever to deliver the letter.

Quietly, she slipped out the front door and around the side of the house. The tears were stinging her eyes, and she blinked hard trying to push them back. Walking at first, and then running, she made her way through blurred vision to the crossover place.

Annie sat down hard on the weeds and ivy-covered stone. She wedged the letter into a stone then texted Jake to tell him she had left something for him. Maybe she should congratulate him, but there would be time for that later.

Annie pulled a weed out of the stone and fingered it while she looked in the direction of the stone house. Even with losing Jake, by coming home she had found so much more. Her grandmother's love and her faith in God, pushed aside for so many years. It was enough to start a new life in this blessed place where her family had been for so many generations. She was brought back here for a reason, and there was deep comfort in that, no matter what the future held.

Annie pushed herself up and walked toward the burned house. She didn't want to be at the crossover when Jake came to get the letter. And, like always, she was drawn to the home of her childhood.

Stones jutted up into the sky like a castle wall where the fire burned out the second-floor room. The fireplace was still stacked, supported by the wall, but went into open sky without a roof nearby. It was hard seeing the old house in such a shape, but thinking about how Stella's life was saved by coming here helped.

After supper, Beulah had offered for Stella to stay with them, but she refused.

"I will be fine at the hotel for the night. Then I need to go back to Chicago and sort a few things out." Beulah wouldn't let her leave without giving her the two thousand dollars back in a check.

"But I burned your house down," Stella had said.

"It's only stuff. You need to work on paying your debts. And we know a banker who might give you counsel if you want it."

A voice interrupted her memory. "It can be fixed," he said. Annie turned to see Jake, a gentle expression on his face, the open letter in his hand.

"I know, it just hurts to see it like this," she said.

"Not the house," he said, taking a step toward her. "I mean us," he lifted the letter.

"I hope so. I don't want you or Camille to be uncomfortable after you get married."

"I'm not marrying Camille. I broke it off the day I took her back to Cincinnati. I think I always knew it wasn't going to work deep down, but I was so close to her family. That was also the day I decided to come back home and make a go of the farm. But there was one thing I couldn't figure out."

"What's that?" Her voice sounded breathless, as if she had the wind knocked out of her.

"Where to go from here with my feelings for you," Jake said, his blue eyes intense and searching. "And then I got this." He held up the letter.

"Yes?" Annie said, stepping closer to him.

"So, now I need to ask you a question," he said, moving close to her.

"Yes?" Annie said, the distance between them now only inches.

He cradled her face in his hands. "Would you go on a date with me? Not as a friend or a brother, but as someone you might fall in love with?"

"Yes," Annie said, and leaned in as he kissed her gently.

Chapter Thirty-Nine

BEULAH SAT IN the kitchen drinking her coffee and listening to the rain on the tin roof, feeling that just as the water was filling up her rain barrel, so was her heart filling up with the blessings of the last two days.

First, Evelyn was back from tending to Dixie, and Beulah took comfort in knowing she was home. Then there was Evelyn's phone call about Scott and Mary Beth's engagement. It tickled Beulah to no end that maybe some of that courting had happened right under their noses over pot roast and gravy. And to think they wanted to be married at Evelyn's home with country ham and biscuits for the reception! They would all be scurrying around like mice getting it together, but what fun it would be.

Of course, some of the talk around town was centered on Scott marrying a divorced woman and not even marrying in the church. But for goodness sakes, Scott's church family was just fine with it. After all, the church's name was Grace, and if ever there was time to dole some of that out, this was it. The new church didn't even have a proper building anyway, what with meeting at the high school for now.

Mary Beth would make a good preacher's wife, Beulah was

certain about that. And maybe once they were married, she wouldn't draw the criticism of the gossips like in some of the more established churches. Some preacher's wives might as well have a target tattooed on their backs for all the verbal arrows shot at them.

Beulah took a drink of her coffee and knew the best news of all was having Annie and Jake both home to stay and courting each other. Her heart overflowed and she had to share some of it or else bust.

Beulah lifted her left knee, giving it a little extra exercise. She was healing up just fine. "Do as much as you are comfortable with," the doctor had told her on her last visit and that was what she intended to do.

Just as the rain was tapering off, she heard Jake drive in. "Jake's here," she called upstairs.

"Coming," Annie said from her room. Beulah made her way to the back door, still using the cane for extra help.

Jake was at the door when she got to it and she held the door open for him.

As soon as he was inside, he kissed her on the cheek. "How are you feeling?" he asked.

"Fine as frog hair," Beulah said as Annie entered the room.

When he looked at Annie, the tenderness in his eyes reminded Beulah of the way Fred used to look at her. And Annie did look awful pretty, the red blouse pulling out the right colors in her face and the silver cross necklace hanging just above the neckline. She almost seemed to glow, Beulah thought.

When Annie smiled back at Jake, Beulah felt like an intruder, feeling an unseen current run between the two that was meant only for them.

She edged back into the kitchen. "Have fun!"

When they waved and went out the door, Beulah took a deep breath and sighed, full of contentment.

Now it was time to share all the good things so she wouldn't split wide open trying to keep it all inside. With her cane, she walked to the back room and found the small metal garden stool. The stool in one hand and her cane in the other, she made her way outside to the Marquis. She put the stool in the backseat behind the driver's side and slid in the front.

It was the first time she had driven since the surgery. Not because she couldn't, but Annie had taken it upon herself to drive her everywhere. It felt strange to be behind the wheel, but she needed to get used to it so she could start being back to her old independent self. Well, almost her old self. Letting go of her pride and allowing others to help her had been a lesson she needed.

She put the car in gear and turned it around in the driveway. As she approached the end of the lane, she saw Betty in her front yard working on her geraniums. Just as she turned onto May Hollow Road, Betty stood and waved as if trying to get Beulah to pull over so she could talk. Beulah waved back, but kept her head straight, set on where she was going. Even Betty Gibson couldn't interrupt today.

She turned left onto Gibson's Creek Road, passing the old stone house on the left. Then she turned into the cemetery lane, pulling her car as close as possible to the wrought-iron gate.

Beulah was even more careful on the uneven ground, but the cane helped to steady her. She got the stool from the backseat and made her way inside the gate. Placing the stool to the side of Fred's grave, she sat.

For a few moments, Beulah enjoyed the silence broken only by the birds singing in the trees above. Then she bowed her head in prayer and thanksgiving to God for all the recent blessings. When she opened her eyes, she looked at the ground next to her.

"Fred honey, you can't believe what all has happened. Annie's home," her voice broke with the words. "That's right, she's back for good." Beulah could feel her eyes fill with unshed tears. "It took us awhile to learn how to live without you, but we finally did."

Beulah knew only Fred's earthly vessel lay below the earth, that his spirit was with Christ in Heaven, but there was some comfort in being close to the place where his body lay. In this peaceful place, she had the freedom to say the things pent up in her heart.

"And guess what else? Jake is coming back to run the farm." Beulah pictured Fred's response in her mind, his eyes twinkling with pleasure, white eyebrows raised, and taking his pipe out of his mouth to grin and say, "Well if that don't beat all."

Beulah reached down and took a handful of loose dirt that was close to the stone. She let the rich soil slip through her fingers back to the ground.

"I hope I'm not jumping the gun, but it looks like there might be a chance to join these two farms after all," she said, finally allowing herself to laugh and cry at the same time.

Acknowledgments

Many thanks to the readers who gave me valuable feedback: Beth Dotson Brown, Jan Watson, Jess Correll, Jennifer Claus, Adrienne Correll, Rachel Correll, Dennis Hensley and the Grassroots Writer's Group.

Thanks to Preston Correll for sustainable farming inspiration; Bruce Petrie for information on Kentucky law; Roni Di Pietro and Spence Closson for airline background from a flight attendant's and a pilot's perspective; Elizabeth DeRossi for the Italian translation; Nancy Sleeth for enthusiasm and encouragement to further the stewardship of this blessed earth; and Jason McKinley for artistic input.

Special thanks to Jenni Burke, my friend and agent, for loving this story from the beginning and John Koehler, Joe Coccaro, and Terry Whalin at Koehler Books for making it a reality.

Finally, the steadfast encouragement to persevere from my husband, Jess, is beyond simple words of gratitude, but I'll use them just the same: Thank you!

Discussion Questions

1. Do you think Annie was really in love with Stuart? Why or why not?

2. Before Annie ever gets to the farm, she notices an old lady in Rome planting seeds on her balcony and she rescues Stuart's neglected plant from his apartment. What do these scenes represent for Annie?

3. Do you sense tension between urban and rural life as it is played out through Annie and Beulah? What stereotypes have you encountered about rural or urban life?

4. What drives Annie to stay with her grandmother when she longs to go back to the city?

5. Jake is interested in sustainable agriculture and local food. What role do you think these issues play in our society today?

6. Beulah teaches Annie how to plant and grow a garden. Should Annie have known this if she grew up on a farm? What skills from your own ancestors would you like to revisit?

7. Beulah and Annie preserve the garden produce through the method of canning. Have you ever canned before? What are the advantages of canning your own food?

8. How does Annie begin to appreciate the history of her family's farm? Do you think we appreciate our elders and their heritage in our culture?

9. Why has Jake fallen for Camille when she seems to have a very different set of values?

10. Do you believe Annie and Jake reconnected by chance at the same time each are about to make life-changing decisions, or do you believe in divine guidance or providence? How do your beliefs affect your daily life?

11. Stella comes into the characters' lives as a desperate and mysterious stranger and then experiences her own grounding through creation. What has grounded you during difficult times?

12. At the end of the novel, Beulah takes a handful of soil and lets it run through her fingers. Have you ever thought about the land as something that connects us with our past? Have you ever considered it to be something God entrusted us to care for?

CPSIA information can be obtained at www.ICGtesting.com
Printed in the USA
LVOW13s1605050813

346368LV00001B/1/P